THE
FOUNDING
FATHERS
RETURN

A Novel

BOOKS BY LAWRENCE ROWE

FICTION
The Tesla Paradox

NON-FICTION
Bubblenomics
Bubblenomics 2

SATIRE
Another Modest Proposal

VISIT LAWRENCE ONLINE

LawrenceRowe.com

THE
FOUNDING
FATHERS
RETURN

Part the First

Lawrence Rowe

New York

Published in the United States of America by MDR Press.

ISBN-13: 978-0-9767668-3-4

The Founding Fathers Return may be purchased at special bulk quantity discounts for educational or promotional use. For information, e-mail: specialmarkets@mdrpress.com.

First paperback printing: July, 2020.

10 9 8 7 6 5 4 3

For My Mother

PREFACE

It is a contentious time in America. Liberty is waning. Present leaders seem unequal to the challenges which America faces. At this precarious juncture in United States history, the wisdom of the Founding Fathers is more relevant than ever.

I have spent years studying America's Founding Fathers via primary sources and am awed by the prescience of their observations, many of which might have been uttered today rather than centuries ago. *The Founding Fathers Return* offers readers the singular opportunity to hang out with the Founders in the present day, to get to know them, and to solve America's problems with them.

America is great, but its problems run deep. True solutions are neither simple nor easy. This journey with the Founders in the present will be a long one spanning several volumes, but it will also be entertaining and enlightening. I hope you will enter the veil with America's Founding Fathers and embark upon their Odyssey with them.

LR
04Jul2020

ACKNOWLEDGEMENTS

America's Founding Fathers are among the greatest individuals to ever trod the Earth. Portraying them accurately is a responsibility I take extremely seriously, one which requires massive time and effort, as well as the help of others.

I prefer privy. The people who have helped me return the Founding Fathers know who they are, what they have done, and how thankful I am.

I am especially thankful to Karie Diethorn, Chief Curator of Independence National Historical Park, who provided information which was indispensable for writing the Constitutional Convention in immediate scene.

INTRODUCTION

A significant portion of *The Founding Fathers Return: Part the First* takes place at the Constitutional Convention of 1787, the seminal event of the last several centuries. No one has ever written the Constitutional Convention in immediate scene as novel chapters—until now. Understanding the Constitution and government that our Founders intended, and how and where it succeeded and failed, is essential to solving America's present problems.

America's Founding Fathers were not Gods, but rather imperfect mortals with foibles. I have written the Founders as I found them in primary sources, warts and all. This includes some curdling portrayals of their racism and chauvinism. My brutally realistic depiction of antiquated norms should not be construed as approval or advocation of them.

Spelling, punctuation, and grammar irregularities in *The Founding Fathers Return* are intentional. Though these irregularities may seem strange to the modern ear, and eye, they are authentic colonial usage.

If you want to know what it was truly like to be a Deputy at the Fœderal Convention of 1787, read *The Founding Fathers Return: Part the First.* I hope you enjoy this one-of-a-kind opportunity to hob and knob America's Founding Fathers and frame our Constitution of Government with them.

Your most humble and obedient servant,
Lawrence Rowe

"We hold these truths to be self-evident, that all men are created equal, that they are endowed by their Creator with certain unalienable Rights, that among these are Life, Liberty and the pursuit of Happiness. That to secure these rights, Governments are instituted among Men, deriving their just powers from the consent of the governed, That whenever any Form of Government becomes destructive of these ends, it is the Right of the People to alter or to abolish it, and to institute new Government, laying its foundation on such principles and organizing its powers in such form, as to them shall seem most likely to effect their Safety and Happiness. Prudence, indeed, will dictate that Governments long established should not be changed for light and transient causes; and accordingly all experience hath shewn, that mankind are more disposed to suffer, while evils are sufferable, than to right themselves by abolishing the forms to which they are accustomed. But when a long train of abuses and usurpations, pursuing invariably the same Object evinces a design to reduce them under absolute Despotism, it is their right, it is their duty, to throw off such Government, and to provide new Guards for their future security."

"Our new Constitution is now established, and has an appearance that promises permanency; but in this world nothing can be said to be certain, except death and taxes."

"I agree to this Constitution with all its faults, if they are such; because I think a general Government necessary for us, and there is no form of Government but what may be a blessing to The People if well administered, and believe farther that this is likely to be well administered for a course of years, and can only end in Despotism, as other forms have done before it, when the people shall become so corrupted as to need despotic Government, being incapable of any other."

"Only a virtuous people are capable of freedom."

"Rebellion to Tyrants is Obedience to God."

"I hope I shall possess firmness and virtue enough to maintain what I consider the most enviable of all titles, the character of an honest man."

"Few men have virtue to withstand the highest bidder."

"I hold the maxim no less applicable to public than to private affairs, that honesty is always the best policy."

"I consider our new Constitution as an experiment on the practicability of republican government, and with what dose of liberty man can be trusted for his own good. I am determined the experiment should have a fair trial, and would lose the last drop of my blood in support of it."

G. Washington

"The Assembly should look forward to a time, and that not a distant one, when corruption in this as in the country from which we derive our origin will have seized the heads of government and be spread by them through the body of the people; when they will purchase the voices of the people and make them pay the price."

"What country can preserve it's liberties if their rulers are not warned from time to time that their people preserve the spirit of resistance? ...The tree of liberty must be refreshed from time to time with the blood of patriots and tyrants. It is it's natural manure."

"When once a Republic is corrupted, there is no possibility of remedying any of the growing evils but by removing the corruption and restoring its lost principles; every other correction is either useless or a new evil."

Th. Jefferson

ONE

George Washington peered at Benjamin Franklin and blanched.

"By Providence! Doctor Franklin."

Washington squinted, causing gash-ed wrinkles to afform between his eyes.

"Good Doctor?" he said.

"In the flesh," Franklin said.

Washington's right hand crossed his body impulsive and made for his Sword, but it found air only and stuttered in its motion, like a person tripping. Washington glanced at his left sword hip and his eyes bulged with Surprize. He scowled and returned his attention to Franklin. Washington approached slow and cautious, a figure of lithe Musculature and a ferocious Visage. He reached out with his left hand, moving it slower as it drew nigh Franklin, as if he thought him a Ghost or mirage.

Franklin knew Washington would never harm him, but bloody Hell was he fearsome.

Right fearsome.

Franklin could not help but step backward.

Washington poked at Franklin. His prod was unexpected gentle given his Strength and gargantuan Hands. Washington seemed suprized to encounter flesh-ed resistance, however corpulent.

Franklin chuckled.

"I said in the flesh."

"You intended for Charon's ferry," Washington said, "some seven annums prior."

"Helpful to know."

"Imperturbable as ever."

"Even in Death," Franklin said.

Washington frowned, encreasing the puffiness about his lower mouth from his false Teeth. Some colour returned to his face though. Or so it seemed. The skin of Washington's face was typical ashen grey, so 'twas difficult to reckon certain.

"My hair came to Attention," Washington said. "Upon my neck especially. I was engulphed in a prodigious Flash."

"A bleu Flash," Franklin said. "As a landspout wrought of electric Fire. And here we are?"

Washington surveyed the surrounding forest.

"Where is here?" he said.

Franklin shrugged.

"The malaria," he said, "smells sweeter than that of Phila-delphiay."

"Scarce the malaria that fouler."

"No smell of shambles here. Nor tanner nor sewer nor garbage. No Shite of horse. Not even a Necessary, 'twould seem. You look elder than when I saw you last."

"Seven years elder?" Washington said

"Perspicacious question. You condescended to incarcerate the Executive?"

Washington but scowled, an emphatick indicator he had.

"You lived to see me inaugurate."

"That a question?"

"Nay."

"Yet I must answer nay," Franklin said. "For I have lived not to see you inaugurate."

Spruce shadows cloaked a Figure as he approached the clearing. He was tall. As a greater portion of him grew visible, his lankiness became self-evident, though 'twasn't that of a frontiersman. To Franklin, the figure's incoordinate lankiness seemed that of a Scholar or Phylosopher.

"Gentlemen?" the figure said.

The voice was soft, so soft 'twas difficult to hear, but Franklin discerned an effeminate quality, even though manifest male.

"How does the afternoon?" the figure said.

The voice was closer, clearer, and Franklin recognized it nigh immediate.

'Twas Thomas!

His old friend Thomas.

As habitual, Thomas had a loose, shackling Air about him. His incoordinate movements conveyed not just joy and optimism, but a youthful Exuberance.

"George?" Thomas said. "Doctor?"

"Yea," Washington and Franklin said in unison.

"How is it," Thomas said, "that you are both still a living?"

"I was about to put the same to Doctor Fr—"

As Thomas Jefferson absented shadow, Washington's reply died and he froze.

"You're antient," Franklin said.

Thomas smiled wistful, showing but little of his teeth.

"Aye, Good Doctor. Antient though thankful not infirm."

Franklin was as intrigued as he was surpriz'd. He was brought to bed in 1706, Washington in 1732, and Thomas in 1743. The Thomas he knew was thirty-seven annums his junior, and middling age-ed.

"I was subsumed in a whirlwind Electric," Thomas said, "Indigo as of Lightning, perhaps tending to a lilac or white. 'Twas fascinating. And affrightening. Not just affrightening, terrific. Right terrific. I felt my hairs a tin—"

Thomas seemed to observe recognition on Washington and Franklin's faces and truncated his intercourse.

"I may be elder," Thomas said, "but you've both been dead for decades."

"I've no memory of dying," Franklin said.

"Nor I," Washington said.

Shock saturated Franklin as he confronted the supernatural implications of his circumstances. Their circumstances. Judging by their consterned visages, Thomas and Washington experienced similar Feelings.

"I must be ripe for Bedlam," Thomas said.

The Priory of Saint Mary of Bethlehem, or The Bethlehem Royal Hospital, was the first lunatick Asylum in Britain. Bedlem or Bedlam were abbreviates of Bethlehem.

"If you are ripe," Franklin said, "then I am rotten, tho' I think both circumstances improbable. I have never heard of a case of collective Lunacy, the delusions of Empire not with standing. Let us meet crisis with Temper and consider rational explanations."

Thomas chuckled nervous

"Our situation," he said, "seems scarce rational."

Washington nodded grim. He peered at Franklin, and into him seeming, with eyes cold and prædatory. Prodigious cold and prædatory.

"When did we first acquaint?" Washington said.

"1755. At the humble Frederick Tavern."

"'Twas pleasing to intercourse alone."

"Nay," Franklin said. "'Twas the French and Indian War. We counciled General Braddock and planned the investment of Fort Duquesne."

"Our first correspondency?"

"1756. About a post Route betweenst Winchester and Philadelphiay."

"My first action when I arrived in Philadelphiay for the Fœderal Convention?"

"You called upon me," Franklin said. "We ha'n't met in over a decade and you wished to renew our Society."

"You hosted a dinner for Deputies in Convention assembled. To what end?"

"To broker a Compromise betweenst the little States and large States upon the mode of Representation."

"What spirits were served?" Washington said.

"A cask of Porter an English friend had sent."

"'Twas marginal, as I recall."

"Nay. The company agreed unanimous that 'twas the best Porter they had ever tasted."

Franklin chuckled.

"Am I in the Cockpit again?"

Washington ignored the quip.

"The Weissenstein letter?" he said.

"A crown Attempt to subvert our Revolution by proffering titles and lifetime pensions to Americay's leaders."

"My pension quantum?"

"The monetary quantums affixed to our Names were left a blank," Franklin said. "'Twas presumed that we were to determine the price of our Principles, draw them in the blanks, and return the letter."

"My Title?"

"If you abandoned the American Cause," Franklin said, "you was to be commissioned a British Leftenant General."

"My observation when we intercoursed of it in privy years later?"

"Ironical," Franklin said. "One of your childhood Dreams was a British Generalship, but you never fancied it would be proffered so ignoble."

Washington nodded.

"Who was Charles de Weissenstein?"

"A pseudonym," Franklin said. "His letter arrived anonymous at my doorstep in June of 1778. French magistrates never determined his identity, but certain phrasings led me to conclude the

letter was drawn by king George himself. Is the Inquisition compleat, George? Doubt you I myself yet? Or shall you construct a
Rack or Pillory and make enquiries at your leisure?"

Washington's eyes softened. Franklin's characteristic wit
seemed to drain his last remnants of Suspicion. Washington
inquisited Thomas, who answered all questions true.

"Neither of you wishes to question me?" Washington said.

Washington pronounced neither in the common stile, as
nigh-ther, that the "nigh" rhymed with high and the "ther"
rhymed with were.

"Your appearance, knowledge, and characteristic Caution are
ample proof," Thomas said.

"Which aristocrat's daughter was the first Sex I seduced?"
Franklin said. "To what University did I matriculate? What
General inspired my second Ballad? When encountred we Mis-
tress Silence Dogood?"

Washington rolled his eyes. Thomas chuckled. Franklin's
early Encounters were with low Women, he had been too Poor
to compleat Grammar School much less attain to University, the
poem he published when turned of twelve was about Blackbeard
the Pirate, and Mrs. Silence Dogood was his first nom de plume.

Washington suffered several more batterys of Franklin's
sarcastic Inquisition, but rebelled eventual, interjecting when
Franklin paused between Phrases.

"Are we in Elysium?" Washington said.

"If we don't remember dying," Franklin said, "heaven would
seem an illogical presumption."

"You presume a person would remember passing," Washington said.

"I must adhere to such Axiom," Franklin said, "until I intercourse someone dead who disproves it."

"Perhaps you do so now," Washington said.

"Perhaps isn't proof."

"Aye," Thomas said. "But how else could you both be live?"

"If we ha'n't died," Franklin said, "the mere act of living 'tis no Marvel."

"Easy argued, Good Doctor," Thomas said. "You didn't live to see me pass."

Franklin wanted to enquire about his "Death," but felt the peculiars, which was to say the particulars, secondary for the moment.

"If this not Elysium," Washington said, "we is vulnerable."

As Washington scrutinized the surrounding forest, his underbite jutted and his jaw set itself in a rigid Line.

Franklin felt a stab of Fear. In uncharted wilderness, Savages were the paramount concern. Every American knew of their Terrours and Atrocities. Savages butchered pregnant Sexes, raped those unseeded, brain'd children, and defiled the dispatched with their infamous Scalping. Franklin and Thomas had associated with Savages in peaceful settings, but only Washington had faced them in Combat.

Franklin imagined Savages lurking the surrounding forest, just without View. Their animalesque war Whoops would pierce the bravest Heart as easy as the air. Savages would sprint effortless through the woods, ducking trees and other obstacles without slowing, as if they were forest appendages rather than men. Franklin and Thomas would have their throats sliced in a Blink, chest cavities hatchet'd like firewood, without Savages breaking stride. If not fortunate enough to expire immediate, they would be scalped whilst still a living.

"No sword," Washington said, "no musket, no pistol, not even a bloody Bodkin."

Thomas fixated upon the forest, scrutinizing it with the practis'd eye of a Naturalist.

"Spruce," he said. "Disperse-ed right sparse. Not a one of Virginia's hard Woods."

"The malaria feels thinner," Franklin said. "And dryer."

"These aren't the forests of my Country," Thomas said. "Nor the East."

By his Country, Thomas meant Virginia.

"Where are we then?" Washington said.

Thomas shielded his eyes with his hand and peered up at the sky.

"The sun is further East and brighter than 'twas at Monticello. For me, morning has become afternoon."

"I need not hazard sidereal Estimates," Franklin said "My Philadelphiay evening is now day."

"Unless my latitude altered," Washington said, "the Spring I left 'tis now Fall. Tho' we have greater Concerns than the climate. The blew Flashes we all seem to have experienced may attract Savages. We must absent this region."

"Could others intend?" Franklin said. "Ought we a wait them?"

"Search as we absent," Washington said. "But absent we must. Immediate."

Military matters were Washington's purview. Franklin obeyed without question, and saw Thomas prepared to do the same.

"We must be wary of Ambuscades of Indians," Franklin said. "From constant practice, they are dextrous in laying and executing them."

"Saint Clair," Thomas said.

"Doctor Saint Clair?" Franklin said. "The Physick?"

"General Saint Clair to me," Washington said. "During my Presidency, I appointed him Commander of an expedition that established a road and chain of military Posts threw the Northwest Territory. I cautioned him to be wary of Ambuscades, but nine Hundred of his fourteen Hundred were decimate by one just before dawn."

"Your Presidency," Franklin said.

He smiled.

Washington scowled.

"Saint Clair's annihilation," Thomas said, "was the worst defeat Americay ever suffered to Indians."

"The deaths was grievous vexing," Washington said, "but Congress' formal enquiry exacerbated the Debauch. I have given ambuscade Warnings to every officer under my command in the Wilderness, and shall now heed my own Counsel. Stay together and keep cluse. We all have questions, but no intercourse. Point if you spot any Thing. And remain vigilant. An instant of distraction may cost our lives."

"Dying twice," Franklin said, "would be malàpropos."

"I should think it in poor taste," Thomas said. "Though Indians might be peaceful, as they were to my Father, I as a lad, and Meriwether and William."

"You sound rotten for Bedlam now," Washington said.

"To strive for peace is Lunacy?"

"I haven't the patience for your Naïveté, this of all days."

Thomas peered past Washington and smiled pleasant, as if Washington hadn't spoke, or had proffered him Praise. Washington scowled and turned away. Franklin wondered who Meriwether and William might be, and why Washington and Thomas seemed at odds, but such matters were secondary for the moment.

As Franklin followed Washington and crept toward the forest, his disease increased. Unarmed, in dress that made them as conspicuous as redcoats, they would be Fodder for aggressive Heathens if any were nearby. Franklin was nigh a Cripple, Thomas now an old man, and even Washington was no match for a small scout Party.

Yet Franklin was comforted by Washington's presence. Washington would face even the direst predicaments with steadfast Valour, and the certain knowledge he was incapable of Fear helped Franklin quell his.

Washington paused momentary at the clearing edge and glared at his civilian compatriots.

"If combat ensues," he said, "expect not mercy. Warring Savages have nothing human about them except the shape."

FRANKLIN FOLLOWED WASHINGTON a short distance in silence. They exited a Break in the woods. A mountain containing four Faces was visible in the distance.

"Stab my Vitales!" Franklin said. "That's you. Both of you. Even a purblind old Fool like me can see sculptures so colossal."

Washington and Thomas gaped at their stone reflections.

Neither man spoke.

Nor moved.

The hilltop remained silent and still, save the shrill whistling of the Wind.

Eventually, Washington glanced at Thomas and then the sculpture of Thomas, alternating his Gaze between man and sculpture rapid and repeated. Thomas did the same to Washington. Neither man acknowledged the other's Glances.

After the comparisons concluded, the silence persisted. Washington and Thomas remained transfixed by the mountain mirror.

Franklin's exclusion enabled him to compare both faces with their sculptures, but this was a trifle a consolation. He realized he was probably viewing a Monument, and though he felt stung by the slight of omission, he could not resent men of Washington and Thomas' calibre in anything but twinges.

Franklin's fascination with the sculptures waned before his companions did, but he spoke not. Doing so seemed sacrilegious. Washington or Thomas ought break the silence.

Franklin watched his two Friends. He wondered what they were thinking, what they would say. He wondered what he would have thought or said, and strangely, had no conception.

As the Wind abated, Thomas turned his head, faced Washington, and waited for him to meet his Gaze.

"We are now Sphinxes," Thomas said.

"You have always been a Sphinx," Washington said.

Thomas smiled, bemuse-ed, without showing any of his teeth.

Washington and Thomas seemed to savour a moment and a Bond that required no enunciation, and was beyond words even if it did.

Like all leaders, Franklin wanted to be remembered, and he knew Washington and Thomas did too, Washington especially. For they knew that History forgets men, even mighty great men. Bloated by the inexorable accumulation of events, it distilled, then pruned, and finally amputated.

Jesus, Buddha.

Socrates, Confucius.

Alexander, Cæsar.

Out of the myriad annals of Antiquity, only a handful of names had survived and remained in the collective human memory. Fixating upon their sculptures, Washington and Thomas had to realize that they were now a part of this Junto, and would stand as a nigh permanent fixture of History. Long after their identities and accomplishments were forgotten, their visages would endure.

"A greater Homage than I might have hoped," Washington said, "even in my most fanciful imaginings."

"Incalculable greater," Thomas said. "We are as close to Immortality as any human ought dare."

"Perhaps cluser," Washington said.

Yet he smiled.

"Congratulations," Franklin said.

"Thank you, Good Doctor," Thomas said. "Though you ought also be sculpted."

Franklin waved a hand dismissive.

"I suspect the answer to this question," Washington said to Thomas. "But I must still put it. Were any of these sculptures begun during your Life? After our Deaths?"

"Sculpting a mountain? The Americay I left could not fashion such a Wonderment. Not with ten thousand Negroes or a hundred Houdons."

Houdon was Jean-Antoine Houdon, the most renowned Sculptor in the World. He had sculpted Franklin, Washington, and Thomas, and other Eminents such as Catherine the Great, Frederick the Great, and Voltaire.

"As I feared," Washington said.

He scanned the forest behind them, and seemed more nervous than before.

"Who are the other two Sculptures?" Franklin said.

Silence.

"Where are we?" Washington said.

Yet another Silence, the longest yet. And a chilling, ghastly Calm. Even the air seemed still.

Franklin peered at Washington and Thomas simultaneous. When he spoke, his words seemed distant to him, nigh Æthereal, as if uttered by another.

"When are we?"

FRANKLIN WAS UNCERTAIN how long he stood dumb-founded. Confronting the possibility and impossibility of intending through Time, he had lost reckon of Time. It might have been thirty Seconds or three Minutes.

Washington's close-mouthed exhalation was more of a Grunt. His nods accelerated, and then he began shaking his head sudden. His eyes grew distant yet intense, as if he were peering into the very fabrick of the sky itself.

"Bloody Hell," Washington said. "'Tis Impossible. It cannot be."

Franklin watched Washington focus on his sculpture, which seemed to refute all he spoke without uttering a syllable. Washington opened his mouth and formed his lips, as if to speak, but closed it sudden and remained silent.

"'Tis but a Dream I shall soon respite," Thomas said, "and laugh about over a crystal of Bordeaux."

Washington and Thomas' denials seemed a compensatory Crutch to Franklin, to ease their Pain of acceptancy, and a half-hearted one at that. Neither man seemed to believe what he was uttering.

"Was I shoed in the head by a horse?" Thomas said. "Resort I too much Laudanum? A hallucination perchance?"

"Are you ripe for Bedlam now?" Franklin said.

Washington chuckled. Franklin joined him, and then Thomas, yet the levity was fleeting. Nervous glances were soon exchanged. The severity of his Predicament, of their Predicament, became manifest to Franklin. Realization seeped into him and memories pierced him, flooding his Mind. Memories Franklin hadn't known were memories until this moment.

Franklin remembered Madam Helvetius, his late-life Love, who he'd left in Paris and always dreamt of seeing again. Also his home in Philadelphia, the city itself, his phylosopher Friends, his daughter Sally, and his flock of grandchildren.

Franklin saw sadness and introspection on the visages of Washington and Thomas. What were they remembering? Washington probably remembered his wife Martha and Mount Vernon, farms he would never ride to oversee again, projects unfinished, and perhaps his step Children. Thomas nigh certain remembered Monticello, probably also his daughters Martha and Mary, and his grandchildren. Had he ever married again? Had he taken a new Wife who he pined the loss of? Probably not.

Franklin remained immersed in his nostalgic Trance for a stretch, and then willed it away. He experienced a string of fanciful Denials more heartfelt than those of Washington and Thomas, yet refused to give them Voice.

"The people and homes we loved are probly gone," Thomas said.

"Permanent?" Washington said.

"What else is gone?" Franklin said

Yet another Silence.

A despondent Silence.

A consuming Silence.

Franklin realized there were more optimistic potentials, but the symmetry inherent in the Sphinx Metaphor was alluring. Not desireable, but alluring. The Sphinx had outlived antient Ægypt. Had this mountain Sculpture outlived the United States?

Contemplation of the American Death was sobering. Franklin, Washington, Thomas, and numerate others had hoped their creation might endure, ushering in a transcendent Golden Age that would spread Liberty, Enlightenment, and Prosperity across the globe. Had such a Golden Age come to America at all? Come and passt?

The silence expanded, and might have become an engulphing Chasm, had it not been interrupted by a child's gleeful Shriek.

"HEY UP THERE!"

The voice was squeaky and prepubescent, yet unmistakable male.

"You guys! Hey!"

Franklin glanced down the hill they stood atop, and saw a lad jumping up and down waving his arms. Two adults stood behind him, but their reactions could not be gauged.

"Shall we treat?" Franklin said.

"But scant choice," Washington said

"Hey up there!" the Lad said.

"Hey down there," Franklin said.

This was all the encouragement the lad needed. Indifferent to the Grade of the hill, he sprinted toward his Quarry.

"The father appears unarmed," Franklin said.

"Appears," Washington said. "I scruple to believe a father goes about forest utter defenceless with his Wife and Childe."

"Gander the lad's Dress," Thomas said.

"Queer," Washington said. "Right queer."

"Never seen such odd cloathes," Franklin said.

"Or even heard tell," Thomas said. "Not even in Arabia or the far East."

The Lad barreled up and skidded to a Stop.

"Great costumes!" he said. "Man oh man. What realistic— costumes!"

His lungs heaved and he spoke in gasps.

"They don't look—bran freakin'—new like—those cheese dick ones—you always see—in parades."

The Lad spat, and then peered up at Washington, whose towering physical Presence commanded his attention first.

Standing 6'3" high, fit and straight-backed even in old Age, Washington had the natural grace of an athlete and a magnetic Stature. He exuded strength. Washington was thick-boned, with unusual long arms and legs, monstrous hands, and a rugged Frame that rippled with muscle. His face seemed engineer'd for Anger; a pugnacious, mountain of a nose rose from the centre of its landmass, pockmarks and sunlines formed valleys, and his hairline receded appreciable atop the continental shelf. Washington's underbite was pronounced, his pursed lips suggested Impatience or Irritation, and his jaw and lower cheeks seemed puff-ed, nigh swollen. But as most everyone who met him observed, his most striking feature was his eyes. Wolfish blue orbs that seemed crueller than Cunningham and were proper murderous.

The Lad gaped while he craned his head to and fro repeated, comparing Washington to his sculpture.

"You look just like him!" the Lad said.

Franklin exchanged a guarded Smile with Washington while the lad compared Thomas to his sculpture.

"Man," the Lad said. "Man oh man. You look just like Jefferson too! 'Cept maybe older. Man, what great costumes!"

The parents seemed a customed to their son's Ebullience and didn't expedite to rejoin him. Strolling at their leisure, they summited the hill after a stretch, and their intercourse could be heard as they approached.

"I can see why Washington, Lincoln, and Jefferson are on the mountain," the father said. "But why include Roosevelt?"

Franklin was familiar with the Roosevelt and Lincoln names. American sugar magnate Isaac Roosevelt had donated prodigious sums to the Revolution, and was President of the Bank of New York at presen—

Franklin amended himself.

Isaac Roosevelt had been President of the Bank of New York in 1787. Major General Benjamin Lincoln was one of Washington's more esteem'd officers. Levi Lincoln was a Massachusetts attorney of some repute, a zealous Abolitionist who had sued for the freedom of a Slave in Massachusetts and won it, thereby effecting Abolition in the state without it legislating. Though Franklin was pleased by the general Abolition, he wondered at the wisdom of the Judiciary in essence legislating. Were the Lincoln and Roosevelt of which the parents intercoursed the distant Posterity of Isaac Roosevelt, Benjamin Lincoln, or Levi Lincoln?

"Who would you replace Roosevelt with?" the wife said. "And if you say Nixon again, I swear to God I'll scream."

Franklin also knew the Nixon name. Brigadier General John Nixon was a Hero of the American victory at Bunker Hill. At the Battle of Bemis Heights, which was reckoned a part of the decisive Saratoga Victory, a cannonball had passed but inches from Nixon's head, popping his ear Drums and deranging his vision permanent. Was the Nixon the wife spoke of the Posterity of General Nixon?

The parents quieted as they neared. Greetings were exchanged. Like their son, they noticed Washington first, compared him to the mountain, and then focused on Thomas.

At 6'2", Thomas was only an inch shorter than the muscled Washington, but lankiness of body and face made him seem slighter. His large hands, gangly limbs, and jutting neck conveyed Awkwardness. Though still well carriaged, he had bent slight with Age, and his stature seemed more aristocratic than athletick. His serene face was angular; its most prominent features were a long, thin nose that was decided large and triangular when viewed from the side, and Freckles that confettied his pale skin. Thomas' introspective, nigh effeminate lips conveyed Kindness and Mirth with subtlety, and his bushy eyebrows stood ready to accentuate expressions of Skepticism or Scorn. His unusual fine hair had once been red, yet was now grey, and he still wore it longer that it covered his ears and neck. Wistful, engaging hazel eyes hinted at prodigious Intensity, Complexity, and Intelligence.

The father compared Thomas to his sculpture.

"The resemblance is uncanny," he said.

He seemed nigh unnerve-ed.

Whilst the family examined Washington and Thomas, Franklin examined them. The father was White but had hair in the stile of a Black, one who had not barbered in some years. The curls of his hair were larger than those of a Black though, and his hair Stile not so uniform spherick as that of a Black. His

Sex seemed unadulterate and plain, as if a farmer's wife, though she was too pale and conveyed too mighty a sense of Ease to be such. Her form was planar and she was exceeding thin. The child suckling her mammaries would want for Milk and be consigned to Thirst, right certain.

Some Thing about the air of the couple made Franklin reckon them Phylosophers or Scholars. Both seemed intelligent, and the trait appeared to have been magnify'd in their inquisitive son, who had his mother's Body and his father's Hair.

The Lad stood before Franklin and examined him. Franklin saw the lad's eyes dart about his form, lingering upon his double Spectacles, cocked hat, knee-length suitcoat, neckcloath, the white silk stock drawers upon his lower legs, his buckled shoes, and cetera.

"You're Ben Franklin," the Lad said.

"I am indeed me," Franklin said.

"We've been reading about you guys in history class."

History class.

Franklin was careful to maintain to an indifferent expression.

"Can I try on your bifocals?" the Lad said.

"Nay," Franklin said.

Bifocal. Having two foci. A curious reckon for double Spectacles, though a pleasing one. Franklin preferenced an industrious word which performed the Labour of two.

"The four half circles of glass look cool," the Lad said. "Archaic. I won't break them."

"If you did, I'd be proper rooked. A grievous rooked. Sorry, Lad, but I'm nigh purblind absent my spectacles."

"Nigh what?"

The Lad laughed.

"Your kite experiment was cool."

"You studied it in history Class as well?"

"Yeah," the Lad said.

"The electric Fluid is fascinating," Franklin said. "I was never before engaged in any Study that so totally engross'd my attention and my time. Tho' I am chagrined we have been unable to produce any Thing of use to mankind from the electric Fluid so a—"

The Lad smiled at Franklin with a certain Condescension, as if he a Simpleton. Franklin truncated his discourse. Some Thing of use to mankind had been wrought from the electric Fluid, it seemed.

"Did you really touch the kite key with your finger?" the Lad said.

"Nay," Franklin said. "I presented my knucle to the key and perceived a very evident Spark."

"Presented? So did you touch the key or not?"

"I held my knucle cluse to the key without contacting it. A Spark leapt from the key to my knucle."

"Lept. You mean leaped?"

"I mean leapt, but yea."

"Yay? You mean yes?"

"Yea. Yes."

"Did the spark shock you?"

Franklin nodded rapid, with vigour.

"I felt the electric Fire."

"When the lightning struck your kite, why weren't you electrocuted?"

Electrocute. Electro combined with acute? Acute meant clever or cunning. Though the electric Fire was indeed cunning when experimented upon, Franklin doubted this the lad's Meaning. Electro and prosecute? Perhaps, Franklin had been prosecuted by the electric Fire, right certain, though thankful never for it. Persecute? Execute? Execute. Electrocute, to execute with electric Fire?

"No lightning struck my kite," Franklin said, "or I would have been dispatched nigh certain, as a Turkey. When Thunder Clouds came over the Kite, the pointed Wire atop it drew the electric Fire from them."

"My history book didn't mention all that. I thought your kite was struck by lightning."

"Had it been," Franklin said, "I would have taken the dirt Nap ere the Revolution."

"Air the Revolution? On TV? That'd be cool."

"Before the Revolution. Well before."

"Wonder what else my history book gets wrong," the Lad said. "Lightning could have struck your kite though. Couldn't it have?"

"Aye," Franklin said. "I took precautions, but aye."

"Man," the Lad said. "You sure are brave."

He smiled at Franklin with admiration, and examined him as he had Washington and Thomas.

Franklin knew he was a pityable Sight, yet was so long accustomed to being so, he had become not just indiff'rent to Embarrassment, but nigh incapable of it. Gandering him, the lad probably saw an amorphous man whose physique hinted at long-abandoned Vigour. Franklin's gut was a Globe, his fingers and calves pudge-ed, and he knew his breech-stretching buttocks resembled ham Halves. The Lad's gaze lingered on the Drapes of chin fat which hunched above Franklin's cravat. And 'twas not as if Franklin was handsome of the face. He felt his enormous, elongate cranium a fitting Capstone to his body, yet was never sure if this more insulting to body or head.

"You know what's weird?" the Lad said.

"A novelty or two certain occur," Franklin said.

Washington's face tensed a trifle.

"Washington and Jefferson kind of look like great Leaders," the Lad said. "You don't."

Franklin let out a Laugh hearty and long.

The Lad seemed confuz'd, perhaps expecting Franklin to grow warm.

"Where's Lincoln?" the father said. "And Roosevelt?"

'Twas an excellent question, by Franklin's reckon. Which sculpture was Lincoln? The face with the mustache or the beard? The mustached Gentleman seemed to passing resemble Isaac Roosevelt. Was the bearded Gentleman a Lincoln?

"Mister Lincoln," Franklin said, "was halfway to Concord yesternight."

"You mean he's on vacation?" the father said. "Travelling to Concord?"

"I mean he was pissed."

"He left for Concord because he was angry? About what?"

Franklin pursed his lips. He saw Thomas smirk ever so slight.

"Mister Lincoln," Franklin said, "imbibed too many strong Beers and spiritous Liquors yesternight. He is oft tardy."

"Oh," the father said.

"Lincoln's a drunk?" the Lad said.

He erupted in laughter.

His father glared at him.

The Lad ceased laughing.

"And Roosevelt?" the father said.

"We know not of Roosevelt," Thomas said.

"Why are you here?" the mother said. "You work for the park?"

"Why are we now?" Franklin said.

"Huh?" the mother said.

"Aye," Washington said. "We work for the Park."

The Lad approached Washington and stood before him. He craned his head upward and looked into Washington's eyes, gulped sudden, then took several Steps back.

"Did you ever tell a lie?" the Lad said.

"Aye," Washington said.

"How many?"

"Scant few."

"Give me an example," the Lad said.

Washington scowled and glared at the lad, who took another Step back.

"We could skip the example. You won't get mad if I ask something personal, will you?"

"Nay."

"You aren't lying, are you?"

Washington scowled and glared.

"Just checking."

The Lad extended his palms outward and backed up. He seemed to want to be certain that Washington wasn't warm, so waited a stretch.

Franklin wondered at the word check, which meant to arrest, stop, retard. Or perhaps used to mean. The Lad seemed to construe checking as asking or appraising.

"Why's your face scarred?" the Lad said.

"The Pox," Washington said. "When turnt of nineteen, I intended to Barbados with my brother Lawrence, where I contracted the disease. Lawrence was ravaged by Consumption and the warm climate was viewed as beneficial."

"The Pox?" the Lad said.

"Smallpox," Washington said.

"Consumption?" the Lad said.

"Tuberculosis," the mother said.

"Tuberkulosis?" Washington said.

"Consumption," Franklin said.

Washington glared at Franklin.

"What's smallpox?" the Lad said. "Is it like chicken pox?"

Washington's stern visage belied Surprize. Smallpox was the world's most fearsome disease. Its epidemics had killed Millions and left Millions more blind or disfigured. Everyone knew of Smallpox.

Or had known.

"Smallpox is sim'l'r to fowl Pox," Franklin said. "Except it w—"

"Except its smaller?" the Lad said.

"Except 'twill oft kill you."

"I was laid low nigh two fourtnights by The Pox," Washington said, "and scarce survive-ed."

The Lad shrugged. His disinterest seemed compleat, as if the Smallpox some irrelevant abstraction.

"What about that scar on your left cheek," the Lad said. "That wasn't caused by pox, was it?"

"Nay," Washington said. "An incision to treat an abscessed tooth."

The Lad's jaw dropped.

"They cut you open like that just to get at a tooth?"

Washington nodded nonchalant.

"Paintings of you don't show the scars," the Lad said.

"Artists can be sycophants," Washington said.

Franklin rolled his eyes.

"And their subjects scarce object Flattery," he said. "My moles were rare painted."

The Lad stared at Franklin overt, the parents discreet. Franklin pointed out the moles on his left cheek and below lip.

"Why aren't you wearing your military uniform?" the Lad said.

"I resigned my Commission long ago," Washington said.

"Long, long, long ago," Franklin said.

Washington glared at Franklin momentary, then smiled serene.

"I'm a Planter now, not a General. Nor President."

"Don't you have a musket or a sword?" the Lad said.

"Nay," Washington said. "Unfortunate that. Grievous unfortunate."

"Maybe they sell them at the gift shop."

"Hopefully."

Washington glanced at Thomas and Franklin momentary.

"And thank you, Lad."

"You're welcome. Say, who do you guys think was the greatest President?"

"Must we chuse a President sculpted upon the mountain?" Franklin said.

Franklin wondered if Lincoln and Roosevelt had been President. Had Thomas?

"Pick any President in history," the Lad said. "'Cept Nixon or Clinton."

Franklin also knew the Clinton name. George Clinton was a Brigadier General during the Revolution and was the present Governour of New Yo—had been the Governour of New York in 1787.

"Why are Nixon and Clinton excluded?" Franklin said.

"'Cause they're like the worst Presidents we've ever had. Duh. Even my parents agree about that."

"Maybe not the worst Presidents," the mother said.

"Top five for sure," the father said.

"Clinton wasn't that bad."

"He was only the third President ever impeached."

"Starr's investigation was a charade."

"If Clinton had a sense of decency," the father said, "he would have resigned and spared the nation the mudslinging."

The parents continued their intercourse, which seemed to denigrate into Agitation. Franklin listened. During a brief moment when neither the lad nor parents seemed to be watching, Franklin exchanged a glance with Washington and Thomas. They seemed as captivate as him.

"I wanna know what the Founding Fathers think!" the Lad said.

The parents quieted.

"Well," the Lad said. "Who was the greatest President?"

"Washington," Thomas said.

"Jefferson," Washington said.

Neither man seemed impassioned of his answer.

"And you?" the Lad said to Franklin.

Franklin feigned deliberation.

"Lincoln," he said.

"Lincoln's my Dad's choice too."

"He did win the Civil War and reunify the union," the father said.

A Civil War? Wrought by regulating Commerce?

Reunify the Union?

"Ought we not term it reunionfy?" Franklin said.

The parents chuckled. Franklin glanced back at Washington and Thomas. They seemed as concerned as him, though careful not to savour of Surprize. Were they true insurprized, or but affecting?

"Why'd you choose Lincoln?" the father said to Franklin.

"The same reasons you did."

"Washington and Jefferson aren't as great as everyone thinks," the mother said. "Jefferson especially. He was too much of a hypocrite to be considered one of the greatest Presidents."

"Thomas Jefferson belongs on Rushmore," the father said. "I agree about the moral flaws, but don't forget the Declaration of Independence, Lewis and Clark expedition, and Louisia—"

"I know what Jefferson did," the wife said.

She glanced at her son momentary, and then whispered.

"And who."

Rare was the man of greater self Government than Thomas Jefferson. He had to be mild disappointed, at the least, yet presented a façade of compleat Indifference.

Rushmore. Montirushmore? Mont Rushmore? Had it been hastened or wrought with superlative Expedition? Perhaps not. There were gentlemen and familys of New York surnamed Rushmore. Had a Rushmore patronized the Monument?

"So Clinton was maligned unfairly," the husband said. "But Jefferson is too much of a hypocrite to be considered a great President?"

The wife rolled her eyes. The husband laughed.

It was right fascinate, to see a Sex so forward, so Frenchify'd. This was perhaps the most glaring proof that they—

That they—

That they were in—

Franklin felt a queer reticence to even formulate the words.

The wife seemed to have alluded to carnal Intercourse.

With who?

Maria Cosway?

Cosway was the beguiling but tragic painter Thomas had fallen in love with while American Minister to France. Franklin knew of no one else embarrassing. Thomas was hardly a Libertine.

But Cosway didn't fit. Though she was married, Thomas was widowed and unbetroth-ed, and they had been in France, where Adultery and Whoring was as ubiquitous as wine. Even if one made the optimistic assumption that the chaste Thomas rogered Cosway, such was no ruinous scandal, and in most instances, 'twould be no scandal at all. Unless morals had grown much more rigid.

Whilst his parents resumed their intercourse with what seemed typical vigour, the lad approached Thomas.

"Would you sign the Declaration of Independence for me?" he said.

The Lad pronounced Declaration of Independency in the uncommon mode, terminating the inflection of Independency as to rhime with pence or whence. He produced a copy of the Declaration of Independency and unrolled it ceremonious. It seemed to be drawn on vellum parchment, yet 'twas too thin to be such, and rather had the texture of paper. Curious thin paper which light penetrated as if a stained church glass. The parchment was also much smaller than that of the original Declaration. A ditto that had been drawn or printed in the knack Shop of which the lad made mention?

Thomas examined the tiny reproduction and smiled, showing but little of his teeth. He was general mild in his expression of emotion, but the triumphant Gleam of his eyes said much.

He seemed elated that the Declaration had survived.

"Have you a quill?" Thomas said.

The father reached within the pocket of his queer cut trousers, which were of a geane Fustian fabrick, or perhaps an inferior Hemp, and dyed of an Indigo that might have been left to fade in the sun for years. The father handed Thomas a thin, cylindrick Object. Glanced but fleeting and superficial, it seemed to be a pencil, a thin rod of black Lead formed into a case of dealwood or cedarwood, for sketching. Except 'twasn't wrought of wood, but rather a darkish substance with a curious sheen the likes of which Franklin had never seen. It wasn't metal, leather, nor even porcelain nor elephant Fang, nor any other material of which Franklin had knowledge.

Thomas held the pen gingerly. His fingers were effeminate and gangly, and seemed to close about the pen as the legs of a wolf Spider about a mouse or bird. Thomas pressed the tip of his finger upon the pointed end of the pen, but no ink flowed.

"You have to click it," the Lad said.

Thomas handed the pen to the lad. He pressed down upon the top of the pen, causing a protrusion without it to retract within. A sound, a click, was emanate by the pen when its protrusion pressed. The Lad released the protrusion, which remained retracted within the body of the pen. The Lad pressed the protrusion again and it sprung back without. He pressed the protrusion again and it retracted within. As the Lad plunged and unplunged the protrusion, for the benefit of Thomas seeming, Franklin heard a series of rapid Clicks.

A clockwork within a quill shaft?

A clockwork pen.

Right ingenious.

Yet also right bewildering. Pens and pencils were fragile and expensive, and were usual kept in protective wood cases, when travelling especially. They were general handled with great delicacy, nigh as China Plate, a delicacy the lad and father had evidenced not. This was common Pens without clockworks, which were not Machines. How was it that the lad and father were indifferent indelicate with clockwork Pens wrought of fantastical materials, pens that must be exorbitant?

The Lad handed the pen back to Thomas. The tip of the pen was now sharper, a nib having been forced out its tip by the plunging Clockwork, seeming. The nib was not triangulate though, as Franklin a customed. Thomas aped the lad, and clicked the pen several times whilst observing it.

"These actors are brilliant," the father whispered. "It's like we just gave a caveman a Bic."

Franklin wondered what a Bick was. He also wondered at the absence of an inkwell. Bick? A Bickern, or Bick Iron? Nay. 'Twas no anvil taper nor tip. Similar to a Wick? As of a chandle? A term for an inkwell within Pen, which wicked ink to the nib by some mode? Whatever a Bick was, and how so ever the ink welled forth, was Pounce still requisite?

Thomas sought a surface to sign upon, floundered, and the lad eventual proffered his torso, forming an L shape with his body, that his back nigh parallel the ground. Thomas laid the Declaration of Independency gentle upon the lad's back, fumbling to maintain it unrolled. Franklin could not help but smirk, contrasting this neckwood Signing to the ostentate Original.

Thomas raised the clockwork pen. An instant before drawing, he paused. Thomas' eyes grew distant, introspective seeming. Remembering the momentous day?

'Twas a far from a pleasant memory. When they signed the original Declaration of Independency, exuberance was tempered by Fear, for the document was a royal Death Warrant as well as a Proclamation of Liberty.

Franklin saw signatures upon the ditto Declaration. Probably printed, not drawn. How had the signatures been etched on to the copper printing Plate? Or did a Civilization that could sculpt mountains and render clockwork pens employ a more modern mode?

Thomas signed the Declaration, slow and careful, so as not to pierce the paper, or parchment, or whatever it was, nor stain the lad's back. When he compleated signing, Thomas held the Pen up, peered at it, and nodded with satisfaction.

Thomas glanced down at his signature and his Expression grew grave. Was he pondering the prolifick Patriots whose signatures surrounded his, contrasting the original Signing with that Present, his exuberance once again tempered by Fear?

Thomas removed the Declaration from the lad's back. The Lad stood. Thomas handed the Declaration to the lad. The Lad examined it.

"Wow!" he said.

His eyes bulged.

"Your signature looks just like the real one! I mean egg freakin' zactly."

The Lad showed the parchment to his parents, who agreed. They did not seem pleased as the lad though. Rather, they seemed a trifle Suspicious. Or was Franklin conjuring Malice where none present?

"Shall I sign the Declaration?" Franklin said

"Who wants Ben Franklin's signature?" the Lad said. "Maybe if I had a kite or something."

"I helped draw the Declaration," Franklin said.

"So what? Jefferson did all the real work. Everybody knows that. Franklin and Adams just proofread. They were like secretaries. Would you sign the Declaration of Independence, Mister Washington?"

'Twas queer to hear Washington addressed as Mister. Franklin could not recollect when he had last heard such Address. People usual addressed Washington as General, General Washington, His Excellency, Your Excellency, and cetera. And perhaps President Washington, or whatever Title the Executive had been stiled.

"I sign'd not the Declaration of Independency," Washington said.

The Lad examined the Declaration.

"Huh. Whaddya know. Why didn't you sign?"

"I was already commanding the Armies."

"Did you sign the Constitution?"

"Aye."

"George Presided the Fœderal Convention," Franklin said.

"You mean the Constitutional Convention?" the Lad said.

"Aye," Washington said.

"Geez," the Lad said. "They put you in charge of everything."

Washington nodded glum.

"Well I've got the Constitution too," the Lad said. "You can all sign that."

"I signed not the Constitution of Government," Thomas said. "I was resident in France serving as American Minister when 'twas draughted."

"I shall sign after Doctor Franklin only," Washington said. "And if we might keep the Pen only."

The Lad acquiesced Washington's terms, and again proffered his back as a makeshift table. Peering at the small ditto Constitution upon the lad's torso, Franklin was affected by a peculiar déjà vu. He felt light in the head, and not just from the excess of Laudanum. 'Twas queer enough to sign the Constitution a second time, and in ditto at that, but what made it grievous unnerving was th—

"Something wrong?" the Lad said.

Franklin held the clockwork Pen, examined the sheen-ed material. It was indeed a species he had encountered not. Some new discovered Element added to the affinity Table? Some alchemy effected with chymical Liquors? The fang or flesh of some novel animal, Fish, or bird? The thin hollow Bones of a bird? Nay. 'Twasn't a bird, Fish, or animal. The pen seemed too regular and symmetrick to be a bone, or wrought of one. Whatever its origin, or nature, the material seemed light yet flexible, and devilish strong compared to the shaft of a fowl feather.

Franklin affixed his signature to the Constitution of Government. The clockwork Pen drew so much smoother than a quill as to defy Reckon. Viewing both his signatures upon the Charta, Franklin experienced the sudden disquieting sense that he had wrought something not mere unnatural, but a proper Perversion.

Franklin handed the clockwork Pen to Washington. 'Twas tiny in his gargantuan Hand. Washington peered at his sculpture a moment before signing.

When the signing compleat, the lad stood, examined the Constitution of Government, and was once again awed by the likeness of the fresh Signatures to the Original. He seemed to favour the Declaration of Independency though, and proffered it to Thomas.

"Can you read it for me?" he said.

"I don't need the Charta, Lad," Thomas said. "I could never forget the words."

Thomas smiled, showing but little of his teeth.

"When in the Course of human events," he said, "it becomes necessary for one people to dissolve the political bands which have connected them with another,"

The parents stood behind their lad. Thomas, Washington, and Franklin were in the foreground of their vantage, Monti-rushmore the background.

"And to assume among the powers of the earth, the separate and equal station to which the Laws of Nature and of Nature's God entitle them,"

The Lad followed along on the Charta.

"A decent respect to the opinions of mankind requires that they should declare the causes which impel them to the separation."

Thomas' voice was unusual soft and quiet, and though he accentuated certain syllables and paused to allow a dramatic moment of reflection between each clause, his was hardly a roaring Oratory.

It didn't have to be. The words themselves were pathetic enough and never failed to evoke emotion. Especially the pre-eminent portion of the Preamble, which resonated like a Thunderclap, causing Franklin to tingle.

"We hold these truths to be self-evident," Thomas said, "that all men are created equal, that they are endowed by their Creator with inherent and inalienable Rights, that am—"

"Wait a sec," the Lad said. "This says certain unalienable Rights."

"Apologies. I made many revisions. As did the meddlesome Congress."

Thomas remained pleasant and smiled at the lad.

"And I'm old."

"Too bad Lincoln's not here," the father whispered to the mother. "I'd love to see him recite the Gettysburg Address."

"We hold these truths to be self-evident," Thomas said. "That all men are created equal, that they are endowed by their Creator with certain unalienable Rights, that among these are Life, Liberty, and the Pursuit of Happiness."

The Lad sprouted a beaming smile and gazed at Thomas with Veneration.

"That to secure these rights," Thomas said, "Governments are instituted among Men, deriving their just powers from the consent of the governed, That whenever any Form of Government becomes destructive of these ends, it is the Right of the People to alter or to abolish it, and to institute new Government, laying its foundation on such principles and organizing its powers in such form, as to them shall seem most likely to effect their Safety and Happiness. Prud—"

"What about your slaves?" the Lad said. "Were they created equal too?"

"Nature, habit and opinion," Thomas said, "have drawn indelible lines of distinction between the two Races."

The Lad's smile fled.

"Why don't we talk about something else," the mother said. "Or to someone else."

The Lad returned to Washington.

"Did you really chop down the cherry tree?"

"I know naught of The cherry tree," Washington said. "I have chopt down A cherry tree. A few in my lifetime."

Franklin knew naught either. Nigh every Farm of the South would have an orchard, including cherry Trees, yet since they bore fruit, 'twas insensible to fell them. Franklin had heard nigh every story of Washington, upon both sides the Atlantic, many of them fabricate. Yet he had never heard tale involving a cherry Tree, fabricate or otherwise.

Washington also seemed confused by the question.

Thomas did not, and smirked fractional.

Was chopping down a cherry Tree, which was to say The cherry tree, some mythology promulgate soon after Washington's death? A mythology of which Thomas aware, but Washington ignorant? Was the chopping down of a—or The—colossal cherry Tree a fable to apotheosize Washington's awe some Strength, Vigour, and Stature?

A cherry Tree seemed a curious choice for apotheosis of Washington's strength and vigour though, as there was far larger species of trees which would be more awe some to fell, as well as numerate actual feats of Washington a far more impressive. To Franklin, Washington's signal attribute was his Character, his Honesty and Disinterest especially, but 'twas not manifest how felling a cherry Tree embody'd these.

"Are your teeth wood?" the Lad said.

"Wood?" Washington said. "Nay. What a ridiculous conceit. Why would anyone suffer wood Teeth?"

"But they're fake, right?"

"False, not fake. Wrought of hippopotamos Fangs, not wood."

"Fangs? Can you take your teeth out? I wanna see them."

Washington stiffened at this.

"Nay," he said.

Franklin knew that removing his false Teeth caused Washington discomfort. Yet Washington had suffered far more grievous Discomforts without objection or complaint. Removing his false Teeth made Washington appear feeble, and liable to be pity'd or railed, which he detested.

The Lad continued to inquisite Washington about his Teeth, oblivious of, or indifferent to, Washington's manifest Irritation. Franklin did his best not to chuckle. He reminded himself that the lad seemed to think Washington an actor, and wondered if Washington was thinking similar.

'Twas a queer intercourse though. All who knew Washington were aware that he was embarrassed of his false Teeth, and were careful to never fixate upon them, nor enquire of them, unless Washington broached the topic. Washington never did so public, and even in privy answers would be exceeding circumspect. No man Franklin had ever known, or even heard tell of, had brass enough to interrogate Washington about his false Teeth, much less ask that he proffer them up for inspection, as one might a new sword, book, or pistol.

"What was Valley Forge like?" the Lad said.

"Every idea you can form of our Distresses," Washington said, "will fall short of the reality."

The Lad asked other questions about The Forge, oblivious of, or indifferent to, Washington's manifest Reticence. The Lad pressed and pressed, invested and invested, enquired and enquired, yet Washington would say nothing more.

"Might I put a question to you Lad?" Franklin said.

"Yeah!" the Lad said. "Heck yeah!"

"May I borrow that pamphlet?"

"Sure. You can have it."

He handed it over and Franklin thanked him.

"Is that the only question you have?"

"Might you reveal the time and date?"

The Lad glanced at his watch. It was a bracelet Watch. Franklin amended himself. An armed Watch.

Franklin knew he was fumbling his language. The fair Sex only went in armed Watches, which were in essence a species of jewelry, and thus stiled bracelet Watches. All males went in common Watches, fob Watches, intended to reside in the Fob, the small pocket afront a waistcoat or breeches. Franklin had seen nigh a Thousand men and Sexes who went watch-ed, but had never seen a male who went in a bracelet Watch, not even in a single instancy. The term bracelet Watch being inapt for a male, effeminate and liable to insult, Franklin resorted to the masculine term armed Watch, but it felt foreign and misappropriate.

Not so foreign and misappropriate as the lad and his armed Watch itself, however.

The watch was undoubted the most advanced Invention in widespread usage at presen—or past as 'twere. Having been invented in the 1500s, the Watch was modern when considered against the long stretch of history and its Inventions. Clocks themselves were exorbitant, but to render them miniature was a supreme Act of Artisanship, a feat which only the most ingenious Master Clocksmiths capable.

A family in America with a Clock in its home was thought prosp'rous if not wealthy, and Clocks were dearer among the labouring folk of England and France. Watches were dearer yet. A man who purchased his own waist Watch was unequivocal wealthy, and familys often bequeathed Watches to their Posterity, fathers to they eldest sons especially.

The most inexpensive, and unreliable, Watches would cost a Labourer a month or two of his Wages, with no allowance for any other expence. An indifferent Watch still fragile and fickle would cost a Labourer a quarter annum of his Wages. A finer Watch, though certain not the crackest Stile, would cost a Labourer in excess of an annum's Wages.

Only adults exceeding wealthy went in fine Watches, and they were proper rareified upon children. Only the son of a king, noble, or merchant of fantastical Wealth went in a fine Watch. There were some three Million total Americans, and Franklin could not recollect more than a dozen children, perhaps a score at the most, who went Watch, discounting a few heirlooms of poorer folk. In all of Europe and Britain, including the Courts of Versailles, London, and cetera, Franklin had not seen a Hundred children who went Watch. Yet here stood a lad who promenaded the most advanced Watch that Franklin had ever seen.

How was the lad still drawing breath? A waist Watch within Fob was without sight, but an armed Watch was right conspicuous. A Lad promenading such a Treasure in America, Britain, France, or any portion of Civilization which Franklin had ever frequented, would have his throat sliced by Priggers or bully Ruffians, right certain.

Franklin scrutinized the armed Watch as best he could. Though circular shape-ed as a typical Watch, it was amputate, absent arms. Also absent were the perm'nent numbers about the circumference of the face which arms would typical spin about and point to. Instead the Watch contained writing within the centre of its face. The time was a number inked upon it!

How in the bloody Hell?

The watch Face contained not glass, but some Thing greyish. Franklin was reminded of an hourglass filled with ink, yet also thought of squarish numbers rendered of numerate halved tooth Picks, as if a child drawing a message upon a beach with twigs. Franklin imagined the electric Fluid, or electric Fire, applied to or permeating ink encased in toothpick shaped hourglasses, mimicking the fire Fly.

Franklin felt his supposition fanciful, perhaps accurate in some small if general peculiar, but mostly a floundering. Within a typical Watch would be gears intricate and fragile, as well as circulate springs which were wound and then dissipate, thereby spinning the gears and driving the arms. What lay within the armed Watch of the lad? A lilliputian Leyden Jar? Wires and conductors? Ink? Essence or organ of fire Fly, or some chymical Liquor substitute? Some other unforeseen, and unforeseeable, mode?

"Its September the fifth," the Lad said. "Two thirty-seven P.M. Don't you have any cool questions?"

The year?

Franklin chuckled.

"Who reckon you the greatest President?" he said.

The Lad grew sheepish right sudden.

Franklin guessed the Reason, and leaned in close.

"You may confide me," he whispered.

"Man you stink!" the Lad whispered. "All three of you. I can't say that in front of my mom cause she'd ball me out for being rude, but man oh man. When was the last time you bathed?"

"1787," Franklin said.

"I believe it," the Lad said.

He was in earnest, and seemed absolute disamused.

"I mean I know you're trying to be authentic and all that," the Lad said, "but holy bajimminy, maybe you should draw the line at not showering. If you smelled any worse, skunks would start humping your leg."

Franklin laughed.

"I ask leave for my Malignance," he said, "and promise to bathe or shower tonight if the opportunity presents. Your favourite President?"

"I don't wanna hurt anybody's feelings."

The Lad glanced at Washington with manifest Fear.

"Or make him mad."

Franklin winked at the parents as he and the lad walked several yards away.

"I shan't repeat a syllable you utter, lad. Even if a Barbar fills my drums with powder and threatens to match it."

The Lad still seemed to scruple.

"Upon my sacred Honor," Franklin said.

"I used to think Washington or Jefferson were my favorite Presidents," the Lad said. "But Washington seems boring and mean, and like honestly, kind of a dick. And Jefferson's racist."

Whatever sort of dick Washington was, Franklin did not think it cheese-ed. The Lad seemed to intend Dick as a derogation, not a generic descriptor of a fellow, nor a ditch, nor a

Will o' the Wisp, and by raceist, he didn't seem to signify that Thomas raced. Franklin none the less thought he inferred the general meaning. Was race-ist a derogation of Slavers, a hearkening to the noun race rather than the verb?

"There's always Lincoln," Franklin said.

"Maybe Washington and Jefferson aren't as great as everyone thinks."

"George and Thomas are not species of perfection, Lad. No human is. But Washington and Thomas are great, and actual greater than most reckon. Prodigious greater."

"Are you sure?"

"Aye," Franklin said. "I am compleat certain of few Things, but this is one."

The Lad still seemed skeptical. He peered at Montirushmore for a long moment, and then affixed Franklin with a pond'rous expression.

"Why weren't you ever President?" the Lad said.

"I was lucky."

"Are you kidding?"

"Nay."

"People want to be President. Don't they?"

"Not the men that ought condescend."

"Did Washington want to be President?"

Franklin could not help but chuckle.

"Nay, Lad. Right certain nay. Washington condescended the Executive as a man drawn to his Quartering. Neither was Thomas enamoured of high Office, I suspect."

As Franklin pressed the pamphlet into the pocket within his suitcoat, he could not help but shift the expression of his face a trifle.

"What's in your pocket?" the Lad said.

"Your pamphlet."

"What else?"

"George's false Teeth. I keep a petrify'd set in reserve, as if the Light Horse, for when he would partake cobb-ed maize, Brazils, chops, and cetera."

"How stupid do I look?" the Lad said.

"I could never deceive a Lad as cunning as you."

The Lad was unconvinced, and continued to press. Franklin continued to tease and lampoon, until the parents decided 'twas time to repair. Goodbyes were said and the family intended, leaving unrealized remnants of their past alone in the Present.

TWO

ashington enforced silence until they repaired to the Safety and Seclusion of the forest. Franklin felt the laudanum he had resorted beginning to subside, and his Gout and Stone reinvesting, and was grateful Washington found a small recess where they respited. The recess containt a small stump and several boulderish rocks. Franklin sat upon the stump, Washington and Thomas the rocks.

Glancing up through a cranny in the tree line, Franklin saw a sliver of sky, and beyond it, Montirushmore. The vantage was less favourable than prior, the view less frontal and the mountain more distant, yet the sculptures of Washington and Thomas were still clear visible.

When Washington lifted the excommunication, Thomas intercoursed nigh immediate.

"We are in Futurity," he said.

"But when?" Franklin said. "I wish the Lad had proffered the annum."

"Speak soft," Washington said. "We mus'n't attract other strangers."

"Futurity," Thomas whispered. "Futurity. Soothing just to utter it. To accept it."

"Or try to," Franklin said.

"Affirming it explicit is sobering," Washington said.

"By what mode were we transported?" Thomas said. "Is such travel common in this Epocha, or is our situation singular?"

"Situation or Predicament?" Washington said.

"Are we marooned," Thomas said, "or can we somehow repair home to the Present?"

"You mean the past," Franklin said.

"Aye suppose," Thomas said.

"If traversing Time were common," Washington said, "the family wouldn't have presumed us Thespians."

Franklin reached inside his suitcoat. He removed the pamphlet and a thick stack of Notes.

"These may provide clues," Franklin said.

"Were the Notes on your person when you arrived?" Washington said.

"Aye believe so," Franklin said. "I didn't discov—"

Franklin froze when he saw his portrait, and handed Washington and Thomas a note.

"You evidence a scant Surprize," Thomas said.

"After Montirushmore?" Franklin said.

He shrugged.

"Perhaps we ought examine the pamphlet ere the paper Money," Franklin said. "It intrigues me more."

"More than notes bearing your Portrait?" Washington said.

"Notes shan't instruct us what to do next."

"Save perhaps spend," Thomas said.

Thomas had never required prodding on this Count, though giving such thought voice would be beneath Dignity.

"We ought pocket the Notes then," Washington said. "Brandishing them may entice Priggers and Rapparees."

Franklin thirded the paper Money, pondering the amputee Watch as he did. He was soon awash in mental imagery of Priggers and Cloves wielding future weapons sim'l'r advanced, and he could not help but reminisce Mr. Pillings.

Franklin pocketed his third of the paper Money, and gave Washington and Thomas a third, which they pocketed. A portion of Franklin thought it more prudential to entrust Washington with nigh all the Notes, only he feared marooning penceless in the dernier Resort.

The pamphlet was soaked with Franklin's sweat. It was unopened, but headings on the back said:

Mount Rushmore National Memorial
National Park Service
South Dakota
U.S. Department of the Interior

"Dakota Savages?" Washington said.

"The Sioux," Thomas said.

He pronounced Sioux proper, that it rhymed with too and sounded as soo.

"I lived to see Americay cement peace with them. In 1815. We planned to cede them an enormous tract west of the Northwest Territory. 'Twas already stiling the Dakota Territory."

"An American Monument on Dakota land?" Franklin said.

"We must have acquired it," Thomas said. "Through further negotiation, I hope. The region may have been split into a North Dakota the savages kept, and a South Dakota which Americay owns. Or perhaps we finally acquired Canada."

"Another item for our burgeoning research Slate," Franklin said.

"What of this Department of the Interior?" Washington said.

"During my Presidency and lifetime there were but four fœderal Departments," Thomas said. "Foreign Affairs, Treasury, Post Office, and War."

"Your Presidency," Franklin said. "A trifle you might have proffered forthwith."

"I was President the Third," Thomas said. "From 1801 to 1809."

"Know you Tom had served," Franklin said to Washington, "when you told the Lad he was your favourite President?"

"Know you who Lincoln was?" Washington said.

Both men smiled.

"The term Interior connotes internal civic Improvements," Franklin said. "And the nomenclature seems to designate this National Park Service as a subdivision of said Department of the Interior. Could there also be a National Road Service? A National Library Service? A National School Service?"

"Surely you mean state Road Services?" Thomas said. "State Library Services? State School Services?"

"Am I to infer opposition to a National Church Service?"

"You're still a clever old Rascal."

"And you're still the devoutest Christian I know."

Thomas chuckled mirth-ed, yet also shook his head.

Franklin laughed.

"Logic and historical precedents such as Rome," he said, "make a modest expansion of fœderal Government seem plausible. A mature Republic would fund public Works. This would account a Department of the Interior."

"For authority to apply Taxes to objects of improvement," Thomas said, "amendment of the Constitution of Government would have been requisite."

"Aye," Franklin said. "All powers exercized must be enumerate. 'Twill be interesting to examine The Const—you seem vexed, Tom."

Thomas glanced at Washington momentary, yet said nothing.

Franklin opened the pamphlet and examined it with his printer's eye. Washington and Thomas stood either side of him.

"The paper is exceeding choice," Franklin said. "And the portraits ... if even àpropos to term them such ... stupefying lifeness ... Michelangelo and Da Vinci could labour in tandem and not equal them ... certain not paintings ... actual scenes must have been captured by some mode."

"An improved Camera Obscura was developing after you both died," Thomas said.

Franklin knew that "Camera Obscura" was Latin. Camera meant chambre, Obscura meant dark. Camera Obscuras were darkened chambres with small apertures that admitted light, creating a shadowed Image within chambre of the scene without. Camera Obscuras had existed since antiquity.

Franklin tapped his forehead with his hand.

"A Camera Obscura," he said. "A Camera Obscura containing a parchment smeared with Schulze's Salts or a sim'l'r eclipsive Chymical?"

In 1727, the natural Phylosopher Johann Heinrich Schulze discovered that chymical Liquors containing salts of Silver would darken when exposed to light.

"Aye," Thomas said.

"I ought have deduced that," Franklin said.

"You just did," Thomas said. "Inventive prognostication can confound even a natural Phylosopher.

Franklin grunted, and then resumed his browsing and read snippets of the pamphlet which seemed momentous.

"A Shrine in the Black Hills … Rushmore was no less than the formal rendering of the philosophy of our government into granite on a mountain peak.' Interesting, but we need dates. Phylosophy is spellt with an I rather than a Y. 'The preservation of the sacred fire of Liberty, and the destiny of the republican model of govern—'"

"My inaugural Address," Washington said.

"Which Address?" Franklin said. "Were there numerate?"

"Address the First," Washington said.

"'We hold these truths to be self-evident …' Yes, yes, the Declaration. Ah, here's the mutton. This Lincoln."

Franklin held the pamphlet up, squinted at it, and then frowned.

"Smear'd and illegible."

Washington scowled prodigious, yet remained silent. Franklin could hazard Washington's thoughts. How could Doctor Franklin sweat so profuse hiking but a few rods?

"Roosevelt," Franklin said. "We, here in Americay, hold in our hands the hopes of the world, the fate of the coming years, an—'"

Franklin expellt with vigour.

"The remainder of that quote 'tis also smeared."

"We are as frustrate," Thomas said, "as Tantalus."

Franklin could not help but chuckle. Tantalus was a persona of Græcian mythology condemned to languish nigh a lake and fruit tree that receded whenever he tried to drink or eat from them. Tantalus' desires was always proximate, yet æternal elusive.

Franklin examined term dates listed below portraits of Rushmore's Presidents.

"Lincoln served as Executive until 1865, Roosevelt until 1909 … The phraze 'Shrine of Democracy' was inaugurate at the 1930 dedication of the Washington sculpture."

"Did you say 'Shrine of Democracy'?" Thomas said.

"Yea," Franklin said.

"Not 'Shrine of Republicanism'."

"Nay."

This was a profund distinction. Fearful of impassionate Mobs and tyrannical Majorities that wrought Havock under The Democracy, the Deputies at the Fœderal Convention had strove to create a more dilute representative democracy, or Republic. Thus, the term "Republican" was nigh always used to denote free self Government in America.

"Has diction mere altered?" Thomas said. "Or have the Constitution and species of government?"

Franklin shrugged, as did Washington.

Dry portions of the pamphlet rustled as Franklin flipped it over. A large image showed suspended workers carving the visage of Lincoln. The lifeness of the image pilfered Franklin's breath.

"Slaves?" Thomas said.

"Difficult to reckon," Franklin said. "The sculptors is indistinct, cloaked in shadow, and their backs only are visible."

"'Twould seem folly to hazard a Houdon," Thomas said, "when one could expend slaves."

"'Dynamite' was used to 'blast' the rock," Franklin read.

"Dynamis is Greek for power," Thomas said.

"Is dynamight futurity's Gunpowder?" Washington said.

Franklin pointed out other advanced tools such an "air-powered hammer." He read a few more snippets from the construction summary, and then focused on a map in a lower corner of the pamphlet.

"'Mount Rushmore is twenty five miles southwest of Rapid City,'" Franklin read. "'And three miles from Keystone … Drive carefully on Black Hill roads … drivers and passengers must wear seatbelts …'"

"Drivers of what?" Washington said.

"Who decreed what drivers and passengers must and mustn't wear?" Thomas said.

Franklin shrugged and continued reading.

"Major airlines and bus rou—airlines?"

Franklin peered up at the sky.

"Airlines?" he said.

Washington and Thomas also looked up.

"Any relevant new inventions after we passed?" Franklin said to Thomas.

"Nay."

"Improvements to the Balloon Invention?" Franklin said.

In 1783, while America's Minister Plenipotentiary to France, Franklin had observed humankind's first manned Ascension, a balloon dismissed over Paris.

"Naught revolutionary," Thomas said. "Stability was enhanced and flight duration and altitude encreased. Balloons remain all the Crack, and though their postulated commercial and military utility rouse Imaginations, they are alas still but hazardous Amusements."

"Or were," Franklin said.

"Aye," Thomas said. "So 'twould seem."

"'Major airlines and bus routes serve Rapid City,'" Franklin read.

He peered at the map. Rapid City was a large square, Keystone a small blip.

"Rapid City," Franklin said, "is the largest town proximate Montirus—Mont Rushmore. 'Tis a logical hub."

Silence.

Franklin immersed himself in rumination. He envisioned fleets of Balloons guided by Tethers, or airlines, but knew this was probably a laughable primitive conception. Balloons were aimless roaming Slaves of the Wind; if used as airbourne coaches, they would require an impetus or motive Force that counteracted air currents.

Washington and Thomas also appeared to be ruminating intense. Were they encountering difficultys similar to Franklin's? Sense they that they should be envisioning some Thing fantastical, yet sputter attempting to assign attributes to such a Wonderment?

"The Balloon," Franklin said, "may have cobbled the way to some discoveries in natural Phylosophy of which we at present have no conception."

Thomas smiled, showing but little of his teeth, and his eyes sparkled with Benevolence.

"I have missed you, Good Doctor," he said. "Lesser natural Phylosophers feign knowledge, but you have the Humility to own ignorance."

"Thank you, Thomas, tho' in fairness, I have scarce other recourse."

Washington asked Franklin what he thought airlines might be. Franklin explained his hazard.

"Lines," Thomas said, "mayn't be literal tethers to Balloons, but rather regular successions of publick conveyances."

"As turnpikes or post Routes," Franklin said, "but in the air, the sky."

It all sounded eminent reasonable. Until Franklin peered up into the sky and imagined conveying across it.

"Are we a thousand Annums in futurity?" Washington said. "Two?"

"Few nations have evidenced such endurance," Thomas said. "Even a millennium seems presumptuous."

"What duration then?" Washington said.

Thomas thought a moment.

"I'd would hazard six, perhaps seven centurys of years in Futurity."

"Ben?"

Franklin answered immediate, with confidence that sur-priz'd him.

"Five centurys of years maximate. Perhaps centurys less."

Thomas arched an eyebrow.

"Your rationale?"

"My hazard, as yours, is rooted in assessments of Invention and natural Phylosophy. Evidence is scant, and we may have erred. But recollect antient Greece and the gothick Enlighten-ment. When wisdom accrues, does it not do so in rapid spurts? If the freedoms we ensconced have endured, and the family, pam-phlet, notes and mountain suggest they have in some modicum, then prospering Republics may have cultivated an Enlighten-ment spanning centurys. Invention and natural Phylosophy may have advanced at a rate beyond our comprehension."

"May have," Washington said.

"A republic plagued by a Civil War and Impeachments mayn't have prospered consistent," Thomas said. "Even if Americay did, your predictions seem optimistic. Rome prospered for centurys and never wrought any Thing as fantastical as that Lad's Watch. Or an airline, whatever it proves to be."

"Natural Phylosophy 'twas an infant then," Franklin said. "The Romans hadn't comprehended electric Fire, wrought an affinity Table, or plied printing presses to accelerate the Diffu-sion of Knowledge. In our time natural Phylosophy was building momentum, like an Avalanche."

"I've lived nigh four decades since you passed," Thomas said. "Your avalanche hasn't struck yet."

"Or perhaps hadn't struck yet."

"Aye," Thomas said. "Our tenses have become proper muddled."

"That my Avalanche hadn't struck after some four Decades," Franklin said, "doesn't signify it requiret some six or seven Centurys."

"I shan't dispute Americay's most renowned natural Phylosopher," Thomas said.

Franklin laughed.

"You just did. Rightness is more important than Reputation."

"You have Reputation," Thomas said, "because you're oft Right."

"That 'tis but the past," Franklin said. "In this Epocha, the dimmest childe prob'ly understands more of the workings of Nature than I."

"We know but little," Washington said. "Scant little."

"We know 'tis at the least 1930," Thomas said. "And we know our approximant location. 'Tis a Start."

Franklin began folding up the pamphlet.

"Speaking of Starts," he said, "I should like to know when you both came from. And your present Ages."

"Present Ages," Thomas said, "would seem an Ambiguity. Is our age the time we have lived, or the time we have traversed? If the latter, I would require the annum to compute my present Age."

"Our Ages," Franklin said, "in the time we were pilfered from."

"Sharing 'tis a prudential admonition, Doctor," Washington said. "Chronological seems logical. You being elder narrate first."

They respited for a Spell. There was scant intercourse. Franklin clused his eyes, breathed in deep through his nose repeated, and let the gentle breeze blow about him.

When Franklin opened his eyes, Washington and Thomas were peering at him expectant.

"I am turnt of eighty-one at present," Franklin said. "Or at past. For me, the date was …"

1787

THREE

Benjamin Franklin was so focused on the imminent Vote he scarce noticed the stabbing of his Gout and Stone. The Convention was nigh compleat. The Constitution was nigh executed, the American Nation nigh established, Liberty nigh secured for multitudes living and unbirthed.

More than forty Deputies was crowded into the East Room, which crackled with anticipation as sure as if a Key were on a Kite. Deputies wore open-front suitcoats over waistcoats, rufflet neckcloaths, knee-length breeches, and stock drawers on their lower legs. They were seated around thirteen green-baized tables which encircled an elevated Speaker's table on a dais near the rear wall.

Thirteen tables, one per state. Except Rogue Island boycotted the Convention. Twelve state Deputations had begun meeting 116 days ago, determined to unify themselves while also preserving sovereignty. Twelve states had entered Convention, one Nation would leave today—if factionalism and warmth were not rekindled.

The final wording of the Constitution had been approved two days ago on Saturday and submitted for inscription onto parchment. Today's approval of the engross'd Charta should have been a mere formality, but the Constitution was a precarious patchwork of counterbalanced Principles and conflicted Interests. Support for it was tenuous, and the Convention could fail, even now in the final instance. If it did, there was scarce hope of calling another, and the Revolution's hard-won Liberty would be lost.

At the Speaker's table, the American Zeus rose from his Chippendale throne. George Washington stood straight as an Indian even in old age. He had the natural grace of an athlete and a magnetic stature, yet looked lanky, cold, formal, an effect accentuate by his white hair and black suit. Washington's height was magnified by the dais.

At a distance Franklin always noted Washington's eye sockets, which painters and sculptors swore were the largest they had seen on a human. Washington's sockets seemed deepset enough to hold billiard balls, and his eyes perched like pheasants in their confines.

Those eyes.

Those fearsome eyes.

Pityless grey orbs that measured men and events harsh, without emotion.

The eyes of a prædator.

Washington flicked open the cover on his silver Watch and peered at it, squinting slight and accentuating the fissures of his face. The watch seemed as small as a shilling in Washington's gargantuan hand. Ever punctual, he had opened the Convention each day at the top of the hour. Today, hopefully the final day, would be no different.

Washington closed his watch and stood so motionless time might have stopped. His eyes became vacant, as if he had been bagged by the British and mounted in king George's throne room.

With each passing moment, more of the assembled Deputies sat, conversation diminished, and the energy in the chambre escalated.

So did the tension.

Was this the quiet before the nor'easter?

The stillness seemed sim'l'r, though there was one key difference.

The heat.

The East Room was forty feet by thirty-nine feet, nigh square, with wooden floors, plastered walls, and a twenty-foot-high ceiling. Unbroke by support pillars, it felt open and inviting despite the crowd. Deputies faced east, and Washington stood with his back to the east wall. Six massive windows consumed the north and south walls, three per wall. Each window was at least four feet wide and extended from waist height to just below the ceiling, with an outer casing large enough for a horse to leap through. Morning light streamed through the upper portion of the south windows, brightening the room considerable.

But also heating it.

And there was no breeze.

The deliberations of the Convention were secret. Even with sentrys, eves droppers could not be chanced. Philadelphia's thousands of horses also shate incessant. Their manure attracted armadas of flies, and to open windows was to invite ambuscade by them, as well as mosquitoes and other insects. Winds would also waft the nauseate stench of the horse Shite, the sewer, innumerate Necessarys, and the garbage upon the streets. Thus, the windows were closed and the chambre was essentially an oven. Deputies glanced at the sunlight ominous, expecting to be roasted as surely as if spinning on spittles.

Washington's eyes sprung to life, becoming cold and fearsome again. As he squinted at his watch, a gash of a wrinkle form'd between his eyebrows across the top of his nose. Washington relaxed his squint and the gash diminished. He closed his watch, looked up and out past Deputies, and his eyes vacated again.

Franklin glanced around at the assembled Deputies. Cognizant of the severity of what was at stake, America had dispatch'd many of its Eminents. Intellect and Reputation litterd the chambre. Even with several Eminents such as Chancellor Wythe absented, and more Coxcombs, Jobbers, and Middlers than 'twas comfortable to concede, the Assembly was still one of the more august Franklin had ever sat in.

Tables were designed to seat two gentlemen situate side-by-side directly a front. Even this was cramped, but three or four Deputies crowded around many tables, organized by state. States tended to choose the same table location day after day, as if tables were territory they had annexed.

The state tables which encircled the Speaker's table—Washington's table—were arranged in two elliptical rows. A central aisle from the west entrance to the Speaker's table cut through the middle of the room, splitting the rows. In the left front row, New Hampshire occupied the leftmost table, Connecticut the middle table, and Delaware the right table. In the left rear row, Massachusetts occupied the leftmost table, New Jersey the middle table, and New York the right table. In the right front row, North Carolina occupied the rightmost table, Maryland the middle table, and Virginia the left table. In the rear right row, the only row with four tables, South Carolina occupied the rightmost table, Georgia the table left of South Carolina, and Pennsylvania the two tables left of Georgia. Being the host, Pennsylvania had the largest Deputation, and had annexed Rogue Island's table.

Franklin sat in the rear row with the Pennsylvania Deputation, at the table just right of the aisle. He occupied the leftmost position at the table and spillt into the aisle.

Direct in front of Franklin and a bit right of him in the front row sat Jemmy, James Madison, mouthpiece of Washington for much of the Convention, and a prime architect of the Constitution. Jemmy had performed an exhaustive study of all antient and modern Confederacies from the Amphictyonic Council to the Swiss Cantons, ascertained their fatal vices, and was determined to design an American government that avoided such erratum and remain'd pure in its Virtue.

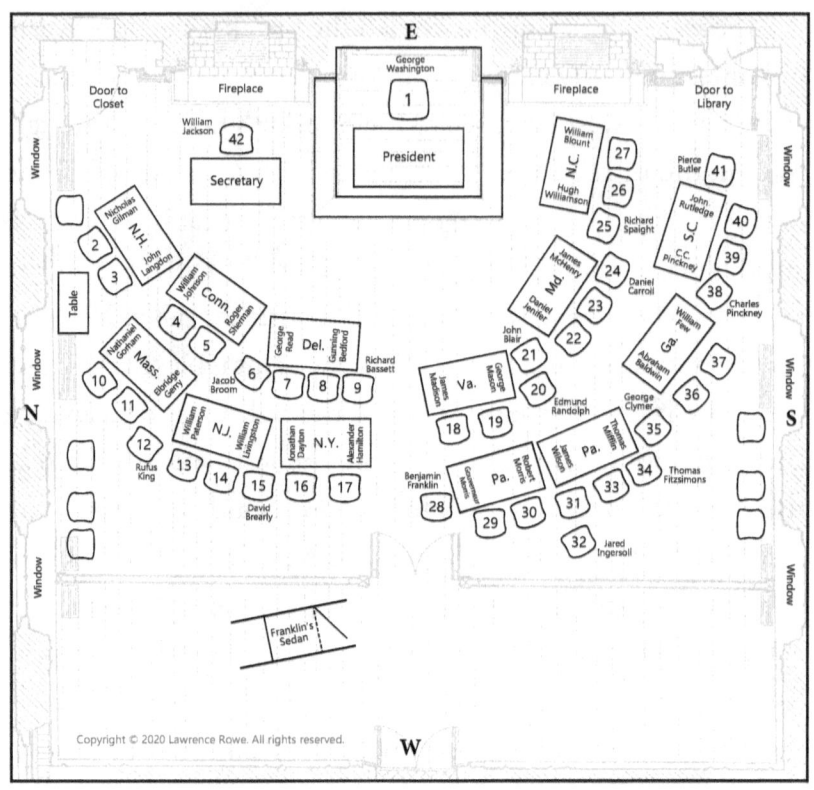

ABOVE: Diagram of the Philadelphia State House East Room on the final day of the Constitutional Convention. OPPOSITE PAGE: Enumeration of Deputys in Convention. FOLLOWING PAGES: Close-up of seating in the East Room.

DEPUTYS IN CONVENTION ASSEMBLED
SIGNING OF THE U.S. CONSTITUTION

Numbers correspond to seats in diagram.

1 – George Washington	22 – Daniel Jenifer
2 – Nicholas Gilman	23 – James McHenry
3 – John Langdon	24 – Daniel Carroll
4 – William Johnson	25 – Richard Spaight
5 – Roger Sherman	26 – Hugh Williamson
6 – Jacob Broom	27 – William Blount
7 – George Read	28 – Benjamin Franklin
8 – Gunning Bedford	29 – Gouverneur Morris
9 – Richard Bassett	30 – Robert Morris
10 – Nathaniel Gorham	31 – James Wilson
11 – Elbridge Gerry	32 – Jared Ingersoll
12 – Rufus King	33 – Thomas Mifflin
13 – William Paterson	34 – Thomas Fitzsimons
14 – William Livingston	35 – George Clymer
15 – David Brearly	36 – Abraham Baldwin
16 – Jonathan Dayton	37 – William Few
17 – Alexander Hamilton	38 – Charles Pinckney
18 – James Madison	39 – Charles C. Pinckney
19 – George Mason	40 – John Rutledge
20 – Edmund Randolph	41 – Pierce Butler
21 – John Blair	42 – William Jackson

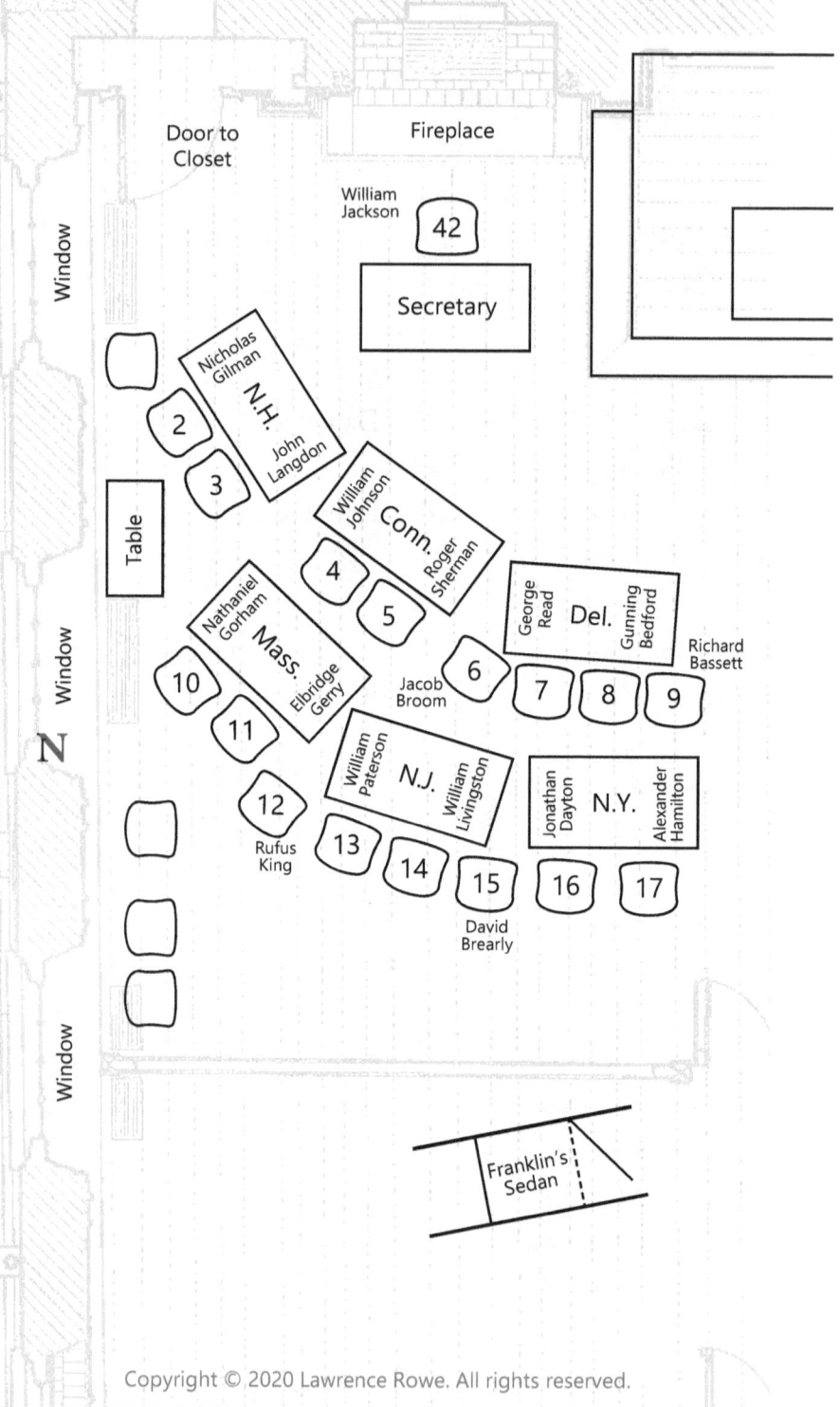

Door to Closet

Fireplace

Window

William Jackson

42

Secretary

Nicholas Gilman

N.H.

John Langdon

2

3

Table

William Johnson

Conn.

Roger Sherman

4

5

George Read

Del.

Gunning Bedford

Richard Bassett

6

7

8

9

Jacob Broom

Nathaniel Gorham

Mass.

Elbridge Gerry

10

11

12

Rufus King

William Paterson

N.J.

William Livingston

Jonathan Dayton

N.Y.

Alexander Hamilton

13

14

15

16

17

David Brearly

Window

N

Window

Franklin's Sedan

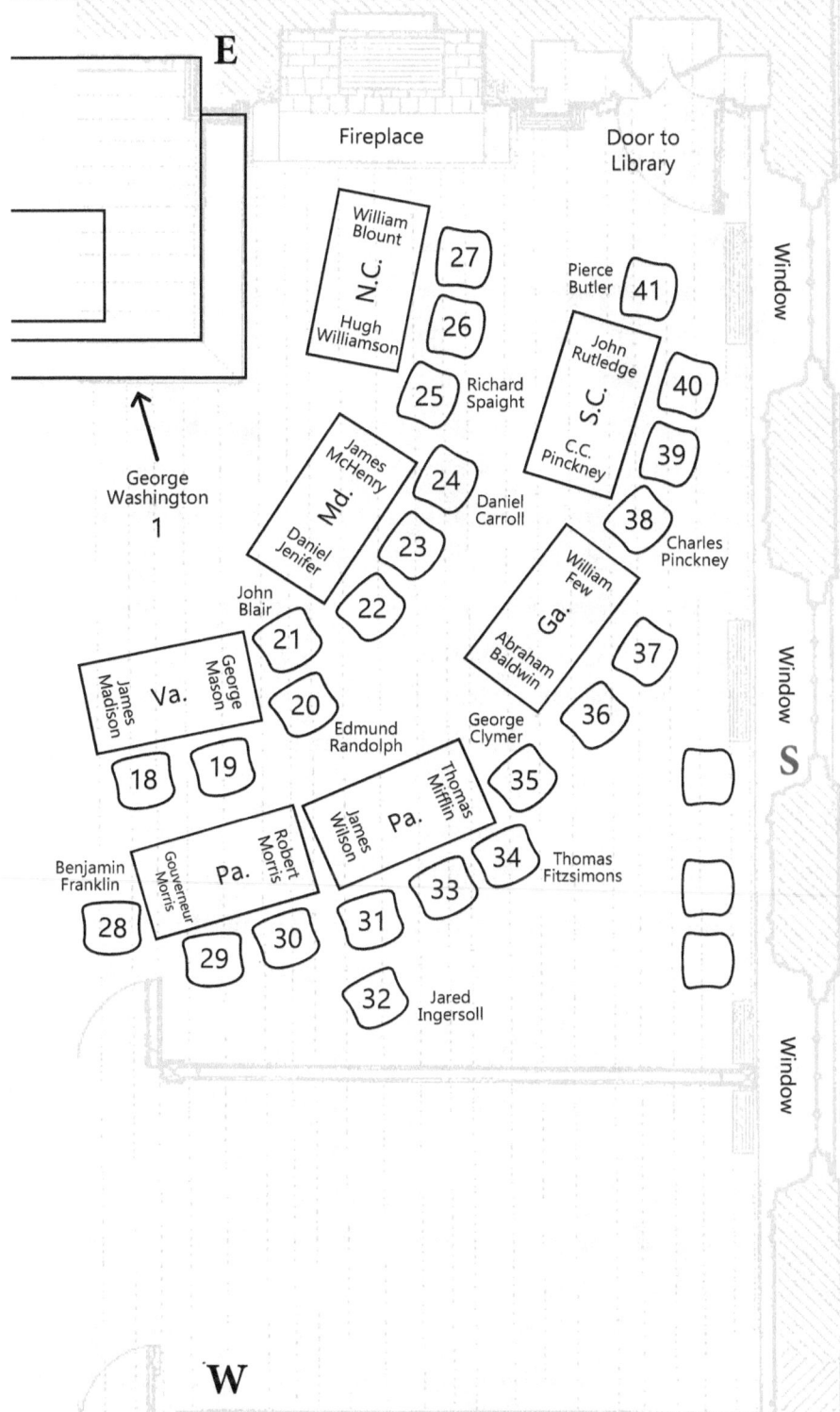

No bigger than a Bar of soap, Jemmy seemed like an amputee without a quill or book in his hand. His feet dangled from his chair, tips only touching the ground. Jemmy glanced leftward, seeming fretful. He had brown hair, bleu eyes, a tawny complexion, scarring of the nose from frostbite, and his hunched comportment suggested shyness.

Directly across the aisle from Franklin, the Little Lion sat alone. Alexander Hamilton was scarce bigger than Jemmy, but possessed an athletick cast and confidence which Jemmy wanted for. His face reminded Franklin of a baby's absent the fat. Hamilton had unblemish'd skin, cheeks as rosy a maiden's, and a high-bridged yet perfect-proportional nose. His nostrils and lips were prim yet hinted at pricklyness, as in a thoroughly-bred horse. 'Twas easy to envision some Sex laying next to Hamilton, twirling the curls in his chestnut hair, mesmerized by his blue eyes and complexion.

Other Deputies were scanning the chambre as sure as Franklin, and when many looked at Hamilton their eyes hardend momentary. Hamilton seemed aware of the darbering glances but unconcerned by them, and simple smirked with cold arrogance.

He had plenty to be arrogant about.

Hamilton was a bureau unto himself and had done more than any man to organize the Convention, though his contributions to the structure of America's government were thankful trifling. His soldiers named Hamilton the Little Lion because he was lean and intelligent, despite the fact that his physical features resembled not a lion, especially not his chestnut hair, which was darker than a lion's and brushed back rather than fluffed about his face like a mane. Yet when Hamilton sat assaying his surroundings, seeming to calculate every Thing with prædatory intelligence, he was as aloof and cunning as a lion, and men were rightful wary of him.

As Franklin dabbed sweat from his forehead with his fingertips, he wished the Little Lion had a tail. Then he could have swatted flies, and the windows could have been opened. Washington could probably kill flies just by glaring at them, which would also help.

Franklin snuck a glance at Washington's vacant eyes, though did so quick, so as not to be caught looking if they sprung back to life. Away from Convention, Deputies speculated what Washington thought while immersed in his vacuous stare. The probable answer was nothing. The consummate man of Deed, Washington wanted the relentless curiosity of the Phylosopher. He was not prone to deep contemplation for the mere love of it, nor for any reason unless necessary to solve an immediate problem.

Washington's dress was among the plainest of any Deputy, though of sterling quality. His suit had black cloathed buttons rather than luxurious metal, was perfect unpleated, had no turn-overs on collar nor sleeve, and 'twasn't figured, watered, or waved. Dressing with exaggerate simplicity was vogue since the Revolution, a refutation of the foppish opulence which prevail'd at European Courts.

Surveying Washington, Franklin felt envy. Washington's height, skeletature, and vigour made him impressive no matter what he wore, a luxury few men afforded. He was right trim from a lifetime of temperance and taking the exercise. Franklin glanced down at his protuberant belly, which droop'd like a four-gallon wineskin, and pursed his lips morose. Washington's suit contrasted his powdered hair, white cravat, white collar ruffle, white sleeve ruffles, and his ghoulish complexion. A moral message perhaps? As if to flaunt the fact that his Character was the only accoutrement he required?

Franklin remembered Washington appointing Commander of the Army in this chambre in 1775. He was damn nigh the same weight now as then. Washington had worn his blue militia uniform to the Congress, in essencey begging for a Commission, though perhaps not Commander in Chief, and once appointed he seemed overwhelmed and cognizant of his want of qualification. Washington was prodigious younger then. Face less lined, hair still reddish, the appearance of middling age even though already turned of 43. 'Twas twelve years since Washington accepted command, but he seemed decades elder. His face had weary'd and his hair had greyed, but the most glaring change was not some overt physical erosion. Washington wore Power more comfortable, was no longer a man overwhelmed or doubtful of his qualification.

A knocker and a small bell were on Washington's left, and the ceremonial mace was on his right, both at his periphery near the far edge of the table. The knocker resemblet a huge Cork or Plug, but with a small piece of metal a fastened to the bottom. The mace was golden, ornate engrave-ed, and its long handle was capped with a head that resembled a goblet. Arcing up from the top of the goblet edges, four equidistant gold strips in cardinal directions formed the outline of a crown, conjoining exact Centre above goblet, with a cross situate atop. Without the crown and cross, the mace would have been reminiscent of an antient Torch. It was nigh an exact replica of the mace used by the British House of Commons, though four feet long only, nigh a foot shorter than the original. This didn't prevent it being an opulent eyesore.

The crown atop the mace symbolized the king's power over institutions of The People. When the colonys resisted British oppressions, the king ordered his colonial Governours to dissolve Assemblies and Courts, asserting the royal privilege to negate elective government and Liberty at his pleasure. This rank act of Tyranny heightened tensions between mother country and colonys and helped precipitate the Revolution.

The ceremonial mace seemed a curious inclusion at a Convention eradicating royalty, but it served a practicable purpose. When the ceremonial mace was on the table the Assembly was formal convoked, but when the Assembly moved into a meeting of the Committee of the Whole the ceremonial mace was removed from the table.

Being a gilded bauble in the British fashion, the mace reflected light, brightening the room unnecessary. Many Deputies seemed irritated by both the glare and the bauble itself. Curious that America had not created some more Republican incarnation, perhaps with a Fasces or some other antient Roman or Græcian symbol. America would probably Republicanize the ceremonial mace at some point, yet for now such tasks was trivialities. At present, the remnant of monarchial privilege had to be countenanced.

Washington's eyes sprung back to life. He squinted at his watch and continued peering at it rather than looking away immediate. Gentlemen situated themselves and chatter subsided. Silence reigned not, however. The State House had a West Room and East Room, with a central Hall between them. The west chambre housed the Pennsylvania supreme Court, and the hall was filled with courtiers. Voices, footsteps, and the bustle of business intruded into the Assembly Room from its rear.

Washington peered at his watch for another half minute, closed it, and plunked it into the fob of his waistcoat with dextrosity incongruous from so large a hand. Washington looked up, surveyed the Deputies, and then peert past them again.

"Mister Fry," he said to the Door-Keep. "Secure the chambre, if you please."

Washington's voice had a raspy, hollow quality, as if it were a weak echoed Growl. This impediment to speech was caused by his false teeth.

Joseph Fry closed the two oversize doors, which shut with an ominous thud. No parole from the tedium now. Fry stood with his back blocking the seam of the doors, at attention. He usual served as the Door-Keep of the Pennsylvania State Assembly. Fry was lean, wore a homespun Suit that was nonetheless impeccable neat, and had the aggressive bearing and hard eyes of a soldier. A worn sword hung low on his left hip and he wore four holstered flintlock Pistols, two per side, one above the other, barrels angled downward towards his rear and handles oriented frontward.

"Mister Weaver is without doors in the central Hall," Fry said. "He stands sentry and awaits Your Excellency's beckon."

Nicholas Weaver was the Messenger. And a Soldier.

"The militia is all at they stations without doors," Fry said. "Colonel Proctor and Captain Markoe of the Light Horse is also without doors lurching round."

The Philadelphia Light Troop of Horse, a self-funded unit of wealthy Gentlemen, had provided two sentries to secure the State House exterior each day. The Light Horse had some times served as Washington's Lifeguard during The War, and his trust in them was absolute. They had also funded the Entertainments of Friday at the City Tavern, the Farewell Dinner for Washington, which still had some heads a throbbing. Franklin wondert how Deputies many had positived the Constitution on Saturday to expedite to their quarters and take respite from barrel Fever.

"Huzza to the sacred Honor of the Light Horse," Washington said. "Thank you, Mister Fry. You may be seated, if you please."

Propriety required the Door-Keep to stand for the entirety of convocation, unless granted leave for respite by the Chair. No Door-Keep of dignity or repute would beg such leave. In granting leave, Washington condescended to extend a courtesy, as he had each day.

As he had each day, Fry remained standing, and curtsied deep. When he compleated his curtsy, he said, "Your most obedient and humble servant, Your Excellency."

Washington curtsied with his head but not his body, tilting forward at the neck without unaffixing his gaze from Fry. Curtsy compleat, as etiquette demanded, Washington shifted his attention to the Deputies.

"Good morrow, Gentlemen," he said. "Tho' the quorum of seven states is clear satisfy'd, the Secretary shall call the roll."

Major Jackson sat at a table on Washington's right, below the dais, direct in front of a fireplace. His was the only table besides Washington's which faced outward towards the Deputies' tables. Jackson's table had been pilfered from the seven on the north side of the chambre, and encroach'd their space, which is why the partition north of the central aisle had six tables only for state Deputations, while the south partition had seven.

On the extreme right of Jackson's table was a small Pile of printed pamphlets, the struck copys of the Constitution of Government. After adjourning Saturday, the Convention had instructed Messieurs Dunlap and Claypoole to strike a several Hundred copys, some four of five dozens of which had been brought to State House, that Deputies might have a definitive text of the Charta. Every Deputy had been given a striking, which some Deputies perused.

Jackson had a face long and sensitive, with dainty eyebrows, delicate eyes, and a bone structure a lady might envy—save for a mainsail of a nose angled enough to intrigue a Mathematic. His whiffer reminded Franklin of Thomas Jefferson's.

Jackson fought with distinction in the Revolution, earning promotion as an aide to Washington's camp, where he excelled. Sent to France to purchase military supplies for Washington using French loans, he had agitated Franklin, America's Minister Plenipotentiary to France, by exceeding his budget and dispencing money set aside for arrears. Franklin's chastizement of Jackson for insubordinating his purview, and Jackson's impolitick Lecture to Franklin about the sufferance of the Army— as if Franklin were unaware the Army malign'd—resulted in a disputation that was excessive warm. Jackson served as one of

Washington's secretarys after The War and was current reading the Law. He asked Washington for the Secretary position
because he needed the pay.

Door-Keep, Messenger, and Stationer appointments were
typical proffered to locals, and had been. Secretary was the only
office at the Convention open to a man wanting in Eminence,
and electioneering for it had been intense among lesser characters desirious of Participation.

Franklin wanted his grandson William Temple to serve as
Secretary. Better than the puddinghead Jackson. Temple served
as Franklin's Secretary in France, during the negotiation of the
Treaty which formalized peace between Britain and America.
Alas, Washington patronized Jackson, at least indirect, and Dep-
uties were inclined to please him where possible.

Temple's burgeoning infamy as a Fop and Libertine abetted
not his candidacy. Nor did his siring of a son in France with Mrs.
Coillot, wife of the famed actor Joseph Caillot. The bastard son
of Franklin's bastard son had sired a bastard son.

Bloody Hell.

Jackson called the Roll. He read aloud the Roll, the list of
states, one by one. The Convention was an Assembly of state
Deputations, not of individual Deputies, and the calling of the
Roll reflected this fact. Jackson proceeded in geographic order
North to South, as always.

"New Hampshire?" Jackson called.

The crafty-eyed John Langdon stood, half-circle eyebrows
tracing a parabolick reminiscent of a rainbow. Procedure required
Deputies to stand before speaking. Officers such as the Chair

and Secretary, Washington and Jackson, were exempt from this requisite.

"New Hampshire present and quorumed," Langdon said.

Quorumed meant that a state Deputation had a Quorum of Deputies, the minimum number of Deputies requisite to cast Votes. The Convention was not granted the Power to set Deputation quorums. State Legislatures appointing Deputations had affixed the number of Deputies and Quorum.

Langdon sat.

"Massachusetts Bay?" Jackson called.

Nathaniel Gorham of Massachusetts stood. He had always been rather lusty and had grown more so with time, his face a-fleshening and figure morphing into that of a pear. Gorham had a forgettable face with nary a distinguishing feature, save a singular Cleft in the lip just below centre of nose. Not a deformity, but rather a dimple.

"Massachusetts present and quorumed," Gorham said.

He sat.

"Rhode Island and Providence Plantations?" Jackson called.

Jackson paused for a right long interim, even though Rogue Island had absented the whole of the Convention. 'Twas as if he expected her Deputies to storm into the State House winded, kick open the East Room doors unannounced, and partake of the final day. Warmth flooded the faces of some Deputies.

"Rhode Island and Providence Plantations absent," Jackson said. "Connecticut?"

Doctor Johnson, William Samuel Johnson, stood, looking the dignifyed Gentlemen as always. He had an aristocratic face save his severe eyes.

"Present and quorumed," Johnson said.

There was something in the Tone of his Voice not pleasing to the Ear.

Johnson sat.

"New York?" Jackson called.

The Little Lion stood with fleet dextrosity, exposing tight-cut breeches and a curious short waistcoat that scarce covered the upper thigh. His suitcoat was square-edged at the bottom and front, like a house Frame, rather than tapering rearward starting at the waist as was traditional. The suitcoat the Little Lion wore over his waistcoat was also curious short, bottom'd an inch or two above the knee. This was the noveau Stile, becoming common in New York and other urbane Centres where men were less vig'rous, less exposed to weather, tended to coaches, and rode distance infrequent.

"Present but absent Quorum," Hamilton said.

States had appointed three to eight Deputies and set a Quorum of one to four Deputies. The Old Dominion, Virginia, the first colony founded by Europeans in America, appointed seven Deputies to the Convention and stipulated that a Quorum of three must be present for its state Deputation to cast a Vote in Convention. Pennsylvania, the Convention host, commissioned eight Deputies, the most of any state, with four Deputies requisite to Vote. New Hampshire—Franklin could not but help remember a liaison with a low Woman from the "old" Hampshire in Britain—commissioned four Deputies, with two requisite to Vote. Connecticut appointed three Deputies, and was the only Deputation which empowered a single Deputy to act for the whole of a State. Connecticut was also the only state in the

Continental Congress that voted against calling the Convention. Delaware, ever obstinate, and ever prescient, appointed five Deputies, with three requisite to Vote, but added the stipulation that it would not partake of any Convention unless suffrage in Convention was one Vote per State. Georgia, America's southern flank, appointed six Deputies, with two requisite to Vote.

And cetera.

Franklin could not remember the commissioning and quorum of every Deputation.

New York had appointed but three Deputies, a parsimonious apportionment given its eminency, with two requisite to vote. Hamilton being the only New York Deputy present, New York could not vote and was not accounted in the Quorum of seven states—a majority of the thirteen—that Procedure required to conduct business. This seemed strange appropriate, as Hamilton, a Bastard brought to bed in the West Indies, never evidenced the intence state Loyalty which Americans born to state bosoms did.

It was, in point of fact, more than a bit surprizing Hamilton had been appointed Deputy in the first instance at all. Governour Clinton was perhaps the greatest enemy of a strengthened fœderal Constitution in the whole of America. He was a State-ist to the marrow, zealous for local Independency and paper Money, and had a Phobia of Consolidation. Clinton certain opposed the appointment of any Deputy of a nationalist bent such as Hamilton. There were moneyed Factions in New York who demanded voice, however, and Hamilton's father-by-law, Philip Schuyler, was wealthy and wielded prodigious Power. Hamilton had probably express'd a desire to be a Deputy to Philip, perhaps with his wife Eliza pouring honey in her pappy's ear, and 'twas only through the weight of the Influence of Philip that Hamilton had been appointed.

Marrying excellent well continued to bear the Little Lion fruit, which made his purported Adultery all the more surprizing.

Nay, not surprizing.

Galling.

Franklin was no Quaker nor Puritan, and had taken a second Sally when resident abroad for long tenure, his wife Deborah petrifying of sailing and unwilling to cross the ocean to adjoin him. It had seemed grievous impracticable to Franklin to spend years abroad absent the gratifications of the carnal Intercourse, which was a curative to the stresses of life, those persistent manifest when he Minister on his third stretch in Britain especially. It also seemed untenable to absent that tender companionship and general softening of nature provided by the fair Sex, for such prodigious durations. Franklin knew his adultery was immoral, but 'twas also spawned of practicable requisites to his Happiness. Yet whilst betroth-ed, he had never taken to the perpetual hounding of Sexes to roger, as if adultery some sport. Franklin hadn't, in point of fact, ever adulterated in America, not even whilst segregate from Deborah traveling the whole of the North of America as Postmaster General, some 1,600 miles, to assay post Roads and post Offices.

To Franklin, Hamilton's purported adulteration of his wife Elizabeth represented base ingratitude for the Station her family and its Wealth had provided him, the same ingratitude Hamilton had evidenced when absenting Washington's service sudden. Washington was damn grueling to labour under, right certain, but 'twas nigh as if the Little Lion saw no more Gain for himself and vacated without concern for the greater Cause. Hamilton's habitual adulteration was indicative of a selfishness, an arrogancey, most of all an impetuousness, which seemed not just intrinsic to his character, but among its most predominate and fundamental traits. Who in the bloody Hell thought they could adulterize so brazen, so persistent and not be caught or given up eventual? Perhaps even Black Mailt.

The Little Lion was not the Phylosopher he fancied himself, often postured as, and which Miscalculates supposed him, but he was inarguable a Partizan, and a right cunning one at that. The Little Lion seemed destined to elevate to Power, but seemed to have a temperament and character ill-suited to it. Though Franklin liked to fancy himself as not Evil, and was discomforted by wishing ruin upon any man, some pragmatick portion of him could not help but hope that Hamilton effect'd his own ruin before he elevate lofty and held Power independent of Washington, to limit the Harm he might visit upon America.

Most Deputies announcing an absence of a Quorum for their state exhibited disappointment, but Hamilton's sonorous voice was conspicuous devoid of it. A few Deputies smirked. Having a Quorum of Deputies meant not consensus, as Hamilton had learned to his chagrin early in the Convention. Once a state had a Quorum, it still needed a majority of its Deputies to vote Yea on a measure for the state to do so. Early in the Convention, the other two New York Deputies, Robert Yates and John Lansing, voted uniform against every proposal for an energetic fœderal government, negativing Hamilton's affirmative votes. Not once had they sided with Hamilton, on even a single vote.

The Little Lion sat.

"New Jersey?" Jackson called.

Its formidable Deputation included its Governour William Livingston, its Chief Justice David Brearly, and its Attorney General William Paterson. They were pressed in a cloister in front of their table, arms of chairs adjoined. Jonathan Dayton, the lone New Jersey Deputy wanting in Eminence, had spilled rightward to Hamilton's table, though he distanced from the Little Lion and sat extreme left, with his Deputation.

Governour Livingston stood. High, reedish, graceless in form and wanting for co-ordination, with facial features harsh and earnest, Livingston exemplifyed his byname, Whipping Post.

"Present and quorumed," Whipping Post said.

He sat.

"Pennsylvaniay," Jackson called.

Jackson pronounced Pennsylvania in the common, tho' not uniform, stile, that the final syllable rhymed with say, and the word sounded Pen-sill-vain-yay.

Franklin was President of the Executive Council of Pennsylvania, in essence its Governour, and the second most esteemed man in America. By titular reckon and that of informal esteem, he was the head of the Pennsylvania Deputation.

"The Deputy begs leave for not standing to address the Chair," Franklin said.

The Gout shot a flare of pain up Franklin's knee, as if to lampoon him.

"Pennsylvaniay present," Franklin said, "and primed to affirm the Constitution of the United States of Americay."

"Pennsylvaniay present and quorumed," Jackson said.

He continued calling the roll state by state. The ranking Deputy of each state Deputation stood and answered. Delaware, Maryland, Virginia, North Carolina, South Carolina, and Georgia were all present and quorumed.

"Twelve of thirteen States present, Your Excellency," Jackson said to Washington. "Eleven Deputations quorumed to vote."

"Thank you, Major Jackson," Washington said. "That majority of states necessary to conduct business presenting, and this fact having been recorded by the calling of the roll, the Secretary shall now read the minutes of the preceding session."

Jackson read his record of Saturday's proceedings. Few Deputies wanted a detail'd Record of what they had spoke in Convention, and with Jackson as Secretary they had scant concerns in this regard. His notes were galling scanty as usual, scarce more than tallys of calling Roll and calling Votes. Deputies seemed thankful for the brevity.

Jackson finished reading.

Washington stood.

"Is any Gentleman," he said, "absent the fresh striking of the Constitution of Government?"

Silence.

All Deputies had attained one of the fresh struck copys upon entering the chambre.

"The Constitution of Government of the United States of Americay having been approved by the requisite quorum and duly engrossed," Washington said, "it shall now be read aloud."

Eyes drifted to the pages of parchment on Washington's table, which were so large they hung off the front edge. Wash-

ington pick'd up the massive parchment. At least something
made his hands seem small.

Washington strode to the edge of the dais and handed Jackson the Constitution. The vellum bristled in Jackson's grip. Made
from calf skin, 'twas tan with splotches of lighter and darker
colouration.

Washington returned to his throne behind the Speaker's
table. Even standing motionless, he carved an impressive figure.

Damn impressive.

Washington sat.

Jackson remained standing. He placed the final three sheets
of the Constitution on his table and kept sheet the first in his
hand. The lower portion of the three sheets hung off the edge
of the table, exposing processions of manuscription.

Franklin pondered his own procession. He had sat at Jackson's table for years as Clerk of the Pennsylvania Assembly. He
had sat in Washington's throne as Speaker of the Pennsylvania
Assembly and as President of Pennsylvania's Constitutional
Convention. Washington was the only man who had sat in the
throne who Franklin considered his Peer. Franklin felt satisfaction that the throne occupied by one so worthy, yet also had to
quell a trifle of irritation. Where he wanted to sit was beneath
his Mulberry tree.

Jackson looked round the East Room solemn. He was about
to read the entire Constitution, but hadn't donn'd spectacles. Ah,
to be that young and vital again. To see and walk unimpeded,
without telescopy of the eyes, or canes and sedans.

Irritation crept onto the faces of many Deputies as they
peered at the processions of words on the parchment. The expres-

sions of some Deputies became right glum, especially that of Dictator John, John Rutledge of South Carolina.

Seated at the at the southeast corner of the chambre near the door to the library, Dictator John looked every inch the genteel of Privilege. He had a softish handsomeness, but 'twas debased by petulant eyes and lips that seemed natural affixed into the precurse of a snarl. Dictator John ouzed enough arrogancy to make the Little Lion seem an epitome of humility. He reminded Franklin of the Barons and Earls he had encountered in Britain, men of talent and inborn advantage who nonetheless overestimated their intelligence and importance, and thought themselves superior to Yeomen and Leather Aprons who tilled land and practis'd tradescrafts.

The irritation of Deputies was perhaps excusable. After nigh four months of analyzing, debating, amending, revising, and often agitating, nigh every word and clause of the Constitution, all Deputies knew what it said. Every Deputy had received a struck copy of the Report of the Committee of Detail, and the Report of the Committee of Stile and Arrangement, and had read these draughts. Many Deputies doubtless felt the reading of the entire Constitution unnecessary, not that any would dare insubordinate Washington. Even Dictator John hadn't that much brass. At least not vis-à-vis, while confronted by the person of Washington.

Procedure mandated that any measure finalyzing by an Assembly had to be called immediate prior. In dishonourable Assemblies, provisions unknownst and tyrannical were often foistered into measures and sprung on the unsuspecting. The reading aloud of a measure to be voted upon was a rampart against such Deceit. Washington would never countenance uncertainty in this regard about a measure of substantial import such as the Constitution. No Deputy would ever be able to pretend he knew not what his Yea, or Nay, positived, or negatived.

So a reading 'twas to be, to the chagrin of nigh all.

Jackson cleared his throat and then read, "We the People of the United States, in Order to form a more perfect Union, establish Justice, insure domestic Tranquility, provide for the common defence, promote the general Welfare, and secure the Blessings of Liberty to ourselves and our Posterity, do ordain and establish this Constitution for the United States of America."

Jackson's voice boomed and had the steady cadence of a soldier's march. Temple could not have read so well. His voice was no match for Jackson's. Had Washington foreseen this? Unwise to underestimate The General.

We the People.

We the People of the United States.

Not the sovereign States. Not bickering States. Not warring States. United States. At last, at long bloody last, a unitary entity!

We the People of the United States!

The phrase seemed nigh melodious. Hearing the words reverberate throughout the chambre chill'd Franklin slight, no trifle in such a sweltering environ.

Franklin glanced at the chair direct right of him, at Tall Boy, Governeur Morris, and nodded respectful. Morris had served on the Committee of Stile and Arrangement tasked with improving the structure and phraseology of the Committee of Detail draught, adding Finish. Morris served the role that Thomas had for the Committee of Five tasked with the Declaration of Independency, penning the Constitution, finalizing the conversion of the structure determined in debate into a documentary architecture. The Preamble of the Constitution was Morris' wording. Would he be destined for fame for his drawing, as seemed to be gradual happening with Thomas and the Declaration?

Morris was portly, with a thick wooden peg Leg that might have been sawed off a dining table. He had arch-ed eyebrows, a nose gargantuan and patrician that should have seemed more unattractive, and the voluptuous lips of a Libertine, which he was. When argumentative or warm Morris' face reminded Franklin of an angry rooster, yet at calmer times like now he seemed more cherubic and his eyes seemed to laugh perpetual. He nodded back at Franklin smiled mischevious.

Morris' Preamble devoided the lofty language of the Declaration of Independency. The Constitution was Law that Legislators, Executors, and Courts would have to interpret, not a Manifesto like the Declaration, and the poetic flights of fancy esteemed in the Declaration was thus inapt. Morris had made the Constitution as elegant as its purpose would suffer, though like Thomas drawing the Declaration, he had eschewed novelty.

Æqual glaring was what the Convention had eschewed. There was no Declaration of Rights prefixed to the Constitution, as in most state Constitutions. A Constitution absent such Prefixation seemed curious at best.

Constitutions could do three main things: enumerate Rights, enumerate a structure of government, and enumerate Powers the government was granted or denied. The Constitution reading enumerated no Rights and thus guaranteed no Rights to

The People. Nor did it specify intentions for the structure and Powers of government that might prevent maladministration.

Would these omissions prove of consequency?

As Law, as a codification of governing principles, what did the Preamble forebode, once the government incorporate and the meaning of the Constitution be haggled?

The answers to such questions were difficult to foresee, often nigh impossible, yet the essence of crafting a durable Constitution. The frequent and discomforting feeling of groping blind, felt so often during the last quarter annum, returned right sudden. Franklin had try'd to peer down the corridors of time and ascertain the effects of Constitutional permutations upon the future structure of government and the Life, Liberty, Property, and Happiness of The People, but at best saw flickers and shadows only, and usually a dark unknown, as now.

In his mind's eye, Franklin drew an alternate Preamble: We the People, in Order to establish Justice, insure domestic Tranquility, provide for the common defence, promote the general Welfare, and secure the Blessings of Liberty to ourselves and our Posterity, do ordain and establish this Constitution for the Nation of America.

Franklin was disquieted by such Preamble, which castrated the States.

But he also could not refrain a contemplating it.

Debate about the fundamental character of the government had been fierce. What was the elemental unit constituting into a government? Was America to be a fœderal compact of States? Or a national compact of People? Political compromise and the need to counterbalance Powers and Interests had begot an alchemy of the fœderal and national forms. At times this alchemy seemed a more potent alloy to Franklin, at other times cheap pewtre, a mere muddling of principles. The efficacy and durability of this Alloy—or perhaps its muddling until it became a cess pool—was something no Deputy could foretell certain.

Franklin was certain of but one res concerning the publica: Every word and clause of the Constitution was a verbial cliff which might unwitting abet Tyranny, careening America into Despotism if ill conceive-ed.

"Article One," Jackson read. "Section One. All legislative Powers herein granted shall be vested in a Congress of the United States, which shall consist of a Senate and House of Representatives."

Such a simple clause.

Deceptive simple.

Fitting it was the first clause of the Constitution after the Preambling, as it was inarguable the most contentious issue of the Convention. Even now, a few Deputies tensed at the mere reading of the clause, especially Deputies from little States, who congregated at the leftmost tables in the chambre as always, as if hoping to attain strength from numbers.

Deputies' inability to compromise on a legislative structure that appeased large States and little States nigh ripped the Convention asunder. Large States demanded a single House in which Representation was proportional to population or each state's Quota of Contribution, its financial contribution, to the fœderal government. Little States felt this structure left them so few Representatives as to be irrelevant, and demanded each state have the same number of Representatives irrespective of population, as under the Articles of Confederacy and Perpetual Union.

Both Factions were intractable and grew warm. Shouting matches ensued, the chasm widened for weeks, and the Convention seemed ready to dissolve—until the Compromise had been broker'd over dinner and copious Lubrication in Franklin's new dining room. It pleased him that it had served some practicable purpose. Two chambres in Congress, a House in which the number of Representatives was proportion'd to population, a Senate in which each state had the same number of Senators. Revenue bills would originate in the House, but require approval from the Senate.

Franklin favoured a single House along the large-state model, and even now the double chambre Congress rankled him, but he nonetheless supported the Compromise because there would be no Constitution without it. No fœderal government without it. No American Nation without it.

All Deputies knew this. Which is why the nervousness of the little States made everyone nervous. The little States were petrify'd of throwing into Hotchpot and swallowing up. Were they entertaining doubts about the wisdom of the Compromise? Was it their intent to scuttle the Convention in the final instancy by retracting support? Deputies of little States had been consulted and were adamant there was no such intention. There was no reason to disbelieve them, but might they nonetheless looze their nerve or decide to follow their hearts as the signing approached and the time to commit irrevocate loomed?

"Section Two," Jackson read. "The House of Representatives shall be composed of Members chosen every second Year by the People of the several States,"

Some Deputies nodded approving. The principle of rotation in office, so fundamental to Republicanism. A House accountable to The People via direct Electoring, allowing Members to be rotated out of office if they implemented not The People's will. A Legislature impervious to the will of The People would thus be impossible—or at the least more arduous for Tyrants to attain than in previous Confederacies.

Pondering Tyranny made Franklin again question the wisdom of rotating but every second Year. In every state but South Carolina, the Members of the first House were rotated annual. In aristocratic South Carolina, rotation was every second Year. A shorter term of more frequent rotation gave The People greater Power to instruct their Representatives and greater controul over government. Rotation annual would have been preferable.

Preferable to Franklin, that was. Some Deputies also wanted annual Rotation, but others wanted rotation every third Year, so the Convention had compromized upon every second Year.

Some of the opposition to direct Electoring had been related to little State fears of Hotchpotting, as direct Electoring typical imply'd proportional representation. The increasing discomfort of little-state Deputies was thus insurprizing, and self-evident. Judge Brearly, the fox-faced Chief Justice of the New Jersey supreme Court, swallowed severe, as if he had a peach pit caught in his throat. George Read of Delaware fidgeted his fingers incessant, like the legs of an industrious insect. Pastry-faced Gunning Bedford seemed ready to vomit creamt filling.

Read's eyes darted towards Franklin sudden. Franklin study'd the chandles on tables. Tall, slender, whitish Chandles that burnt long, placed in weighty brass chandlers that were tough to tip and easy to grip, and whose thickness vary'd through out their height like the curves on a belle's body. The Convention had general met until 3 p.m. each day, adjourning well before can't-see, so the chandles had been as superfluous as literacy to a slave.

Read looked away. A happy man with fortune and family, he nonetheless had a melancholy face, large bags under his eyes, and a retreating hairline that exposed ample forehead. His elongate head might have been compressed in a carpenter's vise, yet the portion of his face below the forehead was pleasing and reminded Franklin of a Græcian drama mask.

Eleven years ago, Read had surpriz'd many by voting against the Declaration of Independency, and though he signed it once it passed to support the will of the whole, he possessed the courage to break with the Majority when he felt principle demanded it. Would today be another such day? Would futurity's historians note that Read was the only American to vote nay on the Declaration and Constitution? This seemed the sort of impotent fact historians loved to tout.

Brearly, Read, Bedford, and of course Paterson. They was assembled on the left side of the chambre with the little States, as always, like infantry amassing for an investment. Read and Bedford sat at the Delaware table at the right of the front row, Read at the left seat direct in front of the table, Bedford the right seat, with the two other members of their Deputation, Jacob Broom and Richard Bassett, left and right of them. Right crowded, the Delaware table. Brearly sat hodgepodged between the New Jersey table at the centre of the rear row and the New York table at its right. Paterson occupy'd the left seat at the New Jersey table.

Brearly, Read, Bedford, Paterson. Not triflers, nor blow-hards like Luther Martin of the Maryland Deputation, who had pleased everyone by absenting himself and repairing to his country a fortnight prior. Read had been Attorney General of Delaware for the crown prior to the Revolution, had served as Speaker of the Delaware House, and had been a Justice on the Court of Appeals in Cases of Capture. Brearly was a hardened veteran of the Revolution, Colonel in the New Jersey Militia, later seeing action with the Jersey Blues of the Army at battles such as Brandywine, Germantown, and Monmouth. Brearly had fought brave, and resigned his Commission only to serve as New Jersey's Chief Justice. The British had arrested Brearly for High Treason during the Revolution, and would have hung, drawn, and quartered him, had an uprising of Patriots not freed him forceful. Bedford served four terms in the Delaware House, three terms in its Senate, was then appointed the State's first Attorney General, and in that capacity was considerd one of the most knowledgeable Lawyers in America.

Read had supported energetic fœderal government through-out the Convention, yet had been equal adamant that he would lead Delaware's Deputies out of the Convention if the rights of little States be trampled by the large States. Would he feel trampled again at the last moment?

Brearly had a strong independent streak, as when ruling on Holmes v Walton, becoming one of the first Justices in Amer-ica to assert Courts' right to negative laws they deemed at odds with a Constitution. A man who had survived some of the bloodiest battles of the Revolution, been damn nigh drawn and quartered, and made audacious rulings as Chief Justice was not easily intimidate. Or even dissuaded.

And no Deputy would ever forget Bedford's infamous threat that little States would ally themselves with foreign Powers rather than submit to a single-chambre Legislature in which representation was proportional to population. Bedford's threat was shouted down as Treasonous by a multiplicity of Deputies!

Men might be prone to ejaculations in moments of warmth, but no formal motion for a partition of America into two or more Confederacys had been profferd by any Deputy. Once the Compromise had been crafted, Bedford had become more conciliatory and reasonable, realizing that the nation needed some sort of fœderal government and that all states must make Concessions. But would he remain that way?

Would Brearly? He was so esteem'd in the Law he could probably piss on the parchment when his time to sign came and still secure a fœderal judgeship, and if he proceeded judicious an appointment to the new nation's supreme Court was hardly unthinkable. Not that anyone really wanted to ride the Circuit.

Brearly was prudential and non-Factional, and had chaired the Committee on Postponed Matters, an important if unheralded committee charged with crafting Clauses for the many issues the Convention had tabled due to uncertainty, confusion, want of time, or inability to compromise. Brearly had a significant hand in drawing Clauses for Taxes, War, Patents, Indian relations, and much of the structure of the Executive. He had been entrusted with one of the Convention's most sacred responsibilities and had proved worthy of that trust. He was sure not the sort of man that would vote against the Constitution at the final instancy.

Was he?

"and the Electors in each State," Jackson read, "shall have the Qualifications requisite for Electors of the most numerous Branch of the State Legislature."

A compromising construction. Electors of Representatives, those electing them by Voting, were to be specified by states, but anyone eligible to elect a state Representative was also eligible to elect a fœderal Representative. The qualification laws each state chose for electoring to its first Branch would thus be apply'd to electoring Representatives to the fœderal first Branch. In most states, a person had to be male, white, and a Freeholder to be an Elector.

A Freeholder, one with a Freehold, a parcel of property free held, or owned, required a different quantum of property for Suffrage in different states. To elector for the first Branch in New York a white man needed a Freehold valued at twenty pounds Sterling. In South Carolina a white man needed a fifty-acre Freehold or town lot. Most other states set quantums between these amounts, some reckoned by a quantum of land, some by a quantum of real Estate value.

In Pennsylvania, any white man who paid Taxes could elector, even without a freehold, the most democratic provision in the whole of America. Other states were beginning to extended suffrage to white males without freeholds who paid a specify'd minimum quantum of Taxes, though some states derogated this as an Innovation and remained steadfast in Property requisites for suffrage. Overall, to elector in America a white man had to be a Taxpayer at the least and a freeholder of fifty acres at maximum. In no state could a white male without property who paid not Taxes vote.

Property requisites in most states were modest, and with land plentyful cheap, any laborious man could meet them and attain Suffrage. In most states, nine of ten persons—of white males—attained to Suffrage for at least the first House, and nigh all who attain'd not to Suffrage dissipated or wanted for Industry.

Franklin nonetheless considered the absence of more diffuse Suffrage a debasement of the virtue and spirit of The People. He would have preferred a Clause in the Constitution that uniformed Suffrage throughout America, granting it to all free white men who paid Taxes.

'Twas simple to proclaim make Suffrage more diffuse and grant it to all white men who paid Taxes. Franklin wanted a Constitution that codify'd this principle with all his heart.

Alas, Politicks were never this ideal.

States such as Pennsylvania that only required white males to pay Taxes to elector would not submit to a national freehold requisite, as this would disenfranchise many Pennsylvanians who paid Taxes but possessed not freeholds. These disenfranchised multitudes would be furious and oppose the Constitution energetic. States such as South Carolina that set prohibitive freehold requisites would not submit to a national qualification with no freehold requisite, a mere Taxpaying requisite, as this franchised many citizens they did not want to have the power to elector.

As with many issues that vexed the Convention, no proposal satisfy'd all States. No proposal could. The Convention had resorted to the best of its imperfect solutions, defaulting to the suffrage qualifications of the States. As with many provisions in the Constitution, no one was under the illusion that it was indefectible, or perhaps even desirable, but 'twas the best attainable.

"No Person shall be a Representative," Jackson read, "who shall not have attained to the Age of twenty five Years,"

More nods and expressions of approbation from Deputies, including Franklin. Men began adulthood and careers at age thirteen or fourteen, so would have at least a decade of experience in the world against eligibility for office, and be adequate seasoned.

Age was a more complex and confounding consideration than it seemed superficial, however. The typickal American could expect a life of some 35 to 40 years, though there was prodigious Variation. By Franklin's hazard, a quarter of Americans lived not to see 25, at least half attained not to 40, yet some, though certain not most, attained to 60, 70, or elder. It seem'd to Franklin that a man who attained to 60 often saw 70 or 80. Individuals turned of 90 or elder were a far from oddities.

Such disparitys were scarce a mystery to Franklin. The stiles of life of the Poor and those of education, wealth, or wisdom could not be more in opposition. The Poor laboured furious can-see to can't-see six days of the week continual, often subsisted on but flesh and drunk to ruin, and had no summer or country homes to take flight to when effluvia and plagues struck. Franklin could not help but think of his Youth, when he abstained all Spirits and flesh, living upon but water and vegetables. How vigorous, healthful, and clear-minded he had been!

There were also regional variations. Life was harder in the South, for labourers in the murderous heat of the deep South especially. In the north States of New England, where the climate cool and temperance enforced by religion, most people expected to live to 35 to 60. In middle states such as Pennsylvania, 30 to 55. In south States, 25 to 35, perhaps 45.

The elder age requisite which some Deputies had favoured would have become increasing prohibitive, and censorable, the further South one traveled, as fewer and fewer could expect to attain to it. With a quarter of Americans not attaining to 25, and at least half not attaining to 40, any age of qualification greater than 25, especially one significant greater, might seem exclusionary and aristocratic, and draw censure from Labourers, Yeomen, and Aprons most apt to expire young. 'Twas equal exceptionable to the wealthy who held most all Offices, who felt that the middling of life an appropriate juncture to elevate to Power, and that any greater qualification impracticable and inadvised.

Deputies glanced at Captain Jonathan Dayton, the youngest Deputy, being turned of 26. Dayton had the face of a frontiersman, even though he wasn't one. He had unusual thin eyebrows, a doorstop for a nose, and cod lips. And woe to the man forced to linger on Dayton's side profile, suffer the long, flat face, the stubborn chin, and one of the most protruding whiffers Franklin had ever seen, with undulating ridges like the Alleghenies. Dayton had his father's face and that was right unfortunate.

Dayton's father Elias was a Brigadier General in the Revolution and had conducted invalueable Espionage for Washington, activity unkownst to the Publick. New Jersey had appointed

General Dayton a Deputy to the Convention, as well the benevolent Abraham Clark, The Poor Man's Councilor, so named because he often defended the indigent. Clark was an excentric Genius who had signed the Declaration of Independency and was one of the most energetic advocates for the common Citizen in all of north America. Clark championed the issuance of £100,000 of paper Money in New Jersey, with land pledged as security, alleviating depletions of the circulating medium that had ravaged commerce. He had stayed in New Jersey to defend the issuance. General Dayton was a leader of the same political Faction as Clark, and absented the Convention for similar reasons, though he perhaps had the additional motive of facilitating his son's participation in the Convention.

Had General Dayton or Clark accepted their Appointment, Captain Dayton would probably not be in attendance. His want of seasoning was egregious enough, and the spirit of Faction in New Jersey warm enough, that his nomination encountered delay, and he did not seat himself at the Convention until late June. Dayton's land speculations had left a swath of stink across the Ohio country, which may have added to delays in his nomination, though in fairness, if shaving in land and securities disqualified a man, the Convention would never have mounted a quorum.

Though a bit of a Jobber, and a man who in darker moments seemed exceeding corruptible, Captain Dayton understood his want of experience and Eminence, and had been prudential enough to speak infrequent. Those few times he had spoke, he had not jestered himself, though neither had he shone the luminary. On occasion he had evidenced the impetuousity of youth, displaying Temper and Warmth injurious to his esteem.

Dayton had been a classmate of Hamilton's at the renowned Academy of lawyer Tapping Reeve, and matriculated to the College of New Jersey at Princeton, but dropped out in 1775 at the age of 15 to fight in the Revolution. Entering the New Jersey Regiment as an Ensign, Dayton was promoted to Lieutenant two years later at age 17, serving as Paymaster. He served under Washington at the Battles of Brandywine and Germantown and suffered the infamous winter at The Forge. Dayton also served under General Sullivan fighting Savages, perhaps the most dangerous and fearsome assignment imaginable. He was later captured by the British, held prisoner for a winter, released, promoted to Captain at age 19, and then fought at the glorious Yorktown victory.

Since The War, Dayton had read the Law, started a practice, branched out into land and securities Speculation, especially in the Ohio Country, and entered politicks. Dayton aspired to serve as a Representative in the new Government. The coincidence of the House age requirement with the age of the youngest Deputy who aspired to be a Representative seemed to attest to the prudence of the requirement.

"Representatives and direct Taxes shall be apportioned among the several States which may be included within this Union," Jackson read, "according to their respective Numbers,"

Deputies nodded with approbation, some rather harsh, especially Jemmy. No direct Taxes would be levied on The People by the national government, but rather would be levied upon states, in proportion to their population, which was to say apportioned. States would then collect direct Taxes from The People in the manner they saw fit. The People might be powerless to check energetic Encroachments by the national government, especially direct Taxes, but not states with Militias. They could stand fast against energetic Encroachments, refusing direct Taxes unless enacted for prudencial purpose and of Necessity absolute.

Energetic Taxation arose in most nations in history even with Representation and other trappings of Republicanism, which were often not the ramparts that political Phylosophers suppose-ed. One of the most challenging tasks of the Convention had been to prohibit the tyranny of energetic Taxation from ever arising in America. Apportionment of direct Taxes among the several States was a critical check on fœderal government Power, one that would limit the Spirit of Levelling, the rise of standing Armies and Empire, and insure that Americans always retained the right of Property.

"which shall be determined," Jackson read, "by adding to the whole Number of free Persons, including those bound to Service for a Term of Years, and excluding Indians not taxed, three fifths of all other Persons."

"Those bound to Service for a Term of Years" meant indentured servants, those who had sold their labour for a period of time, usual several annums, often in exchange for passage to America on a ship, and in rarer cases for land. "Indians not taxed" meant those living in the backwoods in a State of Nature, which was most. "All other Persons" meant Slaves.

The word Slave was conspicuous absent from the Constitution, but not Slavery itself. In enumerating State populations, Slaves would count three fifths a person only, which was as prepost'rous as 'twas Barbary, though also a relic of the Articles of Confederacy, which had contained a similar provision.

This portion of the Clause grated Franklin like John Adams had the French, and it caused a few Deputies to sprout scowls.

But only a few.

It also caused the southern Gentlemen at the right of the chambre to stiffen and glance amongst themselves with mild nervousness. A few southern Gentlemen allow'd triumphant smirks.

But only a few.

The Convention had hazarded the population of America as exact as possible, state by state, and had accounted some 2,776 Thousand. Franklin wondered at the population of America in 2,776, if there still was an America? Some 2,776 Thousand, or 2.776 Million, with 2,256 Thousand being free Persons, and 520 Thousand being Slaves. This was only of the thirteen States which might form the Union initial, not other territorys common reckont a portion of America, such as Kentucket, the Vermont Republic, and cetera.

Franklin had scant confidence in this accounting. America's population had never been enumerate comprehensive, it was not known certain, and he felt there a tendency to under æstimate. The common hazard was a population of some 3 Million. Franklin tended to a greater hazard, cluser to 3.25 Million, and perhaps approaching to 3.5 Million, though not in excess. Franklin had no evidence for such hazard, but this is what his natural Phylosophic intuition told him, and he trusted it. In his mind's eye, Franklin tended to increase the Convention's hazard by some 20 per cent or 25 per cent, usually 20 per cent, though in his mental ciph'ring, he resorted to the Convention hazard, so as to speak a common tongue with all other Deputies resorting to such hazard in their ciphering.

With some 2,256 Thousand persons being free Persons, and some 520 Thousand persons being Slaves, some 19 per cent of the American population was Slaves, nigh one in five. Franklin felt this cipher of the ratio of Slaves to free Persons probably accurate, even if the population greater. Most slaves were in the South, in five States, Maryland, Virginia, North Carolina, South Carolina, and Georgia. At the three fifths ratio, 520 Thousand total Slaves would count as 312 Thousand when Representatives were apportioned. This would increase the number of Representatives of slave States, even though Slaves would not elector and were accounted as Property. Votes of electors in slave States would thus count more than votes of electors in non-slave States.

On plantations, in the low Country of the deep South especially, whites were often outnumbert by Slaves by five to one, ten to one, or more. 'Twas galling to think of a plantation owner who should count as one person for apportionment of Representatives instead tallying his dozens or hundreds of slaves, thereby counting as multiple persons for apportionment and exercising suffrage excessive. Though this wasn't the literal result of the Constitution, 'twas the essential result when slaver States with an excess of Representatives cast Votes in Congress.

Eight north and middle States with few or no slaves had a population of some 1,490 Thousand. Enumerations in the five south slave States were murkyer, but there appeared to be some 1,286 Thousand, 766 Thousand being free Persons and 520 Thousand being Slaves. If slaves were not accounted in enumerations, the South would have some 766 Thousand total Persons against some 1,490 Thousand of the North, but half the population of the North, approximate, and thus nigh half the Representation of the North in Congress. This would be ruinous to the South, resulting in insufficient Representation in the Congress to stave off investments against Slavery.

Franklin perform'd the ciphering in his mind rapid. There was some 65 Representatives in House the First, 35 of the north States, 30 of the south States if Delaware reckon'd one of their Number. This was with the three fifths Provision. Without such Provision, the south States would have some 8 Representatives less, but 22, and would be hopeless outnumbered by the north States and their 35 Representatives, when votes in the House decided by simple Majority.

The south States would not be seating in Convention without the bribe of the three fifths Provision. This would not be the first Bribe in a Congress or Convention, nor the last. Nor was it the only Bribe of this particular Convention.

The effect the three fifths Provision over time might be bloody ruinous. If the South were to maintain Representative parity in Congress with north States, it would have to increase slave population in extant states and expand slavery into new states. If it did not, north States would attain a Majority decisive in Congress and invest slavery energetic. The South would resist such investment and Civil War might result. The three fifths provision was not a prescription for a stable republic. Yet the only construction more instabilizing would have been that which exploded Slavery.

Seating the Convention at its onset, Franklin had known how intractable and energetic south States would be defending

Slavery. He had not been Fool enough to entertain the delusion that a Constitution could unionize North and South states and eradicate slavery simultaneous. Yet 'twas still disheartening to see a Constitution that incentived the diffusion of Slavery rather than setting the nation on a bearing along the opposite tack. Entering the Convention, Franklin had at least hoped for such tack, and in this regard he had been naïve.

Pitiful naïve.

Franklin prided himself on his Knack for finding some Thing encouraging in every situation. But there was little nobility to be found a-contemplating the Constitution's slavery provisions. Franklin told himself that when Slavery exploded final by futurity, the absence of the word Slave or Negroes would leave no suggestion the atrocity had ever existed in the Constitution.

Such rationale rang hollow.

Franklin's glance was drawn rightward to the south Gentlemen again. He envyed their light Camblet dress coats. So much cooler than thick northern suits!

Glancing ahead, Franklin still saw the rear only of Jemmy. Vertical wooden chair rungs enclozed most of his back like the bars of a gaol cell. A vertical arch of wood topped the thin rungs. The chair was rotund, more wide than high, and made of strong hardwood, to accommodate men of girth or corpulence, as many lawyers and scholars were. It could probably bear the weight of a half dozen Jemmys.

Franklin glanced at the dozens of chairs that filled the chambre, each handicrafted, yet all identickal to Jemmy's. Franklin was proud of America's Leather Aprons, those of Philadelphia especially. These American Windsor chairs were a simplified version of the more ornate British Windsor, and the Philadelphia Windsor was the finest American Windsor.

Modern chairs, yet humble chairs, similar to those in homes, shops, and cetera, across America. A stark contrast to velveted chairs of the British privy Council, or the padded leather benches of the House of Commons. Cloath covering or padding on chairs would have made the last months much more comfortable, but Franklin wouldn't have forsaken his humble Philadelphia Windsor for all the Bohea in Boston Harbour. Like Washington's plain dress, the humble chairs was a symbolic refutation of the monarchial excesses of Europe. Fitting that Deputies would sit in Natural Wood chairs while securing Natural Rights.

Chairs.

Mere chairs.

An utter simple Thing, yet thorough pleasing. Franklin had spent more than three decades in Europe, and he had been tempted to stay in France where most of his friends were and take the dirt nap there, but a deep inner yearning told him America was his home and he had to hearken back to her bosom. Some times being home was about the comfort and joy provided by simple familiars like Chairs.

"The actual Enumeration," Jackson read, "shall be made within three Years after the first Meeting of the Congress of the United States, and within ..."

Jackson's words became a drone to Franklin. He shifted his focus to William Paterson of New Jersey, leader of the little State interests. Paterson was a Classic, a Lawyer, an Orator, and possessed of an obstinate morality that tended to the self-righteous.

Attorney General of New Jersey for nigh a decade, he was one of the more formidable legal scholars in America.

Paterson's full head of hair was grey with flecks of black, and cut extreme short, hugging the scalp. Despite being not of a brown hue, it reminded Franklin of beaver fur. Like Washington, Paterson was one of the few Deputies not wearing a wig. Paterson was a man modest and unobtrusive, young faced, with a nose dominant and high-bridged, and gruff eyes and brows that gave his aspect a hawkish cast.

Paterson had been the first Deputy to criticize the Convention for exceeding its mandate. The Continental Congress approved the Convention for the sole and express purpose of revising the Articles of Confederacy and Perpetual Union. With the prudence of a scrupulous lawyer, Paterson counseled that the Convention disband, repair to the States, and obtain a mandate to discard the Articles of Confederacy and Perpetual Union and fashion a new Constitution.

Such a mandate would have been impossible to attain, yet Paterson seemed not to make his proposal as a malicious political tactic. Was he prepost'rous naïve, or intractable in his principles?

Though some Deputies irritated by Paterson might argue intractable, the answer was neither.

So what was he?

The Convention began with Mr. Randolph's large-state Plan and its single-chambre Legislature in which Votes were proportional to state population. Paterson had countered with his own little-state Plan, which called for a single-chambre Legislature in which each state had one Vote.

When had Paterson proposed his plan? The middling of June. The fourteenth? Franklin couldn't be certain of the day. Though only three months ago, it felt like 1720.

Paterson despised Philadelphia. Once the Compromise was attained, he vacated the Convention for the respite of New Jersey, sole for reasons of conveniencey. That was end July, and today was the first day Paterson had attended the Convention since. Had he repaired to but ensure his state mounted a Quorum? 'Twas presumed that Paterson had repaired to affix his Signature, to usurp Honor for work he had absented. But was this his actual intention? Had he repaired to support the Constitution, or to Assassinate it?

"The Number of Representatives," Jackson read, "shall not exceed one for every forty Thousand, but each State shall have at Least one Representative; and until such enumeration shall be made, the State of New Hampshire shall be entitled to chuse three, Massachusetts eight, Rhode-Island and Providence Plantations one, Connecticut five ..."

Franklin could not hear the Number of Representatives enumerate without pondering its augmentation by slavery. The five south slave States had gained nigh eight Representatives via the three fifths provision, about one eighth of total Representatives in Congress the First. One out of every eight votes cast in the House of Representatives would be phantom votes.

The Old Dominion had a population of some 532 Thousand, 252 Thousand being free Persons, 280 Thousand being Slaves. The country of Washington, Mason, Randolph, Chancellor Wythe, and Jemmy owned damn nigh half the slaves in America! The Old Dominion's 280 Thousand slaves represented a Quota of Tax of some 168 Thousand, or nigh four additional Representatives in Congress. This was more additional Representatives than the total which Delaware, Georgia, Rogue Island, or New Hampshire possessed, and was equal to New York's four Representatives.

With slaves accounted as three fifths a Person, a discrepancy between enumerated population and computed population arose. To avoid confusion on this count, the adjusted population after applying the three fifths ratio, the computed population, was stiled the Quota of Tax. The five south States held a population of 1,286 Thousand, but their Quota of Tax was 1,078 Thousand. The Quota of Tax of each state would be utilized when apportioning Representatives and direct Taxes.

Quotas of Tax irked Franklin. Slavery was so nefarious that it debased every Thing it contacted, including a process of enumeration that would have been a simple head count otherwise.

The forty Thousand apportionment was also glaring Large to Franklin. At present, Pennsylvania's General Assembly had 68 Members who represented a population of some 410 Thousand, or one Member for every 6 Thousand, approximate.

Each Representative in the new fœderal Congress would Represent seven times more People than Members of the Pennsylvania Assembly.

This was at the inception of the Republic.

What when there were dozens more states and each state more populous?

The size of the Congress would either grow prohibitive, or Representation become so diluted that The People would surrender the Power to instruct their Representatives. Such dilutions of republican Virtue were why the profund Enlightened such as Montesquieu felt a large Republic infeasible.

Montesquieu was revered, perhaps just, which was concernsome, as the Convention had ignored some of his most strenuous admonitions.

But there had been no other way to incorporate a Republic, a public Thing, bottomed on The People.

Were Montesquieu and other Enlightened Thinkers correct?

Was a large Republic impossible, one of endurance especially?

Franklin knew not, but there was inexorable Logic in much of Montesquieu's reasoning, often devoid of fallacy, seeming.

As the nation grew, the most expedient mode, yet also perhaps the most unwise, would be to affix the size of the House, the number of Representatives, as the Convention had done at 65 during initial apportionment for Congress the First. Over time, an affix'd number of Representatives would nigh certain effect a dilution of Representation so profuse that The People would surrender the Power to instruct their Representatives. There would be the shadow of republican Virtue, of Representation, but not the substance of the res.

Not that Franklin had a better answer.

Or that any Deputy in Convention had.

Franklin felt a curdling Fear. With Senators, Executive, and Justices appointed by modes indirect, and no mode of direct election save Representatives of the House, dilution of Representation would be the death of the Republic.

At what size might the House be affixed in futurity? What was the maximal dilution at which a Republic still feasible? The demarkation of dilution at which a Republic ceased to effective exist?

Franklin envisioned a future population some ten times the current 3 Million, 30 Million. Ignoring three fifths apportionments—optimistic assuming Slavery eradicate—30 Million at one Representative for every forty Thousand was 750 Representatives.

Franklin wanted to whistle.

He wondered how Washington would respond if he did so?

Washington would hardly run him through, but the prospect of affronting Washington still affrighted Franklin. The prospect of incurring the wrath of Washington in any manner did.

How prodigious would the American population grow? In 1751, Franklin had made Observations Concerning the Increase of Mankind, and had presumed the population of America doubling but once in every 25 Years. This estimate seemed general accurate in the 36 years which had transpiret since, though a far from a species of Prophecy. Franklin might adjust the quantum down a bit from 25 Years were he to pen such treatise today.

America at present had some 3 Million, which would double to 6 Million, then 12 Million, then 24 Million, and then 48 Million. If the American population doubled but once in every 25 years, America would attain to a population in excess of 30 Million in more than three quarters a century and less than a century, between 1862 and 1887.

Suppose even greater population increases, to some 60 Million, 90 Million, even 100 Million. At one Representative for every forty Thousand, this was 1,500 Representatives, 2,250 Representatives, and 2,500 Representatives, respective.

Such multitudes was horrifying. A House of Representatives of some Thousands, captivate by the sound of their own oratory, each wanting to show their parts and speak on a measure. Calling the roll would take the worse part of a morning, much less putting a question. If even a fraction of Representatives spoke on a measure, debate on the most incontroversial Law might run weeks. Such a Congress would have to be in session nigh continual, and even then might not accomplish all business.

Bloody impracticable, a Congress so large.

And a larger Congress might eventual be requisite.

Franklin expected the doubling but once in every 25 Years to hold, rough approximate, until America had expanded to occupy all its Lands, at which time he expected growth to slow, the time of doubling increasing to three to five times its present rate, probably at a gradual rate. Or perhaps at an exponential rate, which might require fluxions to compute? How long it would take America to expand to occupy all its lands was uncertain, but Franklin reckoned at least a century.

Any hazard of peopling over the extreme long run was liable to be in erratum to a laughable degree, but it was Franklin's nature to hazard. Franklin hazarded a span of 100 years with the population doubling but once in 25 years, then a span of 100 years with the population doubling but once in 50 years, and then a span of 100 years with the population doubling but once in 75 years, ad infinitum, or perhaps an additional span of 100 years with the population doubling but once in 100 years, ad infinitum, or perhaps a final additional span of 100 years with the population doubling but once in 125 years, ad infinitum ...

Franklin tended to think the 75 years ad infinitum liable the most accurate, yet who could say certain? Plagues and wars might frustrate such hazards, as might vacillations in emigration, but such vagarys could not be foredain'd, so Franklin ignored them. The ciphers of the first 275 years of Franklin's prediction were simple to compute, but then a doubling but once in 75 years had to be computed for a span of 25 years. Franklin was no rapid computer, and disinclined to attempt such arduous exponential Cipher withinst his head, of which he was probably incapable, and would require treatizes in his library, such as those of Bernoulli and Euler.

Franklin computed the simple Ciphers and attained to a hazard of 384 Million total Persons in the Year 2062. This was a fantastickal quantum, more than 120 times the present three Million. If Franklin's prediction was anywhere cluse to the actual value at such time, equal to even three quarters of it, he would count himself fortunate.

Some 300 Million to 400 Million persons, less than three centuries in futurity! That America might endure so long was perhaps more than Franklin had right to hope, but also not prepost'rous when one considered that the Roman Republic had endured more than five centurys of years, as had some Empires.

Some 300 Million at one Representative for every forty Thousand was 7,500 Representatives. Some 400 Million was 10,000 Representatives.

Was it better to have a Congress of some Thousand, or ten Thousand, or more, if even feasible, or to have each Representative representing some fantastickal quantum of Citizens? What was the upper threshold at which the size of a Congress became prohibitive?

Franklin knew not, but the Constitution's want of an upper limit on apportionment concerned him. Franklin envision'd a Clause of greater constrainment: The number of Representatives shall not exceed one for every forty Thousand, nor deceed one for every sixty Thousand, but each State shall have at Least one Representative ...

Such Clause would enforce the House of Representatives to increase its numbers over time, rather than dilute Representation, as it could not have more than sixty Thousand persons per Representative.

Even that was excessive.

Franklin envisioned a Clause of even sterner Constrainment: The number of Representatives shall not exceed one for every ten Thousand, nor deceed one for every twenty Thousand, but each State shall have at Least one Representative ...

To Franklin, the apportionment Clause with one for every forty Thousand made a lampoon of Representation. What Representative could ever return to so large a citizenry and commingle with them meaningful? If a Representative met with a hundred Citizens per diem for instruction, it would take him 400 days to meet all those he served. An over simplistic and brutish estimation, bordering on British to be sure, but one that exemplified the problem nonetheless. This intermixing with the citizenry was unwieldy enough for Members of the Pennsylvania Assembly, who again represented a mere six Thousand each.

Even Great Britain had robust Representation in its House of Commons, owing its trifling geographic extent—Colonys denyed Representation notwithstanding. The whole of Britain, the island proper including Scotland and Wales, contained less acreage than Virginia and Pennsylvania, yet had a population of some 9 Million, nigh triple that of the whole of America. Grievous crowded, plaguy crowded, with land ruinous exorbitant. Yet the House of Commons had some 558 Members, eight and a half times America's 65 Representatives, though that 558 number was affix'd and could not increase. Britain's 558 Members was one for every sixteen Thousand, approximate. America had diluted Representation two and a half times more than Britain! By this reckoning, which was a far from encompassing, America's first House was two and a half times less Representative than that of the British nation, which America had declared Independency from because it was tyrannical and provided not sufficient Representation.

Was the difference between one for every six Thousand and one for every sixteen Thousand the difference between the Liberty that Pennsylvanians enjoyed and the Tyranny that the English suffered? If so, what did one for every forty Thousand forebode?

With the first Branch the only one where The People were empowerd to act Direct upon the government, such questions were critical, and struck to the heart of the ultimate character of the new Republic. If The People's ability to instruct their Representatives be too diluted, rotation would avail them little, they would be excluded from true Direct controul of government, and perhaps be devoted to oppression.

Had the Convention erred fatal in its enumeration and apportionment provisions?

Franklin knew not.

No one knew.

Only time could say.

Nestled among the little-state Deputies was Roger Sherman of Connecticut, who glanced at Franklin, letting nervousness shew in the solemn eyes that dominated his Face. He was seated in the front left row at the centre table, rightward of Doctor Johnson. Sherman was architect of the Compromise that saved the Convention. In 1776, Franklin had worked with him on the Committee of Five that draughted the Declaration of Independency.

Sherman had hair short and brown with streaks of grey, a surly underbite, and thin lips that was perfect horizontal in repose, running straight across his face like a joint in wood. He was dressed conservative in a rust-coloured country suit that was faded and worn to a barkish colour in places. The sort of suit an indifferent Yeoman, a farmer who cultivated his own land, might wear. For a Gentleman it bordered on disreputable.

Sherman was right curious, to be sure, exhibiting one of the oddest shaped characters Franklin ever met with. He was awkward, unmeaning in his face expression, and unaccountable strange in his manner. Look at him too long, in motion especially, and a deep revulsion arrested you. The only word true appropriate was grotesque. Sherman seemed like an apparition that would haunt a crypt.

Like Franklin, Sherman had begun life as a Leather Apron, working as a shoemaker. Like Franklin, Sherman wanted for formal schooling but educated himself by obtaining access to a private library. Skilled with computing, Sherman became a surveyor like Washington, later passed the Connecticut bar despite having never read the Law formal, and was now a Justice on the Connecticut Superior Court. He had also published an Almanack that enjoyt some success, though 'twas not prolifick like Poor Richard's.

Sherman saw larger practicable realities, and along with Washington and Franklin had been part of that minority of Deputies who strove for compromise and harmony rather than jobbing relentless for selfish Interests. Like Franklin, Sherman feared that warmth might resurface, unraveling the Convention, and the frown that resulted natural from his underbite was more severe than typical.

Franklin thanked Providence for Sherman's wisdom and courage. It had been critical that the Compromise upon Representation which required sacrifice by the little States be proposed by a Deputy from a little State, and Sherman had been one of the few willing.

Franklin had appraized the little-state Deputies as best he could. So much uncertainty. 'Twas easy to dismiss the possibility that Deputies would vote against the Constitution. There were myriad reasons they ought not abandon support, and probably would not. Yet Franklin nonetheless fretted, and he would continue to do so until the Constitution was executed and the Convention adjourned Sine Die.

"Section Three," Jackson read, "The Senate of the United States shall be composed of two Senators from each State, chosen by the Legislature thereof, for six Years; and each Senator shall have one Vote."

Franklin pursed his lips tight. The Senate peeved him. A bicameral Congress was like a snake with two heads, pulling in different directions, working against itself at best, disemboweling itself at worst. Franklin had a two-headed snake embalm'd in a jar in his library, and he had peered at it many a night after sitting through cantankerous Convention debates on the Legislature.

Ought Delaware with 37 Thousand persons have the same voting power in Congress as Virginia with its 532 Thousand? It would in the Senate, where a person of Delaware would have more Representation than a person of Virginia. Nigh 14 times more Representation. Even using Virginia's Quota of Tax of some 420 Thousand, which lessened the disparity versus population, a person of Virginia would have one eleventh the Representation of a person from Delaware. How was this any less vile than the three fifths enumeration for Slaves?

Franklin thought of the Preamble. Of the distinction between a government comprized of States versus one comprized of People. More profund a difference than it seemed superficial, once one delved into the detail.

Suppose a Capitation, a direct head Tax, were apportioned among the several States at a rate of one pence per Quota of Tax. The total Quota of Tax for all thirteen States was some 2,568 Thousand, reflecting the accounting of each free Person as one Person and each Slave as three fifths a Person. Some 2.568 Million pence would be raised. Several Hundred pounds shy of eleven Thousand pounds. Ought Delaware have coequal say against Virginia in how such funds be disposed, despite contributing but 37 Thousand pence to Virginia's 420 Thousand pence?

Disproportional representation was a pernicious Injustice to bottom a government upon, one liable to be expanded to ruin. Would not Delaware, and Delawareans, develop a sense of Entitle, expecting ongoing claim to the 420 Thousand pence of Virgina? Might Delaware not press for ever larger Capitations, subjecting Virginia ever more energetic Levelling, draining its wealth away relentless? How was this different from a citizen of Delaware waylaying a Virginian, pommeling them Colcannon, and filching they Purse? Might not all citizens develop a sense of Entitle, seeking to attain more from government than they contributed, precipitating Ruin?

Not with Virginia's proportional Representation in the first House, where a Capitation would also require a majority vote. And not with revenue bills originating in the House, a provision large States had wise demanded. And not with so many energetic restraints on Taxation in the Constitution, direct Taxation especially.

It nonetheless made Franklin sad to forsake a principle so mighty and foundational at the moment of conception. To impregnate a fledgling government with such injustice. How could a government incorporate so misprincipled become anything but more so?

Paterson, Bedford, Read, or Brearly would have argued, and had argued, that voting in the Senate was not disproportional, it was equal—if the voting was by State rather than person.

But what were states?

Legal constructs. Contractual sophistrys.

Sovereign nations, Paterson and others would say. Sovereign nations which had entreated the Articles of Confederacy, and which would check Encroachments and Consolidation of Powers by the fœderal government. Franklin might tend to agree, in measure.

But states laughed not, cried not, bled not, starved not, died not.

People did.

All good Governments were bottomed on The People, not States.

Constitutions ought reflect this fact, the current one more emphatick.

"Immediately after they shall be assembled in Consequence of the first Election," Jackson read, "they shall be divided as equally as may be into three Classes. The Seats of the Senators of the first Class shall be vacated at the Expiration of the second Year, of the second Class at the Expiration of the fourth Year, and of the third Class at the Expiration of the sixth Year, so that one third may be chosen every second Year;"

With a third of the Senate rotated every second Year, it would take six years to rotate the entire Senate out of office. Most Deputies considerd this Delay beneficial, a rampart against rash impulses of The People.

But Six years could be a veritable æternity.

Much longer than the decisive portions of most Revolutions.

If government became corrupt, which all governments had eventual, could The People be supposed to rise up three times, at two-year intervals, to enact Reformation without resort to the Sword? If government stoop'd to Tyranny, why should The People wait six years to end it? Or even four years, the time required to rotate a majority of the Senate?

The very tempering and counterbalancing effect that most Deputies saw as the prime advantage of the Senate seemed to Franklin its prime deficiency.

Franklin envisioned a different Constitution reading, by Temple rather than Jackson: All legislative Powers herein granted shall be vested in a Congress of the United States, which shall consist of a House of Representatives.

No Senate.

Franklin knew he was being petulant. A sore Compromiser. Some Deputies were doubtless engaging in similar fancy. Hypothesizing a Constitution with all provisions they fancied, which they envisioned to be superior to that reading.

Jemmy doubtless saw his Council of Revision and a Congress with an inviolate Negative upon all state laws. Caledonia James perhaps saw a President direct electored by The People, or at Least electors direct electored by them, as he advocated, rather than the convoluted mode chosen. Southern Gentlemen nigh certain had visions of clauses perpetuating Slavery ad infinitum. Governeur Morris, the most vocif'rous and principled opponent of slavery at the Convention, probably saw a single succinct clause exploding slavery immediate and permanent, imposing a one-time Capitation to purchase all slaves from owners, manumit them, expel them from America, and pay for their equipage and Transportation back to Africa, the Carib, or south America. Colonel Mason had so many objections to the Constitution he probably struggled envisioning them all, but his chief grievance was the absence of a Declaration of Rights, which he doubtless fancy'd prefixed before the preamble. Little

States perhaps envisioned the mirror opposite of Franklin's fancy, a single-house Congress in which only States voted.

At least Senate votes would be by majority of individuals, rather than majority of States, as under the Articles of Confederacy. This was Consolation, though a trifle of one.

Viewed at present, through the narrow medium of state Jealousies, the Senate seemed to many a right clever construct. Adding a second House to the Congress had facilitated the addition of a dizzying array of counterbalances upon other Branches and the first House. Many Deputies supposed this a defence against Tyranny. And it was, in some measure.

But Franklin was one of the few Deputies who had actual stood before Parliament, both the House of Commons and the House of Lords, and even the king and his dastard Bastard Privy Council. Doing so, Franklin learnt a simple lesson: the Corrupt ignore all Laws.

A Constitution could say whatever it wished. If the men in Power implementing the Constitution were not honest, 'twas all for naught. In his encounters with Parliament and the British nobility, Franklin had seen the naked exercise of Interest that was not just dishonest, not just corrupt, but god damned Evil.

Devilish Evil.

The Convention should have given more focus to ensuring electees Honest, and to empowering The People to rotate them if Dishonest. Every suggestion Franklin had made to address this problem, such as denying electees pay, had been dismissed by Deputies as naïve or Utopian.

Franklin looked forward in time to a government brimming with not just the dishonest, not just the corrupt, but the evil.

The Devilish Evil. To suppoze men Devilish Evil populating all offices of government would somehow counterbalance each other and produce honesty was preposterous. Yet this seemed to be what the Constitution was tending towards.

Franklin told himself he was just being ornery.

And Vain.

Supposing himself wiser than all others.

But that didn't mean he erred.

Or that he wasn't wiser than most others, much of the time.

Franklin feared the intrenchment of a Senate that was an insurmountable blockade to the will of The People. Over time, a large number of unpopulous states need only incorporate, be admitted to the Union, and they would have a sufficient Faction in the Senate to block any action of the populous majority in the House, approval of House of Representatives and Senate in tandem requisite to positive any Law, and each Branch of the Legislature thus in effect possessing a negative upon the other.

In the first House of Congress The People were represented, in the second House of Congress the States were represented. Even with Compromise, large States feared for their Money, and little States feared for their Liberty. Franklin feared that the interest of The People might have been trampled amidst the jockeying of little States and large States.

A Legislative structure born of political Compromise might not be, and probly wasn't, the best to secure natural Rights and Liberty. How much would this political Compromise of the present cost Futurity? Franklin was no Delphi Oracle, and scrupled to prognosticate, but it concerned him.

Jackson moved his hands down the parchment as he progressed, that the Clauses reading were direct in front of him and discernible. As he progressed, more and more of the upper portion of the parchment draped downward and frontward. Franklin discerned the giant calligraphic "We the People," as well as a smaller but still oversize calligraphic "Article. I." Both were inverted.

"The Vice President of the United States," Jackson read, "shall be President of the Senate, but shall have no Vote, unless they be equally divided."

The bloody Vice Presidency. Perhaps the most impotent office ever conceive-ed. The Vice President was of as much use as a sword or whore to a Quaker. Being an officer of the executive Branch, the Vice President's grant of legislative Powers was right curious. He seemed to have been placed at the head of the Senate so he would have some formal purpose besides standing fast in case the President was to die—or conspiring to ferment such eventuality with his abundance of leisure. How long would it take for a designing Vice President to Assassinate a President, as with the heirs of the monarchys of Europe?

Like most constructions in the Constitution, the Vice President was not an original one. In New York, the Lieutenant Governour was President of the Senate. At least the Vice President hadn't been stiled Lieutenant President.

Franklin would have preferred to annex a Council to the Magistracy, as in Pennsylvania, to give weight and inspire Confidency. He would have preferred leaving the Senate to their business, and the Executive branch to its, so the segregate Powers which Deputies claimed to so cherish remain plantate. If the President of an Executive Council died, a replacement was simple elected from amongst the remaining members. America might one day be a vast nation—too vast for one man to effective act as Executor. An Executive Council could be expanded as the nation grew, and would allow the accumulation of wisdom and expertise, making the execution of laws more effectual. An Executive Council was also a rampart against an energetic President that might become an elective Monarch. An Executive Council was a rampart against Tyranny.

This was yet another construction where the Convention had ignored Franklin's admonitions. Deputies favoured the dispatch and accountability of a single Executive, the risk of Monarchy or a tyrannical Executive be damned.

"The Senate shall chuse their other Officers," Jackson read, "and also a President pro tempore, in the Absence of the Vice President, or when he shall exercise the Office of President of the United States."

The Latin phrase "pro tempore" was right conspicuous to Franklin. President pro tempore meant President for the time being. The Constitution was English, except for a few Latin phrases. The Latin seemed appropriate, as 'twas the language of the last great Republic, Rome.

Jackson continued to enumerate the Senate. Nigh every syllable grated Franklin. He told himself to be wise. Not to grow frustrate. To play the role required of him.

It was hard.

Like watching a Grandson you loved, born of an estranged Son you despized, reject all attempts at guidance and become a Fop and a Libertine.

"Section Four," Jackson read. "The Times, Places and Manner of holding Elections for Senators and Representatives, shall be prescribed in each State by the Legislature thereof;"

Jackson continued reading. To hear the Constitution was to relive the last four months, the warmth, the frustration, the fatigue, the exultation. 'Twas impossible to relive the last four months without travelling further back, to dark times, to the signing of the Declaration of Independency in this chambre, the appointment of Washington as Commander of the Army, the train of events long and improbable that led the states to unite, rebel, and create a Constitution.

On July 4, 1776, America declared Independency and each colony became a sovereign Nation. These sovereign Nations realized they must co-operate, and on July 12, 1776 they began drawing Articles of Confederacy and Perpetual Union. Franklin helped draft the Articles. A crude Constitution, they created a single-house Congress in which each state had a single vote, regardless of its geographical size, population, financial or military contribution, or number of Deputies.

Like a marriage in which the wife was co-equal, the Articles of Confederacy proved defective and impracticable. They were a Treaty among sovereign nation states, not a Consolidation of those states into a Union. The Continental Congress under the Articles had no ability to levy Taxes or compel states to pay them. Amendments of the Articles required the unanimous Vote of all member States, which was impossible to attain. The sole Branch of government under the Articles was Congress. Congress passed measures, but states refused to pay for them, and there was no Executive to administer measures even if Taxes were paid.

There were myriad testaments to the impotency of the Confederacy, but none more galling than The Forge, where soldiers languished shoeless, coatless, freezing in literal Dead of Winter, while American locals sold Supplies to the ample-funded british army for ready Specie. America had the resources to equip its Army, and Congress requisitioned Funds, but states refused to pay.

"The Congress shall assemble at least once in every Year," Jackson read, "and such Meeting shall be on the first Monday in December, unless they shall by Law appoint a different Day."

Denying the Confederacy the Power to make States pay Taxes, or make States do anything, seemed wise in 1776 after declaring Independency from a tyrannical Parliament and king. Taxes were an especially prickley issue. The Revolution began as a Tax dispute. No Taxation Without Representation was a motto of the Revolution, but in truth, Taxation With Representation didn't seem so appealing either. Why fight for Liberty from an energetic Parliament and king only to replace them with an energetic Congress and Executive?

Thus, America remained thirteen nations even though its problems increasing required a single nation. Britain, France, and Spain were encroaching, filching the boundless cornucopia of the West, making sport of the separate states, wooing many to become protectorates. Savages were marauding the frontier with audacity, scalping and raping, emboldend by the want of a united defence from supposed United States. The barbary Pirates of Algiers, Tunis, Tripoli, Morocco, and cetera, continued their wanton reign of Terrour. States were discriminating each other with tariffs and duties, acting more like the petty nations of Europe than Allies. In time, if tensions continued to mount, War amongst States was not unthinkable.

If not War, then some of the several states might dissolve in civil Disorder. At best, the Confederacy would grow inexorable weaker year by year, until effective nonexistent. America would then be divided against itself as separate nations. Three nations, most probable, one comprized of the New England states, a second comprized of the south slave States, and a third between comprized of middle Atlantic states. Portions of the western frontiers might also become separate nations. 'Twas difficult, if not damn nigh impossible, to envision these separate nations not warring eventual, aping the carnage of Europe to ruin.

The situation was scarce one of encouragement, but Franklin was disinclined to the alarmism that deranged many Deputies. Perhaps he was biased because Pennsylvania was one of the few well governed states and had flourished without a fœderal government. As a prominent leader for decades, and recent elevating President of Pennsylvania's Executive Council, Franklin made certain of that. Franklin had also survived enough crises to know they were not always as dire as they seemed. Yet even he conceded that the States were growing inexorable less United, and that their pressing problems had a continental Character which required a Union more powerful than the Confederacy.

Some of the wisest men in America had come to Philadelphia to create one.

"Section Five," Jackson read. "Each House shall be the Judge of the Elections, Returns and Qualifications of its own Members, and a Majority of each shall constitute a Quorum to do Business; but a smaller Number may adjourn from day to day, and may be authorized to compel the Attendance of absent Members, in such Manner, and under such Penalties as each House may provide."

English tradition gave Houses controul of their own procedural workings. The Convention had adhered to this tradition. Provisions such as these also allowed Branches to maintain their Independency from one the other, keeping Powers segregate.

Absenting Congress to prevent it from conducting business would not be countenanced. In dishonourable Assemblies, such stalling tactics became common Place and proliferate. The Congress was not to be such an Assembly.

"Each House," Jackson read, "may determine the Rules of its Proceedings, punish its Members for disorderly Behaviour ..."

At any chosen moment, several Deputies would be glancing at their struck copys of the Constitution, some reading the words Jackson spoke, others reviewing specific Clauses which tickled they fancy or perhaps irked them. At present, Richard Spaight of North Carolina, Daniel of Saint Thomas Jenifer of Maryland, and George Clymer of Pennsylvania were doing such. All were seated right of Franklin. Jenifer and Clymer seemed be reading the words Jackson spoke, while Spaight, a younger Deputy turned of but 29, seemed to be perusing diff'rent Clauses, those of Slavery perhaps.

This simple Act of consultation of a Charta said much.

Franklin pictured the Convention trying to incorporate a government without a written Charta. He peered at the parchment in Jackson's hands.

The Constitution.

Not just The Constitution, but A Constitution.

A foundational assumption 'twas easy to overlook. Or even take as a grant.

America was to be a Constitutional Republic. A written Constitution would specify fundamental Principles that would create a republican Form of government. In a Republic, The People govern'd not direct, but rather elected leaders to represent them in government.

Elected leaders could violate the Natural Rights of The People as sure as a king, Nobility, or Democratic Mob. Constitutions were therefore critical. In a Constitutional Republic, elected officials could not do any Thing they pleased. They could exercise only specific powers granted by the Constitution, powers that protected the Natural Rights of The People. To prevent abuses of power, well-crafted Constitutions explicit forbade government from exercising powers that violated the Natural Rights of The People. Thus, a Constitutional Republic was the palladium of the Natural Rights of The People, Liberty especially.

Whilst Franklin glanced at his struck copy of the Constitution, eye lingering upon the enlarged first letter, a capital W which dropped down and fill'd three rows, Jackson plodded through the other Clauses of Section 5. As with Section 4, most Clauses were administrative and incontroversial. As incontroversial as any Clause in such a contested creation could be.

The oversize W reminded Franklin of his humble beginnings as a Printer. He had been forced to take on a partner and contract grievous debt to attain to his first press and type Set, of a facing rendered by William Caslon.

The Convention had been in session less than an hour, yet the chambre already seemed hotter.

Much hotter.

Unsurprizing, the sunlight streaming through the windows on the south wall seemed brighter.

Much brighter.

Franklin glanced without the north windows, saw Promenaders strolling leisured upon the side walk which was nigh direct a front the State House. Also numerate folk in working Dress, walking with more vigour and purpose. Beyond the side walk, Franklin saw traffic upon Chestnut Street, men riding horses, and carts, carriages, and coaches drawn by them.

The Promenaders and Workers nigh all gawked at the State House, peering withinst at the Deputies assembled. All of Philadelphia knew the Convention intended to execute the Constitution of Government this day, and the city was ripe with Anticipation. Franklin also spied the back of a bluecoat militia Sentry who stood to attention a front the centre window of the East Room, and seemed right vigilant in preventing anyone from approaching the State House to eavesdrop.

Despite the city Commissioner having laid gravel upon Chestnut Street to lessen the clacking of hooves and wheels upon the cobblestone paving, such noises were audible and persistent, as the gravel had been steady thinned and worn away. Franklin had long ago learned to disattune such distractions, but some Deputies had not acquired such faculty.

Franklin wiped his forefinger and middle finger across his forehead, felt warm sweat, glanced at the fluid on his fingers, and pondered his Experiments with perspiration and condensation.

How diffuz-ed water in the atmosphere? How diffuze it in air, adhere to air? If Franklin could shrink himself down to miniscule size, become a Lilliputian to a Lilliputian to a Lilliputian to a Lilliputian, and do so Swift, that the bead of Sweat on his finger was the size of a horse or House, what would he see? At such miniscule size, what would the electric Fluid look like? The electric Fire? Cold? Heat? Magnetism? Gravity? Matter itself? Franklin frowned. No time for such fascinations today.

Franklin felt excretions building in the pits of his arms and couldn't help glancing at the fireplaces on either side of Washington's dais. Their worn bricks were recessed behind a marble enclosure which merged into a plaster façade.

Fireplaces!

In this heat.

The cruelest of jokes, even unlit.

Not a novel observation, one Franklin had made hundreds of times over the decades while seated in this Chambre, yet which remained irresistible.

The fireplaces was massive, as wide as Washington's larger table and higher than the head of the seated Jackson, reminiscent of the under Side of a small bridge, designed to provide significant heat during winter. Though one might have a hard time convincing Deputies who had sweltered here for a quarter annum creating a Constitution, especially those that had absented the first few weeks, the chambre could be freezing. The Forge was but twenty miles nor'west, a mere half day's ride.

Franklin thought back to the opening of the Convention, in late May, when Washington was elected President—that would hopeful happen again—and the rules of Procedure were drawing. 'Twas cold enough that fires burned in the hearths at least a portion of each day until the beginning of the second week of June, when the hottest summer in nigh half a century descended.

Franklin had been under the weather Bow on the opening day of the Convention, forsaking his chance to nominate Washington as President and see him elected. He was determined to languish in life duration enough to partake of Washington's next inauguration.

During the previous week and much of the summer, it'd been grievous humid. Right suffocating. It had rained on Saturday and the Sabbath and the morning dawned cool, teasing Deputies, making them hope that the mild weather prevalent at the beginning at the Convention might be enjoyed at its conclusion.

But 'twas not to be.

The weather had once again become unconstitutional.

Franklin closed his eyes, breathed in deep, felt warm air rush through the wheat fields of hair in his nose, fancied himself sneezing fresh ovened bread crumbs rather than buggers. The fireplaces had not been used in months, but the smell of burnt wood and soot never vacated the chambre, and aromas of Stain, Plaster, Paint, and Sweat always linger'd at the periphery. The one smell the chambre clamoured for, fresh air, was absent. No scents of grass, flowers, pollen, or lavender, though no horse Shite either.

Franklin knew that the air in the room had become impregnate with snuff of candles, soot, Stain, Plaster, and Paint. Miniscule particles of these substances had become dissolved in air and did so continual. The smell lingered because this air was not replacing with new air, or the dissolved particles were not undissolved or otherwise evacuate. If Franklin the Lilliputian were standing near the horse-sized bead of Sweat, might he deduce a way to undissolve the impregnations? Could such knowledge be made of practicable use once he returned to his usual elephantine size?

"Section Six," Jackson read. "The Senators and Representatives shall receive a Compensation for their Services, to be ascertained by Law, and paid out of the Treasury of the United States."

One of the most deplorable Clauses in the whole of the Constitution, to Franklin. If the Clause had to be kept, then there ought have been some qualification, as in many state Constitutions. Maryland's Constitution required every elected leader to take an oath that he would not receive, direct or indirect at any time, any part of the profits of another office, nor part of the profits arising on any agency for the supply of cloathing or provisions for the Army or Navy.

The Corrupt might ignore such Clauses, but including some direct negative of Profiteering would have nonetheless been beneficial, to pave a constitutional Avenue that facilitated prosecution and made graft overt Fugitive. The Maryland Constitution's ban on Profits Indirect, in peculiar, could be interpreted broad, and acted to deter Profiteering by leaders in that State. Franklin envisioned such a Clause in the Constitution reading, but worded more energetic, so as to ban Profiteering in any form, not just from supplying cloathing or provisions for the Army or Navy. However, the best course, and in truth the only prudential course, would have been a total ban on Compensation and Profiteering, as the one liable to morph into the other.

Franklin was apprehensive—perhaps too apprehensive—that the government of the United States might, in future times, end in Monarchy, perhaps elective Monarchy, yet Monarchy nonetheless. But this catastrophe might be long delayed if America sowed not the seeds of Contention, Faction, and Tumult by making its posts of Honor into places of Profit.

Franklin would have outlawed all public salarys, direct and indirect, except for Judges. Deputies imagined offices without recompence a utopian Conceit, believing Americans could never find men to serve them well without paying them well for their services. Deputies also feared that with no Pay, only the moneyed would serve, resulting in Aristocracy.

Franklin conceived such reasoning to be an errour.

In this single Clause alone, even if all others proved prescient and prudential, might the ruin of America be sown.

"Section Seven," Jackson read, "All Bills for raising Revenue shall originate in the House of Representatives; but the Senate may propose or concur with Amendments as on other Bills."

Bills dispencing money had to originate in the House, for this was where representation was apportioned by population. This insured against the Minority plundering the Majority. Insured against the Spirit of Levelling. Franklin's thoughts had galloped ahead of the reading and he had pondered this provision previous.

This was yet another Clause pilfered from the state Constitutions. Its wording was nigh the exact same as that of the Massachusetts Constitution. Most all state Constitutions had similar constructions.

Jackson now held the parchment nearst the bottom, one hand each side. The upper drooping portion was most of the parchment and contacted the table which he stood before.

"Every Bill which shall have passed the House of Representatives and the Senate," Jackson read, "shall, before it become a Law, be presented to the President of the—"

Jackson placed parchment the first of the Constitution down quick but careful and picked up the second. The parchment rustled as he did. Jackson cleared his throat once, gulping hard, and then gulped again as he switched pages.

"—United States," Jackson read. "If he approve he shall sign it, but if not he shall return it, with his Objections to that House in which it shall have originated, who shall enter the Objections to that House in which it shall have originated, who shall enter the Objections at large on their Journal, and proceed to reconsider it."

Glances of Deputies linger'd on parchment the first. A few pursed their lips or shook their heads fractional. Dictator John expelt wind through his nose.

Washington's eyes sprung to life and swivelt left in their sockets. They affixed on Dictator John, and then narrowed ever so fractional, growing prodigious colder and even more fearsome. Dictator John met Washington's gaze a moment, and then he withered and looked down right sudden. A few Deputies sprouted smirks, though many clear tried not to do so, with scant success. Washington's eyes remained affix'd on Dictator John for several seconds, and then once again faced forward and vacated.

No one else expellt wind or complained, but Franklin could none the less feel the impatience in the air. But a quarter of the

Constitution read. Maybe as much as two fifths if one accounted the blank portion of the final parchment.

Right murderous, any reading of an entire Constitution.

"If after such Reconsideration," Jackson read, "two thirds of that House shall agree to pass the Bill, it shall be sent, together with the Objections, to the other House, by which it shall likewise be reconsidered, and if approved by two thirds of that House, it shall become a Law. But in all such Cases ..."

Jackson's words became a Drone. Franklin knew the meaning of the convoluted Clause and did not truly listen to the words. Congress could positive laws with but a simple Majority in both Houses. The President was granted the power to negative laws of Congress. Congress was granted the power to ride over the Presidential negative, via a two thirds supra Majority in both Houses, a calling of the roll in both Houses requisite for such Votes, that Members of Congress could be held to account.

As with so many Clauses, this one was a far from pioneering, a virtual copy of that in the Massachusetts Constitution. Massachusetts was the only state that gave its Executive the power to negative Laws passed by the Legislature, owing the influence of John Adams, who mistrusted The People. New York's Council of Revision, comprised of supreme Judges and Governour, could also negative Laws passed by the Legislature. In every other state, such Power was absented. In both Massachusetts and New York, Legislatures could ride over a Negative of a Law via a two thirds supra Majority of both Branches.

The ability of the Legislature to ride over an executive Negative was illusory, as a two thirds supra Majority in both Houses of the Legislature would be damn nigh impossible to attain. In practice, in most instancys, America would have a three chambre Legislature, with the third Chambre compriz'd of but a single person, the Executive.

Franklin had seen the royal Governour of Pennsylvania abuse his negative prior to the Revolution, negativing laws passed by the Assembly solely to extort renumeration for himself. As the royal Governour had possessed an absolute negative which the Assembly could not ride over, bribes to the Governour had been requisite to pass any law.

The President was not a royal Governour appointed by a king, but rather was electored indirect by The People. This was scant comfort. Even perverted by a Senate, the Congress was the purest distillation of The People's will. Congress ought pre-eminate the President, not the opposite. It was more arduous to corrupt many men, a Congress, than one man, a President. Argument, again, for an Executive Council. Pennsylvania had no Executive Negative upon laws which its Assembly positived, yet it prospered.

These facts mattered little to Deputies. Nor did other exclusions, which were right glaring to Franklin. Under the Articles of Confederacy, a supra Majority of nine states was requisite to pass most Laws. Nine of thirteen states was nigh two thirds of States, a much more exacting requisite than a simple Majority. Franklin object'd not to this simple Majority requisite in the Constitution reading, but it was a stark change from the Articles, one that might beget a proliferation of legislation.

The south Gentlemen on the right side of the chambre looked right glum, which was right rare, given the energetic protections of Slavery, and inactions upon Slavery, they had foistered into the Constitution.

Franklin glanced at Dictator John, who met his glance even, eyes a-flaring, as if grease had been spilt into a fire. Dictator John was unaccustom'd to having terms dictated to him, and was mighty perturb-ed. So was the diminutive Charles Pinckney, who was seated at the left outside edge South Carolina table, appearing as a sort of deep-south Articulation of Jemmy. Also Colonel Mason. And gentlemen on the whole right portion of the Chambre, which constituted the south States, save gentlemen at the Pennsylvania table.

South States had wanted a two thirds supra Majority vote of Congress requisite for Navigation Acts, those which would regulate intercourse with foreign nations. This was the portion of the Constitution where such a Clause might have been placed.

Had the South been willing to cede more on Slavery, the North would nigh certain have ceded the supra Majority for Navigation Acts, perhaps at a lesser three fifths rather than the two thirds which the South desired.

With a three fifths or two thirds supra Majority requisite for Navigation Acts, mischief against Slavery or southern Commerce would have been difficult, nigh impossible. With but a simple Majority, the eight North or non-South states would nigh certain ruin the five South states eventual, investing slavery upon its flank via Navigation Acts.

Many who detested Slavery seemed happy to see it invested by any mean necessite, but Franklin felt this foolish. A direct frontal investment, a direct Abolition, was the prudential mode.

Franklin wished the Convention and its Deputies had shown more wisdom. He wished he were immune to baser urges, but he could not quell an image of Dictator John dragging behind a horse through mud, the horse a shiteing as it went. Dragging, dragging, dragging, until Dictator John so black with Shite that he could be sold into Slavery in the darkest nethers of the deep South.

"If any Bill," Jackson read, "shall not be returned by the President within ten Days, Sundays excepted, after it shall have been presented to him, the Same shall be a Law, in like Manner as if he had signed it ..."

This Clause was also a nigh exact copy of those in the Massachusetts and New York Constitutions. New York's Council of Revision had ten days to negative bills, and if not return'd either approved or negatived, such bills defaulted to Law. Massachusetts set the time at five days, lessened because a single Executive would decide rather than a Council, with more dispatch, presume-ed.

Both the Massachusetts and New York Constitutions used the exact same wording in their Clauses: And in order to prevent any unnecessary delays ...

With the time for the Executive or Council to return bills then specified.

John Adams had literal copied portions of the New York Constitution when writing the Massachusetts, and the Convention had in a more roundabout and indirect mode done the same sort of copying. There was nothing wrong with drawing wisdom from others, but at times Franklin felt the Constitution more cribbed than an act of statesmanship.

The ten-day negativing period also troubled Franklin, for it was the only constraint on the time requisite to pass a Bill. If the Congress passed a bill hasty and the President signed it rapid, it might become Law in mere days, without The People even informing. As travel and transmission were slow, ten days was insufficient time for all Americans to even hear of a Bill.

To prevent mighty great mischief, and Tyranny, delay in passage of Laws was indispensable.

Such provision was also less than ideal for Washington. Though sure in conclusion, he was slow in reckon, and made his worst decisions when enforced to expedite.

British Parliament had long required Bills to be read three times in each House before passage. Reading involved the literal calling aloud of the entirety of the text of the bill on the floor, in open public without doors, not within doors in privy. Reading also involved free Debate upon the Bill after it was called, Debate which occurred not once, not twice, but thrice. States had long adhered to this thrice-reading Mandate, but newer state Constitutions had begun to discard it, as the Massachusetts Constitution of 1780 had. Right ironic that America maligned the tyranny of the British system while crafting a Constitution that discarded one of its most democratic aspects.

Franklin would have preferenced not just a three-reading requisite, but even stricter provisions to ensure that The People could instruct their Representatives. The Pennsylvania Constitution mandated that the doors of the Assembly remain open to the public, but the Constitution reading contained no such requisite. The Pennsylvania Constitution mandated that votes and proceedings of the Assembly be published weekly, whereas the Constitution reading specify'd only publication "from time to time," a period indeterminate.

To prevent machinations and hasty determinations, Pennsylvania required that Bills be printed for the consideration of The People prior to passage. In Pennsylvania, a law could also not be passed in a current session of the Assembly, even when read in Assembly and printed for The People. Rather, it had to be voted upon in the sequel session of the Assembly, after another bout of electoring and rotation.

With The People acquainted of proposed Laws timely, and able to rotate leaders out of office before proposed Laws were voted upon, they were able to rotate out leaders who proposed tyrannical Laws, thereby preventing their passage in the sequel Assembly session. Laws passed in Pennsylvania thus had to be approved by The People and serve their Interest.

Deputies despised these Democratic provisions, which in effect made The People a second House of the Legislative Branch and gave them a direct controul of government perhaps singular in history. Modern history, at the least. Regardless, better The People be a de facto House of the Legislature, rather than a single Executive electored by a mode Byzantine.

The Constitution reading enumerated an oath for the President only. The Pennsylvania Constitution included one for Members of the Assembly. Members swore not to propose or assent to any bill, vote or resolution which was injur'ous to The People, nor to consent to any act or thing whatever that had a tendency to lessen or abridge The People's rights and privileges. The Corrupt would of course violate any oath, but Franklin still felt it important to have Assembly Members swear an oath to

The People, so as to be held to account easier if they became perverted and served any other Interest. Franklin would have had such an oath in the Constitution reading, and would have had it address indirect Misbehaviour and Profiteering, as well as direct, making all explicit Fugitive.

Overall, to Franklin, the Constitution as read seemed insecure where Legislation concerned. In peculiar, the Power to Legislate with expedition, virtual unchecked by The People, was grievous terrific to Franklin. What oppressive and venal Laws might the Congresses and Presidents of futurity pass without The People having an inkling?

"Section Eight," Jackson read. "The Congress shall have Pow—"

He paused and cleared his throat.

"The Congress shall have Power," Jackson read, "To lay and collect Taxes, Duties, Imposts and Excises to pay the Debts and provide for the common Defence and general Welfare of the United States; but all Duties, Imposts and Excises shall be uniform through out the United States."

Many Deputies who had slouched a bit or sprouted vacuous Expressions sat up straighter and focused. This Section granting specific Powers to Congress was the mutton of Article the First.

Power to pay the Debts.

Mozart to Franklin's ears.

And those of America's creditors, once the Constitution disseminate.

To lay and collect Taxes.

Five plain words.

A simple Clause which Leaders of the Revolution had been fighting to codify for nigh a decade. Voluntary payment of Taxes was a ludicrous principle, or want thereof, to bottom a government upon. During the Revolution, states usual paid Taxes only when british Forces neared their territory. Once menacement abated, so did revenues. States made repeated Promises for funds, materials, and men, yet were Niggards when pressed to honour their commitments. Powerless to force states to comply, the Congress could do little more than beg.

The Congress resorted to paper Money, as many states now was. Paper Scrip was not in its nature flawed, as many a Deputy suppose-ed, though insecure and emitted without restraint, it was rapid ruinous. To meet the prodigious funding needs of the Army, prodigious Continental Scrip was printed, until the worth of a Continental was nil and merchants rejected them. Congress then resorted to emitting Bills upon Credit, which people purchased, in effect issuing loans, but overissuance again destroyed Confidency, and additional Bills that were but promises to repay debt could not be circulated. The only remaining course was to borrow in Europe at ruinous interest. Franklin had personal negotiated such Loans, with France especially. John Adams and Thomas had also done so, Adams in peculiar with Holland. Franklin had looked Financiers in the eye and pledged upon his sacred Honor that loans would be repaid.

The Army had disbanded and no longer had to be supported, but Interest was accruing on the Loans at a rate right harrowing. Payments on the Debt had come due two years ago, in 1785. No one knew the debt totality a-certain, as much of it was disperst among the several States, but by Franklin's æstimation coarse and brute, America was in arrears some $40 Million, with some $8 Million owed to Holland and France.

Horrifying sums.

America could not even pay the interest on most loans, much less the principal, and forebearance from France, Holland, and other lenders would be limited. America's creditors expected it to organize and tax, to honour its Commitments. Default on Loans so large, and America's reputation would not be mere razed. France and other Powers would send Armies to collect, presume America itself to be collateral on the loans, and foreclose upon it. Franklin had confidence in his powers of Diplomacy and Persuasion, but he scrupled to think he could negotiate loans from France to wage a war against France.

The loans to France and Holland could not be defaulted upon.

Allowing this to happen was bloody unthinkable.

This practicable Necessity, much more than Shay's Uprising or other domestick concerns, motivated Franklin to support the Convention and Constitution. That and his understanding, derived from prodigious experience in Europe, that the several States would be conquered by the nations of Europe eventual if they United not. Fear of default also motivated states, especially those in Arrears who were also calling upon by France and Holland to honour obligations, inducing them to cede Power of Taxation they had long been loathe to divorce.

Mozart, indeed. Though not his armonica concerto.

So many men within this chambre—and without it—had struggled so mighty to keep the Cause cobbled together without revenue. 'Twas a miracle they had prevail'd, but a government could not rely on miracles indefinite. Expecting Washingtons and Franklins to wrangle military and diplomatic victories out of air, to accomplish everything with nothing, for æternity, was folly.

By the time Army officers stood ready to mutiny at Newburgh in 1783, most had not been paid in bloody years. A nation purporting to revere Liberty could not recompence the very men who had bled to secure it. Only the Character of Washington prevented Newburgh from burgeoning a Mutiny that extinguished Liberty in America.

Earlier the present annum, when Shay and some four Thousand destitute yeomen attempted to enforce relief of Taxes and Debt by overthrowing the Massachusetts government, many wanted a fœderal Army to quash them. Congress was amenable, but had no funds. A charitable subscription had been taken up, and it funded a militia that put down Shay's attempt at Revolution.

A charitable Subscription to quash an Uprising!

The restoration of civil Order funded as a Poor House might be.

One could scour the histories and scarce find such absurdity.

What if no one had subscribed?

No longer would the funding of Government be a ragged quiltwork!

Yet the joy of many a Deputy seemed tempered.

Taxing was perhaps the most important of any Power that could be granted to government. It connected with all other Powers, and in the process of time, drew all other Powers after it. It was the great mean of Protection, Security, and Defence in a good government, and the great engine of Oppression and Tyranny in a bad one.

All Duties, Imposts and Excises, all Taxes, would be uniform throughout America. Equal applying of the Law to all under it was crucial. One Tax rate for all, rather than arbitrary Preferences that stoked the Spirit of Levelling and wrought the opposite of what the wishful suppose-ed. Franklin had observed the prodigious Corruption wrought in Parliament by abandonment of this elementary yet profund Principle.

All Deputies understood the intrinsic Risk in consolidating a government and giving it Power to draw revenue from states and The People, but hearing the words "Congress shall have Power To lay and collect Taxes" read with Finality nonetheless chilled one a bit. Especially because there was scant Limitation placed upon the Power direct. If Deputies' wisdom in constructing the Power To lay and collect Taxes was wanting, generations living and unbirthed might subsist in indentured Servitude to government.

George Mason shook his head back and forth fractional yet rapid. He was sitting at the Virginia table in front of Franklin's, right next to Jemmy. His head froze right sudden, and he exhalt deep. Though Mason made effort to froth quiet, the expellation could be heard. The acoustics of the Chambre were such that most any utterance could be heard by other Gentleman, even utterances Gentlemen did not want heard. The Chambre had been designed to make Oratory auditory, not afford Privy. Likewise, every Gentleman could observe the expressions on any gentleman's Face, if they were facing him and within View.

Franklin could not see Mason's face, only the back of his head and body. Mason's wig was long and white, his suitcoat dyed artichoke, brighter than the forest but darker than the lime, as if he'd suffered the table baize to fade for decades and then fashioned a suit from it. Franklin pictured Mason with the head of a bull, breathing heavy through the nose, saliva frothing, eyes growing bloodyer with each word read.

Mason raised a paper upon his desk and peered at it with disgust. 'Twas a Report, but one whose paper worn, not the fresh struck final Charta. 'Twas either the Report of the Committee of Detail or the Report of the Committee of Stile. The Committee of Detail Report of early July, the first working draught of the Constitution, had a generous left margin equal to some two fifths of the page width, that Deputies might have ample space to pen notes and Amendments. The Committee of Stile Report of last week, a more finalized draught of the Constitution, had a more modest left margin equal to some one fifth of the page width. The modest left margin of the Report which Mason held, equal to some one fifth of the page width, marked it as the Committee of Stile report, as did the lighter, tanner hue of its paper.

Franklin glimpsed the oversize type on the uppermost line of Mason's Report, which he squinted and could discern: We, the People of the United States, in order to form …

The Committee of Stile Report, right certain. The Committee of Detail Report read: We the People of the States of …

It then enumerated all thirteen of the several States.

The Preamble of the Committee of Stile Report was superior to that of the Committee of Detail Report. The comma between the words "we" and "the" in the Committee of Stile Report had been removed from the final draught, also an improvement by Franklin's reckon, even if less correct and precise to a finn-icker of Grammar.

As Colonel Mason flipt the Committee of Stile Report over and placed it upon his table, Franklin glimpsed the writing upon its back momentary. Mason had filled a third of the page with his Script neat and small, which extended to the extreme right edge in most instancys, and had but a trifle of margin upon the left. 'Twas as if Mason felt that a mere four pages, the length of the Committee of Stile Report, an insufficiency, and sought to cram as much as possible upon each page.

Mason grabbed a quill from the Stand upon the centre, rear portion of his table. Like nigh all feather Quills, this one had the barbs shaved cluse to the shaft on the in side, or inner vane, which contacted the webbing of the hand between thumb and forefinger. On the out side or outer vane, opposite the webbing the hand, the barbs had been cut to less than an inch, and tapered toward the shaft moving upward. The quill was perhaps nine inches of length, with the lowermost three or four inches com-pleat smooth and absent barbs, as if wrought of bone.

Franklin glanced about at the pens, the quills, which the Sta-tioner had placed upon every table in stands. Goose quills, nigh all. Though a few goose pens were longer or shorter, they were uniform in most other respects, and at the more distant tables 'twas hard to ascertain the barbs or that they were even feathers.

A few tables had smaller darkish crow quills, used for fine work, fine lettering and numbering, such as a counting ledgers, of which Deputies in Convention assembled had but scant need in most instanceys. Franklin thought he spied a larger white goose Quill at Jemmy's table. Such Quill would be used for oversize

Lettering. Whether Jemmy had brung the goose Quill, or Mason, or it had been provided by the Stationer, Franklin knew not.

Mason moved one of the inkstands close to the Committee of Stile Report. He opened the inkwell, dipped his goose Quill tip in it, and began penning feverish, as he had also done Saturday.

Governeur Morris glanced at Mason and then back at Franklin, his expression ominous. Mason wasn't penning an ode to the Græcian Virtues of the Constitution, damn certain. Rather, he was probably quilling venom, documenting his Objections to the Constitution of Government. 'Twas nigh certain that his Venom would be transmitted to other enemies of the Constitution and make its way into the Papers.

No Deputy had thought the Constitution would be floated to ratification upon a goose pillow, but seeing a Gentlemen as prominent as Mason working open against it in Convention, before the parchment had even been given the Sanction of their names, was right sobering. The campaign for ratification would be bloody contentious.

"To borrow Money on the credit of the United States;" Jackson read.

Power to contract Debts.

Less symphonic to Franklin.

Robert Morris could not nod quick enough. Nor vig'rous enough. The fat of his chin pressed up and down, in and out, in cycles, as if his neck were a pastry Bag and he were trying to excrete butter cream Frosting from his Adam's apple. Robert Morris was seated right of Governeur Morris, so Franklin received a closer view of the apastryment than he would have preferred. He gripped his drooping chins reflexive, felt the ample corpulence, and quellt Disgust. He and Morris could frost a sweetmeat together.

Some of the borrowing of the Revolution had been on Morris' personal credit, and that of his firm Willing Morris & Co., and his finances was still a shambled because of it. No man was more pleased with this Provision than Morris, as it meant that future Patriots would not have to extend personal credit for the Cause.

Franklin had become a Gentleman through Thrift and Industry, manumitting his time for electric-fluid Experiments, inventions, and public service. He hoped America, and Americans, would avoid debt and the indenturement it represented, choosing the manumission of Thrift and Industry instead.

"To regulate Commerce with foreign Nations," Jackson read, "and among the several States, and with the Indian Tribes;"

In his mind's eye, Franklin placed "The Congress shall have Power" before each Clause now read. The southern Gentlemen again sprout'd severe expressions, tho' not warm expressions. This Clause was another of the Prices they had paid for the Protections of Slavery within the Constitution, and to keep Encroachments upon Slavery and Manumission without it.

It was a steep Price.

Congress would have the Power to regulate south Commerce in Staples, in principal crops such as rice, tobacco, indigo, corn, wheat, and cetera, which accounted for nigh all the Income of the South. The south Gentlemen had wanted the Power to regulate Commerce more resident in the States, but the north Gentlemen were not to be played for bloody Fools. They had not surrendered Slavery without wresting a mighty emolument in exchange.

Here the debate had a national character as well. England and France did not let counties and providences set independent intercourse policies. Uniformity of Navigation Acts and intercourse within and without the nation was requisite if foreign Powers were to view America as a single Nation, and if it were to ultimate be one.

It was nonetheless easy to envision Slavery becoming more odious as time passed and the Congress regulating Commerce so as to cripple south staple Markets. Ruinous duties on Staples might be imposed as a flanking manœuvre against Slavery. Or the Congress might assert dominion over slave Property under the guise of Commerce. In case of such Prosecutions, the South would resort to the sword, nigh certain.

What would begot then? Either the Death of slavery, the Death of states, or the Death of the nation. Or perhaps some mingling of the three?

Long after the slaves were manumitted and expelled to Africa, the commerce Power granted as a concession against Slavery would endure—if eradicating Slavery scatter'd not the Republic to the winds. Right ironic that the most lasting effect of slavery upon the Constitution might not be slavery itself.

"To coin Money," Jackson read, "regulate the Value thereof, and of foreign Coin, and fix the Standard of Weights and Measures;"

Approbation showed on the faces of most all Deputies. One money coined by a national government, perhaps not immediate, but eventual. The money's Value, the weight of gold or silver it contained, regulated to ensure it constant, unshaven, and true. No longer thirteen separate state money Units, plus a Hotch Potch of foreign and private, including the Spanish Dollar. A single medium of intrinsick Value irrevocate, circulating through out all of America, unifying its commerce and finance!

How would the money appear?

Washington's visage in some incarnation, to be sure.

Franklin fancy'd himself on a lesser denomination. Washington on the largest denomination of gold Specie, him the next largest? Washington on the gold Specie, Franklin the silver Specie? Would smaller denominations be preferable despite their decreased stature, owing their larger circulation?

Or would the Congress slight Franklin again, showing continued ingratitude for his many services to Country?

Probably.

If Franklin could not attain to a few scraps of Land and but a single low appointment for Temple, expectation he might be honoured upon the circulating medium was phantasy.

Franklin chided himself for such ignoble thoughts. He was acting the Adams. More than a Little Lionish. But what man was immune to a trifle of vanity? Not even Washington could lay such claim.

There was a certain proportionate Quantity of Money requisite to carry on the Trade of a Country freely and currently. A quantity much less than this was exceeding detrimental to it, especially if the quantity dwindled rapid. Many of America's current problems, including Shay's Rebellion and the general Crisis of commerce ravaging the states, could be traced to such Scarcity of the circulating Medium. To solve this problem and

coin the proper quantity of circulating medium was to elimi-
nate much of the suffering in America and lay the foundation
for prosperity.

If specie, coined Money of precious Metal, could solve the
problem.

Gold and silver were not to be plucked from trees like figs
and minted prodigious.

Over time, Franklin feared Specie would prove itself ever
more indurable, owing the spiraling extremity of its scarcity.

States had resorted to emissions of Bills of Credit to remedy
a Scarcity of Specie. Bills of Credit were paper Bills or paper
Notes—any paper circulating as a medium of exchange—not
backed by Specie, not backed by Gold nor Silver, nor convert-
ible to Specie, to Gold or Silver, at a rate, a weight, fixed and
unalterable. The States had general proved incompetent to the
task of emitting Bills of Credit, emitting ruinous quantities that
balloon'd Prices and made a Lottery of Property. Pennsylvania
was a notable Exception, in part because Franklin had helped
it address the problem decades earlyer.

The Committee of Detail draught of the Constitution gave
Congress the Power to "emit bills on the credit of the United
States." Having seen paper Money cause ruin throughout Amer-
ica and history, many Deputies possessed a mortal Hatred of it.
The clause was struck out with some vehemence.

Many Deputies thought striking out the obnoxious clause
insufficient security, however, and wanted to disarm the government of such Power with a firm Negative, preventing its
assumption. Other Deputies were cognizant that they could
not foresee all Emergencys and were unwilling to tie the hands

of the Legislature. The late Revolution was funded by Bills of Credit, Continentals in peculiar, and could not have been carry'd on if such Prohibition existed. Better to give Congress some discretion on the point.

Especially because Yeomen and Aprons were energetic in Favour of paper Money and the moneyed Class was energetic in opposition. The current construction, or more proper the absence of one, was also a political Compromize that helped make Ratification of the Constitution feasible. In neither enumerating nor disarming Bills of Credit, Deputies did not fatal alienate money'd Interests who opposed emissions, nor common Citizens who desired emissions.

The expressions of many Deputies seemed more thoughtful than during previous portions of the reading. Some probably lamented the absence of an energetic Negative upon the power to emit Bills of Credit, and desired one.

Franklin did not.

He had been enquiring into the nature and necessity of a paper Currency at intervals for more than half a century. Absent a negative, the power to emit Bills of Credit would be assumed eventual. Thinking other wise was pitiful Naïve.

Like Colonel Mason, Franklin would not have a Power exercised unless it were expressed—enumerate explicit in the Constitution. If expressed, the Power to emit Bills of Credit could be limited and counterbalanced, checking Abuse. If unexpressed, if absented from the Constitution as it præsent was, the Power to emit Bills of Credit could be usurped and exercised without Limit, leading to the ruin that caused such a mortal Hatred of paper Money in Deputies.

Franklin feared a repetition of the great convulsions over Bills of Credit presently taking place in individual states, a repetition that might one day ravage the entire nation uniform. Franklin feared a future in which Financiers, moneyed Men, and perhaps even Yeomen and Aprons, abused the Power of emission and revocation of Bills of Credit to ruin.

Counter to intuition, such Ruin might be averted by a Grant, a limited Grant, of the Power that Deputies rightly feared.

Franklin would have preferenced an additional Clause to the Constitution granting Congress the Power to emit Bills of Credit, but also imposing inviolate Limits upon Emissions. Franklin understood the Politicks, yet it remain'd stupefying—to him at least—that with several of the states in convulsions over emissions of Bills of Credit throughout the Convention, the Constitution was virtual silent on the question. It could ill afford to stand mute on a matter of such import.

But it did.

"To declare War," Jackson read, "grant Letters of Marque and Reprisal, and make Rules concerning Captures on Land and Water;"

War.

Irrepressible War.

Indispensable War.

Until some future when there might be a Congress of Nations, and Articles of Confederacy and Perpetual Union amongst them, mankind would not be manumitted from War. And probably not even then.

Franklin wished he could be young again, re-embrace the naïve Delusions of the Metaphysick, and believe that man was something better.

Instead Franklin faced the truth.

Something intrinsic in man inclined him to Barbary.

Depravity innate and irrevocable. This was the Essence of man, his Constitution. No written Constitution could negative this Essence, nor transmute it.

Deputies not fancying themselves Alchemicks, debate on War had been cooler than on other topics and conspicuous devoid of the fallacys persistent on other matters.

Most Deputies had experienced the desolating horrours of War. More than half the Deputies present in the Chambre had listed the Army. Killed the Enemy in close Quarter. Stared men in the eyes as they ended them.

Even those Deputies who had not listed the Army nor risked themselves direct in Combat had tasted the Ravagement which War wrought. Amputate limbs piled up without physick tents as if they was a Shambles. Gangrenous wounds that ouzed viscid fluids and smelt of festering cheese. Men a-floundering like landed Fish as they expired in prodigious Gushes of their own blood. Survivors so deranged they became incapable of the Pursuit of Happiness, Ripe for Bedlam.

The historium of Europe, and of all the great Confederacies antient and modern, was of rulers fermenting Wars that glory'd and enriched them, and destituted The People. Even mighty Empires such as Rome that wrought Luxury through Plunder, butchering Foreigners to enrich a despotic People, were at the last governed by this Law.

Never in history, neither antient nor modern, had a People rose up spontaneous and advocated strenuous for War. Not even during the late Revolution, or Washington would not have been perpetual deficient Listees.

To declare War.

A mere twelve letters.

But oh what Suffering they might portend.

All government needed Power To protect. Such Power could not be absent'd from the Constitution, thereby absenting War miraculous, as much as Franklin longed for such Fancy.

How to provision the Power then?

Prevent its perversion into Empire as in antient Rome, or the wanton Carnage of modern Europe?

Congress would have the Power to declare War, meaning The People, via their Control of Congress, would decide the question of War or Peace. The military would continue to follow the example Washington had set, that of prostrating itself to the civil Will. The People and their government would command the Army, not be ruled by it as in most nations to ever exist.

Or so 'twas hoped.

The Constitution removed the priv'lege to make endless war from Monarchs, who long assumed it as a noble birthright. This was so radical an Upheaval as to nigh defy reckon.

All Deputies sensed it.

Kings 'round the world would read the Constitution, or listen to Reports upon it, with eyes a narrowed, right certain.

What when the Power To declare War applied to actual conflict, actual Armies, actual Alexanders? Actual corruptible men? The Devilish Evil?

Tyrants and Profiteers had historically been disconcerned with the niceties of Constitutions and willing to resort to any Encroachment or Lie to ferment War.

Might Armies stand without a Declaration of War? Might encroachments certain to ferment War, and force Congress to a Declaration thereof, be undertaken whilst pretending peace? Might a Congress cowered by a Standing Army declare war imprudential?

How would future Courts arbitrate such questions? Future Congresses? Presidents? Future Peoples?

Franklin did not necessarily think an explicit enumeration of the Power To declare Peace was necessary and proper. Yet it remained curious to him that the Power of Peace so much more difficult to exercise than the Power of War. The absence of War was not necessarily a proper Peace, and Designers might exploit this Fallacy.

Would mankind ever know an end to War?

Whatever mankind's fate, America was not to be an Empire, a Plunderer. It was not to war incessant. Executives would no longer determine the question of War solitary and unilateral, Powers unto themselves, as in a Monarchy. A Congress beholden to the will of a People who were disinclined to War would in theory declare War infrequent. This was the desire of most all Deputies, Washington especially. Whether the Constitution as enumerated would realize such Desire, or whether such Desire could be realized by any Constitution, none could say.

"To raise and support Armies," Jackson read, "but no Appropriation of Money to that Use shall be for a longer Term than two Years;"

Yet another controul over the Army, and the Power to War, entrust'd with Congress, rather than Monarchs as in most nations. Another radical Upheaval. Throughout all Europe, and all history, Armies Standing at the Ready under the pretext, and Prætexta, of defending a nation had enslaved The People. In attempting to subjugate America, Britain had placed a large army Standing at the Ready within it, and even forced Yankees to quarter such troops within their Homes. This standing military Force had been used to inflict Terrour upon America and remained vivid in the mind's eyes of all Deputies and Americans. The hope of Deputies was that clauses such as this would prevent standing military Forces in America from putting The People to the domestic Yoke and becoming instruments of Tyranny.

Colonel Mason the Minotaur looked prodigious dour again, at least from the rearward. He emitted another deep expellation through his nose, discernable to all Deputies, though not so volumed as to be lewd.

Perpetual revenue must of its nature subvert the Liberty of any country. This was an acute fear of Mason's, and he had desired a limitation on all provisions of Perpetual Revenue, not just those for Armies. He was perhaps envisioning a more general revenue clause that no Appropriation of money shall be laid for longer than some specify'd term of years, the public Credit perhaps excepting. Mason doubtless favoured the shortest term, but a year, and envisioned a Congress that could not shackle a future Congress or its Posterity with unfunded enactments of the Present. There had been several Deputies of Mason's thinking, considering such clause a Palladium of Liberty.

Colonel Mason was perhaps envisioning a corrupt Congress enacting Laws that imposed minimal expence on the Present, yet much burden upon future Congresses and Posterity. 'Twas difficult to know with Mason. So much about the Constitution warmed him that ascertaining a narrowed purview of his discontent could be right vexing.

"To provide and maintain a Navy;" Jackson read.

Deputies seemed to wince a bit. Without French naval Support, America could not have bested Britain and would still be under her Yoke. America must have a strong Navy eventual, including Ships of the Line. But a road to Las Californias a-paved in sugar cubes and Ivory might be less a dispence.

"To make Rules for the Government and Regulation of the land and naval Forces;" Jackson read. "To provide for calling forth the Militia to execute the Laws of the Union, suppress Insurrections and repel Invasions; To provide for organizing, arming, and disciplining, the Militia, and for governing such Part of them as may be employed in the Service of the United States ..."

Jackson's voice became a Drone again. To repel Invasions. Might that day never hearken. But what nation existed epochas without conquistadoring? Franklin was not so vain to think America immune and might not succumb to Invasion. If it endured.

As Jackson continued to read, he continued to inch his hands down the parchment, slowly lengthening the portion which hung down in front of him. Section 8 filled the upper middle portion of the parchment. Franklin saw the leftward calligraphic flourishes of the letter S in Section. 8., which curled back upon itself like one of the Little Lion's locks. Squinting through the upper hemisphere of his double Spectacles, Franklin saw the conspicuous space between letters in Clause the First of Section 8. He could not discern the script, but knew the Clause:

The Congrefs shall have the Power To lay and collect Taxes, Duties, Imposts, and Excises, to pay the Debts ...

Numerous additional Clauses were indented below the introductory Clause, each beginning with To. Clauses were indented above the introductory Clause, in actuality, as the parchment was inverted.

Franklin saw a long procession of indented clauses initiate with To, with flourishing curls atop and bottom of each calligraphic T. A neat column, stretching vertical down the parchment. In his mind's eye, Franklin again conceptualized each To clause preceded by The Congrefs shall have the Power.

Franklin glanced at Dictator John, who met his glance even, allowing a smirk ever so fractional. A vague enumeration of Powers had predominated when the Committee of Detail had been convoked and charged with converting the decisions in Debate into a workable Draught. Dictator John had chaired the Committee of Detail, and the Draught it returned had replaced the vague enumeration of Powers with a specific list of Powers.

All Deputies understood that only Powers enumerated were to be exercised, else an enumeration was useless, and so was a Constitution. This doctrine of Enumeration pleased Deputies such as Colonel Mason, who wanted limitations upon the Powers conferred to the general Government. It also pleased south Deputies. As regulation of Slavery was not a Power enumerate, it would be the position of the South forevermore than Congress had not the Power to regulate it, absent an Amendment which they could easy thwart.

Much would transpire in futurity that no Deputy or Convention could forecast. What was to happen in such instance? As Congress was only to exercise Powers enumerate explicit in Section 8, were the Republic to endure into distant futurity, simple Amendments to Section 8 would be expected, granting additional requisite Powers

To the Congrefs.

Franklin wondered what errata the Convention had made. What else ought Congrefs have the Power To?

Jemmy and Charles Pinckney had both drawn lists of Powers which they thought should be granted To the Congrefs. These had been submitted to the Committee of Detail, were reckon'd similar, and thus combined.

Both Jemmy and Mr. Pinckney wanted Congrefs to have Power

To establish a University. All great nations had a national University, usually in the Capital.

Like Colonel Mason, Jemmy and Mr. Pinckney wanted clauses restraining the Legislature of the United States from establishing a Perpetual Revenue.

Jemmy wished Congrefs to have Power

To grant Charters of Incorporation. This reflected Jemmy's distrust of the wisdom and virtue of state Legislatures, who exercised such Power at present.

Franklin wished Congrefs to have Power

To cut Canals, which usual required chartas of Incorporation. Chartas of Incorporation were granted for durations short and for but specific Projects, with expiration when Projects compleat. States had grown a customed to the Power of Incorporation, and were loathe to surrender it even in portion, but some Allowance of Incorporation for fœderal projects had seemed prudential to Franklin.

Jemmy also wished Congrefs to have Power

To dispose of the unappropriated lands of the United States. States were unwilling to countenance such Encroachment.

Mr. Pinckney wished Congrefs to have Power

To establish Rewards and Immunities for the promotion of agriculture, commerce, Trades, and Manufactures.

Mr. Pinckney further wished Congrefs to have Power

To secure all creditors under the new Constitution from a violation of the public faith.

Colonel Mason wished Congrefs to have Power

To enact sumptuary laws. Mason feared The People would become luxurious, enslaved to Sumpture and Pleasures. Right ironic for a man who lived voluptuous by the labour of Slaves.

None of these Powers was in the Constitution reading. Would any of these omissions prove to have significancy? Other omissions Franklin could not recall? Omissions the Convention had not been wise enough to foresee?

Franklin knew not.

No one did.

"To exercise exclusive Legislation," Jackson read, "in all Cases whatsoever, over such District (not exceeding ten Miles square) as may, by Cession of particular States, and the Acceptance of Congress, become the Seat of the Government of the United States,"

The fœderal Capital.

In Pennsylvania, Franklin intended.

But pondering this seemed a-putting of the cart before the horse, a way to nemesis the looming Vote inadvertent.

"To exercise like Authority," Jackson read, "over all Places purchased by the Consent of the Legislature of the State in which the Same shall be, for the Erection of Forts, Magazines, Arsenals, dock-Yards, and other needful Buildings;"

"And," Jackson read.

He paused momentary, with a sense of drama, as if he were acting Shakespeare and the next line climactic.

Misleading.

There was nothing climactic about the Clause depending. Nor of acute import. But 'twas the final clause of Section 8.

"To make all Laws," Jackson read, "which shall be necessary and proper for carrying into Execution the foregoing Powers, and all other Powers vested by this Constitution in the Government of the United States, or in any Department or Officer thereof."

The Little Lion smirked appreciable, as south Gentlemen had for Slavery.

Deputies sprouted expressions of perturbation.

The Little Lion was a designing man, to be sure.

And Washington's most trusted Aide-de-Camp for the bulk of The War. Difficult to envision Washington condescending to accept the Presidency without the Little Lion prominent.

This Clause had been added to the Constitution by the Committee of Detail. Ever desirious of a more energetic national

Government, Jemmy had wanted an addendum specifying that Congress shall have the Power

To make all laws and establish all offices which shall be necessary and proper for carrying into Execution the foregoing Powers,

Jemmy's desire for implications of Powers was insurprizing. As Deputy to the Continental Congress, he had argued that the Confederacy under the Articles possessed an implied Power to enforce states to do what so ever it wished.

Fearful of proliferations of offices akin to Aristocracy, the Convention rejected Jemmy's addendum of "establish all offices" to the original Clause, and approved the original Clause with nary a word of Debate, the Yeas being unanimous.

Jackson paused and cleared his throat several times. Phlegmy sounds. Manly sounds. Yet when Franklin focused in on Jackson's face from eyebrow to lower lip, he might have been looking at a Sex. What sort of Lady cleared her throat so crude?

"Section Nine," Jackson read. "The Migration or Importation of such Persons as any of the States now existing shall think proper to admit, shall not be prohibited by the Congress prior to the Year one thousand eight hundred and eight, but a Tax or duty may be imposed on such Importation, not exceeding ten dollars for each Person."

The Tendency of every government antient and modern had been to consolidate all Powers not denied explicit. So denied Powers Deputies had. Section 9 of Article I denied Powers to the fœderal Congress, Section 10 the state Congresses and States. Herein were some of the teeth of the Constitution, though they were perhaps in need of a sharpening, and at times false as Washington's.

The position of the Importation Clause at the head of Section 8 attested to its importance.

But not its approbation.

It was odious to most every Deputy, North or South, Slaver or Abolitionist.

To Franklin the seasoned politician, this signify'd it an effective Compromise.

Which indeed it was.

Yet odious none the less.

Grievous odious.

The wording assaulted Franklin.

The Migration or Importation of such Persons as any of the States now existing shall think proper to admit,

Does thou mean Slavery? Franklin wanted to shout this at Dictator John, the de facto President of the South Deputations, and their Paladin protecting Slavery.

Franklin would never allow himself to be so ungovernd. And Dictator John was too shrewd to respond even if Franklin reverted to a State of Nature. No south Gentleman would do so. They had prevail'd on Slavery, knew it, and were not inclined to risk their Victory by rubbing the noses of north Gentlemen in the Shite.

The Migration or Importation of Slaves could not be prohibited by Congress prior to the year 1808. But a Tax could be levy'd upon imported Slaves, as with all other staples, Manufactures, commodities, wares, and cetera.

Governeur Morris appeared right roosterish, not cherubic. His left fist had clenched and he was squeezing it tight. He cast a recriminating glance rightward, towards the Deputations of the South. They met his glance even, were impervious to it, and a few simple smirked, as if trying not to laugh.

Governeur looked away from the southern Slavers sudden and peered at Franklin. Franklin tried to soothe Morris with his Glance. He understood Morris' warmth, even though he did not feel it as acute. As with compromising Representation and Tax clauses, this clause had hardly been sprung on the Convention, yet hearing it read with finality and realizing it might soon be law had a powerful effect upon Franklin. Clear Governeur as well. 'Twas right curdling to seat mute as the natural Rights of more than a half Million humans were bargaind away like the Fish and fruit on Market Street.

Yet seat mute they must. Slavery was a vein that simply could not be re-opened. Franklin was unsurpriz'd Governeur Morris struggled in this regard. The sobriquet Tall Boy had been bestowed upon Morris by his criticks. His liaisons and tendency to wear his sensibilities on his sleeve were viewed by detractors as evidence of immaturity. Morris often wanted for self Government and was ruled by his passions, and not just in matters of the Sex.

Morris cooled, the rooster transmuting to the cherub before Franklin. The Tall Boy's eyes become pools of sadness rather than Fire. His smile was too sanguine for a Boy though, one of jaded resignation rather than childish innocence.

Slavery was usually a distant Injustice a world away in the South, one northerners could rightful pretend they did little to energize.

Until today.

To sign this Constitution was to strengthen the institution of Slavery, not weaken it.

To seat at a Convention convoked to secure Liberty and extinguish it for so many was damn nigh unspeakable.

Providence have mercy upon them!

And America.

Franklin looked around at the Deputies, seeking the same warmth Morris exhibited, and which he felt in lesser degree.

Franklin found little.

Perturbation etched the expressions of some Deputies.

In a few, it even stretched to irritation.

But not outrage.

Assuming the Constitution ratified within a year, by 1788, which might very well be a misbelief, it would impoze a twenty-year Prohibition on eliminating the Trade in Slaves. The South preferenced a permanent Prohibition, and the North would have exploded the trade immediate if unconstrained. In theory, the North could pretend a victory, as it would be able to govern the trade in slaves eventual, in 1808 or thereafter. Yet the South would import hordes of slaves against such Time, enough to keep it supply'd for centuries should it be unable to prevent a Prohibition on Importation by the Congress. Thus a Clause which might seem to the Ignorant an eventual investment of Slavery, and which might be, would have the present Effect of proliferating Slaves prodigious.

All Deputies knew this.

With slaves accounted in Enumerations, they would be rode harder to multiply, as this would increase Representation of south States in the lower House. Prodigious slave multiplication would also be enforced to increase populations should Importation be banned. The Constitution thus encouraged the proliferation of Slavery in multiple, reinforcing ways.

All Deputies knew this.

Franklin envisioned a Clause more energetic and direct: Slavery shall not be prohibited by the Congress prior to the Year one thousand eight hundred and eight. A Prohibition not on the Importation of Slaves and the Trade in them, but a Prohibition upon slavery itself.

Franklin rebuked himself caustic. At present, envisioning the word Slave in the Constitution was utopian Phantasy, much less a Clause manumitting slaves or even allowing for the contingency. If such Clause was in the Constitution in even the most diluted Form, no south Deputation would be present in Convention and there would be no United States. In truth, all such a Clause would ensure was a resort to the sword in 1809. Or whatever time the North might amass a plurality in Congress and a President inclined to a Prohibition or flanking Tariffs.

It was right grievous that the Convention made no general action on Slavery itself, yet also right telling, and in the end, right understandable.

"The Privilege of the Writ of Habeas Corpus shall not be suspended," Jackson read, "unless when in Cases of Rebellion or Invasion the public Safety may require it."

Colonel Mason's entire body seemed to cool, like a balloon draining of its fluid. He advocated a prodigious List of restrictions such as these, a Declaration of Rights. Most were not in the Constitution, and this was the primary reason Mason opposed it.

"No Bill of Attainder or ex post facto Law shall be passed," Jackson read.

He adjusted the Constitution in his hands. It rustled.

"No Capitation, or other direct, Tax," Jackson read, "shall be laid, unless in Proportion to the Census or enumeration herein before directed to be taken."

Colonel Mason nodded vig'rous. Other Deputies also nodded, more than on perhaps any other Clause. Franklin joined them.

This was the sort of Clause that made one feel a part of something right noble. A desired sensation, after the Slavery clauses.

Capitations, direct Taxes tallied per Person, were to be Proportional to population. Government might levy a Capitation that required each person to pay a pence, a shilling, or a pound of sterling Silver. Government could not levy a Capitation that made one person pay a pence, another a shilling, another a pound of sterling Silver. This Clause also governed direct Taxes besides Capitations, such as those on wages, income, or property of a Person. Such Taxes had to be the same for every person.

The enumeration of a principle in the Constitution was oft found not in a single Clause, but in many Clauses. Limitations upon direct Taxes were such Provision. Deputies had already required that direct Taxes be apportioned among the several States, in Section 2. The United States Government could not levy Taxes direct on People, but rather upon States only. Even if the United States Government pass'd a law that required every Citizen to pay a pence or shilling or pound of sterling Silver, perhaps to fund an Army to repel a marauding Invader, a requisite for which ordinary indirect Tariffs and Duties might be insufficient, it could not plunder citizens direct for this Tax.

In total, protections against abuse of the direct Tax powers that were constructed into the Constitution were right stringent. Not stringent enough for Franklin's liking, and fraught with ambiguity that might grant prodigious latitude for abuse, yet stringent nonetheless. This was one of the most careful conceived Ramparts in the whole of the edifice, and for proper reason. The Power of direct Taxation was prone to grievous Abuse and had contributed to the ruin of nigh every Confederacy and Nation, antient and modern.

Government would chafe under the direct-taxation Shackles which Deputies had effect'd meticulous. Woe unto The People be they ever so destitute of Sense as to hand the shackle screw to the gorillæ Monster, unchaining it.

"No Title of Nobility," Jackson read, "shall be granted by the United States: And no Person holding any Office of Profit or Trust under them, shall, without the Consent of the Congress, accept of any present, Emolument, Office, or Title, of any kind whatever, from any King, Prince, or foreign State."

The last Clause of Section 9. Making a fugitive of Nobility and its trappings seemed a fitting punctuation. As did insuring against the dangers of foreign Gold. Many Deputies nodded emphatick.

Except Colonel Mason. In addition to a Declaration of Rights, Mason had wanted an explicit hard Limit on Taxes, a ceiling never to be exceeded; an explicit hard Ceiling on Debt; an explicit boundary on the Power To declare War including a supra Majority requisite of both Houses; an explicit hard Ceiling on Revenues allocate to Armies; and cetera.

"Section Ten," Jackson read. "No State shall enter into any Treaty, Alliance, or Confederation; grant Letters of Marque and Reprisal; coin Money; emit Bills of Credit; make any Thing but gold and silver Coin a Tender in …"

Jackson held parchment the second nearst the bottom, one hand each side. The upper portion of the parchment drooped and contacted the table. Jackson's voice became a Drone to Franklin. Section 10 denied Powers to States, general those which had been granted to the United States Government and which it was imprudential to also have States exercise concurrent, or Powers denied to the United States Government that States ought also not have. Little controversial hither, except perhaps the Prohibition upon the emission of Bills of Credit, of paper Money, by States.

The same could not be said of Section 9. Like Washington, it could stand the addition of teeth. Colonel Mason would have so a-teethed Section 9 as to make it a great snarling Beast. This demand might prove prescient. Mason wanted a list of emphatick negatives on government actions that violated Liberty—A Declaration of Rights.

But there were other clauses not in a Declaration of Rights which Deputies had wanted to include. Jemmy had wanted a Clause stipulating

That funds which shall be appropriated for the payment of public creditors, shall not during the time of such appropriation, be diverted or applied to any other purpose.

The absence of a Ban on perpetual revenue also remain'd right glaring, though not so glaring as the sun streaming into the chambre with increasing intensity. Deputies peering towards windows were now forced to squint.

It was possible to enumerate a thousand Clauses negativing every Debauchery and Tyranny known to history, and myriad more unhatched which designing men might conceive. Yet therein a quagmire. 'Twas impossible to foresee every Abuse and negative it. Nor desirable. Were there to be clauses saying the Army shouldn't rape and pillage and torture? That Presidents shouldn't be stabbed in the back et tu Brute? That men oughtn't shite in their hat?

A Constitution wasn't a county statute nor a personal Contract, intended to enumerate every contingency and morsel of minutiæ with exacting specificity. To craft a Constitution in such mode, as if prescribing instruction for a thick child, was certain folly. A Constitution drawn proper laid its shoulder to the great points.

In drawing the Constitution, the Committee of Detail had determined to insert essential Principles only, lest the operations of government be clogged by rendering provisions permanent and unalterable, when they ought to be accommodated to Time and events. The Committee of Detail therefore aimed for language simple yet precise and general propositions, according to the example of the state Constitutions.

Franklin had often seen natural Phylosophers conducting Experiments presume a precision of measurement with their instruments which was impossible to attain, creating a fallacious Sense of exactness. The Committee of Detail had wise avoided such folly in the current political Experiment, but that did not mean a more extensive List of negatives simple yet precise wouldn't have been beneficial—and perhaps nigh indispensable. More energetic Limitations upon government Powers might secure The People against Tyranny more firmer, without clogging the canal of government. Colonel Mason had wanted a Clause stating that all Powers not explicit granted to Government defaulted to The People and could not be assumed by Government. Franklin would not have object'd such Clause, though Tyrants and Designers would but ignore it.

Yet a Constitution could effect only so much, no matter how clever conceive-ed. Mere words were a tool pitiful inadequate for trying to check the innate Depravity of Man.

As time progressed, it would be tempting to observe any a rising corruption and pretend it should have been negatived in the Constitution, condemning its drawers for want of prescience. Franklin made no claim to infallibility, but in the end, all governments were bottomed on the Virtue and Character of The People and their leaders. The Devilish Evil would ignore any Negative and presume any Power wanton through Slithers of language.

Jackson continued reading, continued enumerating the Republic. Tho' his forehead had begun to glisten with sweat, his voice remaint resounding, and the cadence of his words staid steady.

Right steady.

Footsteps could be heard above, hollow clanks that seem'd to come from a great distance hence and were vague reminiscent of clacking horse hooves. Also more stuttered Scrapings as Chairs were dragged or moved. The Pennsylvania Assembly was in session above stairs in the Great Hall. It was wise enough not to seat throughout the blistering humidity of summer and had convoked on September 5th. The Convention was seated in the Assembly Room that was the usual meeting Place of the Pennsylvania Assembly, but it had ceded the chambre, which was exceeding gracious, especially given that Congress was not even being charged to let the room. No one expected that a Convention begun in May would still be in Session in September, so contingencies had not been made in this regard. The Assembly had been assured their chambre would not be filched for more than ten days, yet it was two past the Fifteenth.

The clacking and scraping overhead continued, but Jackson stopped reading not. He simple increased the volume of his Voice.

Franklin minded the noise not.

Any sound besides the pontification of Deputies was welcome.

Franklin glanced up at the crystal opera lustre, the chandeler, that hung from the ceiling just in front of the President's Table. Glass arms curled down and upward like the tentacles of an octopus, holding unlit chandles. The commotion above stairs caused the chandeler to jiggle a trifle. It also caused Deputies to glance at Franklin. He had been running Pennsylvania before and after hours as a second occupation, and many Deputies seemed to peer at him with respect as they were reminded how diligent he had been working. With an Executive Council, Franklin had been able to delegate most responsibility to other council Members, who had been more than accommodating, though responsibility was still responsibility. Franklin's Situation was another reason he favoured an Executive Council for America rather than a lone President. It seemed a far from preposterous to envision an overburdened President in distant futurity who struggled to oversee a massive Republic. Especially if The People foolish enough to let government grow Energetic.

The overhead noise heightened brief, becoming a cacophony of Clacks and Scrapes, and then it ceased.

The intrusion by outsiders, even those unseen above Stairs, made Franklin revisit a fundamental Question, one he had asked himself numerate times, and one Deputies had discussed numerate times, yet had never truly answered with satisfaction.

What would the world think of the Constitution?

To someone who had not seated at Convention but read the Constitution, the most singular aspect would probably be the degree to which Power resided with The People and emanated from The People. Most of the world expect'd some form of Republicanism to emerge from the Convention, but not a government so controlled by The People and answerable to The People. To Franklin's thinking, the Constitution did not transmit enough Power to The People, yet he had started life among them, which most Deputies had not. Franklin embraced and trusted The People in a way most Deputies would never. Franklin was a far from enamoured of the Constitution, yet even in its dilute Form, with its myriad Bufferings and Insulations of government from the will of The People, 'twas a radical upheaval. The singular degree to which the Constitution empowered The People would nigh certain shock the world.

Despots worldwide were depending the results of the Convention anxious, sneering with derision at the conceit that the common rabble had Natural Rights or could govern itself. Despots were hoping with desperate fervency that America's Constitution would be ill conceive-ed, that the government it constructed would crumble in Chaos, so the innovation that people had natural rights and could govern themselves could be laughed off with finality.

For several shining centuries in antient Rome, the belief that men ought be free and could govern themselves had taken root and been implemented on widespread Scale. Yet the Roman Republic had succumb'd more than 1,700 years ago, and human Liberty had died with it.

Nations such as Holland, Portugal, Belgium, Switzerland, Iceland, Italy, Germany, et cætera, had dabbled in Republicanism since Rome, and bristled at the notion that America was a resurrection of Republicanism, but in truth, there had not been a Republic of Substance in more than 17 centuries.

'Twas tempting to think that Diffusion of Knowledge had enlightened human conceptions, and that demands for Liberty would persist even if America failed. In Franklin's estimation, this reflected a want of appreciation for how fragile and elusive Liberty actual was. Some naïve Phylosopher in late-stage Rome had probably presumed that Liberty would arise again in just a decade or two, maybe a century or two at most. Yet here Rome's distant posterity was, still struggling to resurrect it.

So many Nations and Empires litter'd History, so many Generations had lived and died, and so few, so frustrating few, had ever truly been free! Liberty was easy to espouse, but history taught that it was exceeding difficult to secure.

If the political phylosophy Experiment called America succeeded, Republicanism might become the standard, despotism the derangement that the world sneered at. If America failed, if the Constitution reading was fatal ill conceive-ed, Liberty might vanish from the world for another thousand years or more. For another fifty generations or more, millions would continue to suffer under the Yoke of Tyranny, serving as oxen for the sordid Avarice of despots.

Franklin sigh'd deep, careful to do so quiet. The stakes were so profound as to nigh defy Comprehension, and made any wise man necessary uneasy. Like most Deputies present, Franklin was wise enough to be damn uneasy.

"Article Two," Jackson read. "Section One. The executive Power shall be vested in a President of the United States of America."

A curious discomfort swept over Deputies, as it had when the Executive had been debated in the Committee of the Whole. Washington's election as Executive the First was a certainty, which made debating the Executive in his presence awkward for most everyone.

Except Washington. He continued to sit motionless with martial Grace and Temper. His face conveyed no emotion, and as he peered past the Deputies his eyes assumed that vacuous quality again. The same detachment he had shown during the

Debates on the Executive, to make Deputies as comfortable as possible that they might speak with Liberty.

Franklin felt a manly Love for Washington. He saw the same Love on the faces of most other Deputies. Save perhaps Thomas Mifflin of Pennsylvania, and the Little Lion.

The Little Lion and Jemmy had machinated behind the curtain to organize the Convention, but 'twas Washington's prestige that gave it credibility. Had Washington refused to attend the Convention, it probably would have convoked not and there would be no Constitution.

Such was Washington's fame and Influence. And for all the Esteem heaped upon him, he deserved more. Washington spent nigh six years in the field securing America's liberty.

Six bloody years!

And the total tenure of Washington's Commission, from the moment he accepted Command of the Army in June of 1776, to when he surrendered his Commission in December 1783, was some seven and a half years.

Franklin was Minister Plenipotentiary to France during The War, and saw French Générals pore over maps analyzing Washington's actions, astonish'd that he could overcome such insurmount odds, especially given his want of formal military training and amateurish Mistakes. This was when the Générals presumed Washington's forces was actual supplied. Once French officers joined Washington in the field and reported the truth, that his "Army" was little more than Vagabonds, amazement became utter reverence. Especially because all French officers who served with Washington, even those disdainful of his want of professional military Training, reported the dignity with which he suffered

hardship, his unwavering obedience to the Congress despite its
rank Incompetency, and most of all his courage and utter fear-
lessness in Battle.

Phylosophers might have stood in salons for another thousand years pontificating about the Natural Rights of man and
the resurrection of Republicanism while Tyranny flourish'd. The
singular opportunity to resurrect Republicanism had been won
not with rhetoric, but with blood, balls, and steel.

Won with Washington.

Despite his want of innate military brilliance, want of recruits,
want of Supplies, want of nigh every Thing, he had fox'd one of
largest, best-trained professional Armies in the world.

Only because of the courage and perseverance of George
Washington was there an America. Only because of his Integrity had the Revolution not been subverted, like most Revolutions in history. George Washington was not American, he was
America. To separate his identity from the American was like
trying to shake salt out of seawater.

And yet the more famed he grew, the more responsibility
that was heap'd upon him, the more equal he seemed the task.
Franklin had never seen a single action from Washington that
lessened his approbation, and most every Deputy present felt
the same.

Most any esteemed Figure from the Revolution could have
been eradicate and victory still attained.

Except Washington.

The improbability of his victory still defy'd comprehension,
and perhaps always would, even in distant futurity.

"He shall hold his Office during the Term of four Years," Jackson read, "and, together with the Vice President, chosen for the same Term, be elected, as follows"

Impatience and frustration creased the faces of many Deputies. The Clause enumerating the Election of the President and Vice was so lengthy it seemed a Constitution unto itself. It would be right torturous to hear read and was bloody Murder to contemplate.

As was the Executive.

Concern was also evident in the gaze of many a Deputy. The mode of chusing the Executive proved one of the most vexing Issues of the Convention. It was symbolick of Deputies' pervasive uncertainty about what the Executive should ultimate be.

Americans were deranged by a Phobia of Executives, having been oppress'd and nigh subjugate by one. The long train of abuses that the Declaration of Independency cited were Executive abuses. Yet the excess of reaction of the Articles of Confederacy, a government with a Congress but no Executive, was deplored by most all Deputies.

America must have an Executive of some species.

On this Deputies were virtual unanimate.

But this was nigh all they could agree upon. At least six hours a day, six days a week, for damn nigh a month in the sweltering heat of summer, they had wrestled the conundrum of the Executive, knotting themselves repeated, like a drunken snake. The Executive was first considered at the onset of June and had not been resolve-ed until last week. In truth, it lay unresolved-ed in the final Constitution reading.

Even Jemmy, having read every syllable penned on government, and usual so certain he knew what Structure best, acting as if descending upon the Convention with commandments in the stile of Moses, enter'd the Convention with no clear idea on the Executive. Like most Deputies, Jemmy presumed a mode of selection by Congress, and once this rejected, he was stumped.

The mode of Congress electoring the President had been the embarkment point of the Convention, advocate by the Pennsylvania and Virginia Deputies in the Virginia Plan they used to ambuscade the Convention at its onset and arrest the initiative. This was the only proven mode of chusing an Executive, outside monarchy. Many Deputies favoured this Structure, wanted the President a mere Prime Minister, subordinate to the Congress, electored by it, removeable at its leisure. This was the mode in nigh every state Constitution, meant to check against Tyranny by the Executive.

As President of Pennsylvania, Franklin was remov'able at the leisure of the Assembly should they be displeased with him. The Assembly had significant power to monitor Franklin and exercised it with vigour on occasion when concerned about his actions. He chafed not under this Power nor considered it an affront, but rather thought it prudential.

The only act of Despotism that Franklin envision'd as President was forcing every citizen of Pennsylvania to labour feverish in search of a remedy for the Gout and the Stone. Yet even if Franklin tended to the Tyrant, he had scant recourse to do so. The Executive Council must either conspire with him, or would report him to the Assembly, which could remove him by a simple majority Vote of nay confidence should he evidence Tyranny, Incompetency, Derangement, Senility, and cetera.

Authority tended to pervert men.

Absolute authority tended towards absolute perversion and Absolutism.

Why grant a single man authority then?

Especially that nigh absolute Authority which executives had long abuse-ed?

Franklin felt a replication of the structure of the Pennsylvania Executive Council the most effectual for a fœderal Government. Absent an Executive Council, a Council of State comprised of Secretarys and perhaps the Chief Justice of the supreme Court ought be attached to the Executive, to both assist and monitor him.

Franklin felt an energetic Executive dangerous—grievous dangerous—and liable to morph into elective Monarch. The Constitution ought not be impregnate with the Fœtus of Monarchy. Mr. Randolph was also of this opinion, and the structure of the Executive was one of the Reasons he might not give the Constitution the Sanction of his name.

Most Deputies shared Franklin's Phobia of Monarchy, the elective species especially, yet disagreed with Franklin about how to best secure against it. The Convention rejected the notion of an Executive Council or Council of State, and a President that was mere Minister, favouring a single President of vigour and dispatch.

The Convention's view was that a President elector'd by Congress would beget corruption—especially if re-eligible for second or multiple Terms, which they felt he must be. Who wanted

Washington, who might live decades more, rotate after but a
term? After Washington, a President beholden to the Congress
for re-election might be extort'd by them for re-election. It was
not possible to reference Washington direct in the Constitution,
drawing, "All Presidents except George Washington shall ..."

Deputies favouring Congress electing the President envisioned a single Term of seven years, with no re-eligibility. Such
term was deem'd too long, certain to beget Corruption. As President of Pennsylvania, Franklin faced rotation each and every
year. So did most other state Presidents and state Governours.
Franklin thought of his current Term being seven years and
wanted to groan. Surely America would never elect a President
so decrepit as him? Were Washington to succumb in coming
months, would Franklin be proffered the Presidency? Nay, owe-
ing the slanders of Adams. Regardless, Franklin would refuse
the burden.

Smitten by the doctrines of segregate Powers and counterbalances, many Deputies insisted upon a supreme Executive, one independent of the Legislature and Judiciary. For the
Executive to be truly segregate from the Legislature, it could
not be appointed by it, nor serve at its leisure and be removeable by a simple majority vote of the Congress. Yet if the Executive were too remote from the Will of the Congress, he would
likely morph into monarch. A delicate counterbalance, one nigh
impossible to effect. And if the President be not beholden to
the Congress, chosen by it and removeable by it, then chosen
and removeable by who?

Most nations on Earth had kings. In monarchies, the lottery
of Birth chose the Executive, the eldest son of a king succeeding

upon his Death. Even if America inclined to king Washington, there was no guarantee his son would have Virtue or Talent.

The powder in Washington's munitions also appeared whet and his want of Heirs would cause concern were he to be king. No Deputy wanted a king, not even a king Washington, and that included the Deputy that was Washington. America would not have a Monarch, at least not immediate, so monarchial precedent was of scant aid in this regard, save as an exemplar of what not to be. The Executive must be chosen, not by matriculation from the womb indiscrim'nant, nor inbred Station, but on Merit.

Who ought chuse an Executive of merit then?

The People.

The People?

The People!

There was scant Precedent for this. Damn nigh none, in point of fact. In the whole of the world, and the entirety of its histories, precious few examples of Executives electored by The People could be found, save in localities and city-states. This was true even of antiquity, where analogues were inexact, and any direct comparison necessarily distorted and strained. To have an Executive electored by The People across the whole of a large Republic was untried. Deputies were rightful wary of stooping to Innovation.

Fools liked to laud the novel. Novelty had its place, in natural-Phylosophic experimentation, in literature, in the baubles of Fashion and the baubles that worshipped it, when wenching, and in the bedchambre. But in crafting a government novelty was less desired. Novelty was Risk. Novelty might be Ruin. Novelty was at times necessary, but not for the mere sake of novelty.

Fortunate then that there was so little novel in the Constitution reading. Only the Ignorant or Thick could or would ever think so. This absence of novelty was a strength, not a weakness.

Yet a Novelty the Executive was in some Respects.

And unfortunate, also perhaps an Innovation.

Franklin could not help but think of Caledonia, the Convention's great Contrarian on the Executive. He was the only Deputy in the whole of the Convention who felt the Executive should be elector'd direct by The People, and he even wanted the Senate direct electored. Governeur Morris also inclined to Caledonia's view of the Presidency at times, but ever fickle in his predilections, not with constancy. Caledonia seemed to have contemplated and conceptualiz'd the Presidency more than any other Deputy, though the Convention often rejected his notions as too radickal.

In Votes specifying direct election of the President by The People, Pennsylvania had been the only state to vote yea.

Some Deputies felt The People incapable of chusing wise, without their local sphere especially. Fearing excesses of The Democracy, many Deputies also opposed having The People elect both the President and lower House direct. One portion of government elector'd direct, the lower House, was more than sufficient by Deputies' reckoning, any more deemt insensible. Distance and slowness of travel also made direct election across the whole of America cumbersome at best, and more realistically impracticable, especially once America sprawled west and comprehended the continent.

Franklin detested much of this thinking. Experience, in New York and Massachusetts especially, showed that an election of the first Magistrate by The People at large was both a convenient and successful mode. To have a Convention convoked to fashion a government for The People—or was it the States?—evidence so little faith in The People was right Sardonick. Yet most Deputies had noble Intentions in some Portion, and believed they were protecting The People from themselves—or was it Themselves from The People? In all nations in history, there were but two Factions, Rich and Common. Every Deputy present was Rich, relative to the Common. Franklin saw no absence of Nobility in the Convention, no Conspiracy to destitute or enslave The People. Yet neither did he see a seating of Saints total divested from their Interest, not even the most disinterested leader he had ever known, Washington.

The Constitution was both a lewd enumeration of Interest and a noble striving for a government that secured Liberty. Franklin had sat in enough Councils and Assemblys to know that noble striving was often compleat absent and Interest the only Concern. Some might fixate on the lewd enumeration of Interest, condemning it viceous, but expecting a total absence of it any proceeding of men was the height of folly. More realistic to expect Angels to descend a quills in hand and draft a Constitution. To Franklin, it was amazing that the Constitution was as principled and noble in intention as it was, even conceding its horde of lewd Interests and vast Imperfections.

Franklin was prone not to angst, but pondering the Executive caused his chest to tighten ever so slight. The Convention envisioned a President of energy and Supremacy who was also beholden to The People, Congress, and States, and counterbalanced by them. An Executive of Dispatch and Vigour that became not a tyrannick elective Monarch.

But how to make this seeming Chimæra into something viable and real? Single or plural—lone Executive, multiple Executives, or executive Council? Appointed by Congress or other council, or elector'd by The People? If elector'd by The People, direct or indirect? If direct, what suffrage requisite? Direct electoring for the fœderal lower House could default to the lower House requisites of States, but many states did not elector Executives direct, and thus had no suffrage requisite for Executives which could be defaulted to. If the Executive was electored indirect by The People, by what mode? What term of rotation for the Executive? A single term? Re-eligibility? Affixed number of Terms? Perpetual re-eligibility via successions of Terms? What length of Terms? Uniform Terms, or of different length? Tenure during good Behaviour? What of removal from office? Of Powers granted the Executive? Powers deny'd? Eligibility requirements to be Executive? How energetic should the Executive be? How energetic would he be?

Deputies had agitated all these Issues, and myriad others. They had considered every mode conceivable. Two Presidents, with the concurrence of both necessary to conduct business, each thereby possessing Veto over the other, in the mode of the Roman Consuls. Terms of one year, four years, seven years, fifteen years, and cetera, even life. Seven years with no re-eligibility had been the initial mode, but it had been altered to four years with perpetual re-eligibility at the last moment.

And cetera.

Designing the Presidency had been murderous.

Right murderous.

There had been no monolithic contending Factions, as with Representation and Slavery. No North versus South, large State versus little State. No opposition'd Deputations with simplistic Interests easy appeased. Views was more dispersed among differing ideologies of Deputies, with different Deputies placing emphasis on different facets of the Executive. Personal phylosophys jostled. No simple Compromise could reconcile them, as with Representation and Slavery. This made forming consensus nigh impossible—but also made Franklin think Jemmy's prediction about an absence of national Factions might prove valid. Regardless, there was greater variation and vacillation in opinions of Deputies about the Executive than any other construction the Convention took up.

Uncertainty about the Executive, and the want of historical precedent for the Executive, led to uncertainty about how to segregate Powers and counterbalance Branches, actions which were also relative untried. Change the term of President, or the mode of his Election, and corresponding changes in other Branches and Clauses were also requisite to keep the government counterbalanced. This resulted in much inefficiency and backtracking, and increased uncertainty, as the Convention groped towards a structure of government never before tried.

The Executive.

Murderous, indeed.

Bloody murderous.

The ambivalence in the air was right palpable.

No Deputy was certain the Executive enumerating would prove efficacious. That it might not devolve into elective Monarchy or even barbary Despotism. It might fall to Posterity to Amend the Presidency to make it viable.

"Each State shall appoint," Jackson read, "in such Manner as the Legislature thereof may direct, a Number of Electors, equal to the whole Number of Senators and Representatives to which the State may be entitled in the Congress: but no Senator or Representative, or Person holding an Office of Trust or Profit under the United States, shall be appointed an Elector. The Electors shall meet in their respective States, and vote by Ballot for two Persons, of whom one at least shall not be an Inhabitant of—"

Jackson placed parchment the second of the Constitution down quick but careful and picked up the third. The parchment rustled as he did. Jackson cleared his throat once, gulping hard, and then gulped again as he switched pages.

"—the same State with themselves," Jackson read. "And they shall make a List of all the Persons voted for, and of the Number of Votes for each; which List they shall sign and certify, and transmit sealed to the Seat of the Government of the United States, directed to the President of the Senate. The President of the Senate ..."

The language become gibberish to Franklin, like a nagging wife, once again a Drone.

Seasons might come and go; crops sprout, tickle the sky, and dwindle; Empires a rise and fall, in the Time it would take to read the mode of chusing the President.

The crux was that each State Legislature would specify a Manner of appointing Electors, whose number would be equal to its total Representatives and Senators in the fœderal Congress.

Each Elector would Ballot the two men he thought most worthy of President, at least one not of his State. The votes of Electors would be tally'd. The white man having the greatest number of Votes would be President, and the white man having the second greatest number of Votes would be Vice President. If a tie, or if a Vote was unequivocal with no white man receiving a simple Majority, the House of Representatives would chuse by Ballot, but such resolving Votes in the House would be by State, each State having but a single Vote.

No Elector would cast a Vote for Vice President. Rather, each Elector would select two men he thought ought be President, with the second in the aggregate Presidential voting being Vice. Nor could any Elector differentiate a preference in his two choices, in case of Tie, placing partiality with one. Some Deputy, Franklin could not recall who, had wanted each Elector to have three Votes to split among two men, with two Votes for the preferred Ballot, and one Vote for the secondary Ballot.

Franklin wanted to shake his head. The People would elector State Legislatures, which would appoint Electors, which would then chuse the President. Could The People be any more segregate from chusing the only public official that would represent them in totality? Perhaps the mode of chusing should have been routed through the great Indian Chiefs by smoke signal and then the Icelandic Legislature, to render it even more cumbersome, remote, and disempowering to The People.

Woe unto The People should a President turn Tyrant, or the office itself become Consolidate and Tyrannic. The People would have to wade through state Legislatures, hold their feet to the fire to chuse new Electors, and then hold the Electors feet to the fire to chuse a new President. This was damn nigh impossible and all Deputies knew it.

And who would the Electors be? The very men in this chambre, or a Faction similar. The totality of men who had attended the Convention as well as those who had been appointed but refused deputization. Also a few lesser men, a few Daytons. A clique of the Moneyed and Interested would be Electors, with but few exceptions.

Champions of The People would surely be found amongst Electors, but not in plentitude. State Legislatures would tend to resort to the same small pool of virtued and talented men when chusing Electors, a seeming Benefit superficial, but a stout rampart to Reformation when once The People desired it. For the same old Electors would continual chuse the same species of men as President. This was beneficent now, with Washington poised to assume the helm and the virtue of the Revolution pervasive, but what when the Spirit of '76 antient and virtue corroded? What when The People desired a revolutionary Departure and a clique of Electors moneyed and interested refused? The People would have to hang state Legislators and Electors, else resort to violence, or submit. History suggested that Submission was more to be expected.

Franklin's view was again contrary. The Convention's concern ran in the opposite. Deputies feared The People would be duped or corrupted into elevating a Tyrant, and felt Electors a rampart against this tendency.

And even this rosy appraisal assumed no Tie, in which case the House of Representatives would be resorted, not by the desirous mode of proportional Vote, but rather the ruinous mode of voting by state. In such case, Delaware's 37 Thousand total Citizens would again have the same Electoring power as Virginia's 532 Thousand or Pennsylvania's 360 Thousand. In essence, the Vote of a Delaware citizen would count more than one from Virginia or Pennsylvania, and the strength of this Disparity would increase the smaller a state was, a grievous counterweight to popular Will.

In case of Tie, with a proportional Vote, a large quantum of Electors voting as individuals would rapidly chuse a candidate, but with a mere thirteen States, a mere thirteen Votes, achieving sufficient Consensus might prove right difficult. A mode which already accrued dangerous counterweight in little States might anchor its counterweight, when state Deputations were split or cluse decided and a single Vote would swing them. And what of States with an even number of Representatives, equal split in their Vote? Were they to abstain, the suffrage of their Citizens—and three fifths of slaves—nullified? In such situations, a few Representatives from a few deadlocked or contested states might in effect chuse the President and might extort concessions as Renumeration for their Vote. A few states might well hostage the Will of the Majority—of The People—and render the selection of the President nigh aristocratic, via such mode.

This inclusion for resolving Ties was a concession to the little-state Interests, another replication of the Compromise that mangled the Congress. If the main mode of chusing the Executive by state Electors be largely proportion'l to population and favoured large States—granted two Senators were added to the number of Representatives, deviating from pure proportion'l Representation to the benefit of little States—then why shouldn't the provision for resolving Ties be by State and favour little States? Such had been the reckoning of the little States, and they were a formidable enough Faction—owing to the voting by States of the Convention itself—that they had to be appeased.

Meeting prior to convocation of the Convention, and conspiring to seize its initiative and render it little more than a Caucus, with admirable success, the Pennsylvania and Virginia Deputations had wanted to open the Convention by enforcing a proportional mode of Vote for the Convention itself. Each Deputy's Vote would be accounted individual, or each Deputation's Vote would be proportioned to its population, rather than voting by the mode of States. A much sounder Constitution would have resulted, a fact surmised then and proved true by experience in Convention. Yet the Pennsylvania and Virginia conspirators had also proper surmised that little States would never have countenanced such an Encroachment. Delaware's Legislature even foresaw this machination, disallowing participation under such condition in its instructions to its Deputation. If faced with such a measure, little-state Deputations would have absent'd Convention as sure as the south Deputations if manumission proposed.

It might take iterations of revision over Epochas, by a People and government progressive more national and democratical, to arrive at a sound Provision for the Executive. In mighty great measure, the Convention had been hostaged by the mode of voting by States. 'Twas impossible to disempower States beyond a certain extent when States were themselves voting the measures and slicing they own throats. And 'twas impossible to disempower the Moneyed and Interested beyond a certain extent, when they were themselves voting the Measures. It might never be possible to disempower southerners on Slavery, save by the Sword.

Franklin again try'd to discern the murky future. Over time, as state populations ballooned, and the number of Representatives increased relative to Senators which were fixed in number, the mode of Electors chusing the Executive would tend more towards proportional election—save in case of Tie. But like a fluxion of Mathematic, such mode would never produce honest exact proportional representation, only approach and approximate it. The mode of resolving Ties was apt to prove ruinous if the Lottery of electoral voting invoked it often, producing counterweighted results in opposition to The People's Will. By such mode, a President the majority of The People or even Electors supported not or chose not could be elevate.

And what of Faction? When the two Eminents in the nation were Whig and Toy, Whig elected President and Tory his Vice. A President might have his staunchest political enemy as his second, a profound inducement for Assassination, or machination at the least. It would be foolish to think the nation might not be factioned, along little-State versus large-State lines, or Slave versus Abolition lines, or some other Lines unknownst at present.

Jemmy hoped a larger nation with copious regional Factions would evidence an absence of large-scale Factions, dissolving into the gaiety of homogeneity, but Franklin was skeptickal. What when the President was a south Slaver, the Vice a north Abolitionist, and a key Bill energizing Slavery required signature? Or a versa of Vice, an abolitioner President, a key Bill manumitting Slaves, and a south Vice President who Assassinated the north President to prevent passage and perpetuate Slavery? To anyone who had read a history, such suppositions were a far from fanciful.

One could also reason that having two Factions elected would lend stability, as both could pretend equal stake in government, or some stake. In crafting the Executive, Deputies seemed too inclined to presume that men would put Faction and differences aside. The same might also be true of the Constitution.

Parliament's proceedings were scarce more than Feuds of Faction, and Auctions to Interests. Without some accounting for Faction in the Constitution, America might suffer the same fate.

'Twas enough to make one's head ach. How in the bloody Hell had such a serpentine mode of chusing the Executive been chosen? The dismaying answer was that the Convention had to decide some mode and knew not what else to do. In shunning monarchy, refusing to have the President electored direct by The People, and disdaining his appointment by the Congress, the Convention had cornered itself unintentional. No viable avenue remained save indirect Electoring by The People, but Deputies had disparate opinions about how to best effect this mode, fretting so many multitudinous details, admitted of import, as to leave one dizzy. This was especially true of the mode of settling Ties or votes unequivocal. As bad as the final Provision in the Constitution was, it seemed bloody brilliant contrast'd with many considered.

The Convention had considered having State Executives, Governours and Presidents of Executive Councils, chuse the national Executive. It had considered the mode of State Legislatures electoring the President direct. Also the fœderal Senate, the fœderal House of Representatives, or a joint ballot of both Houses. Every potential mode was contemplated, no matter how obscure or absurd, save letting the kings of Europe chuse the President, hosting Duels for the office, or shooting Dice to select him. The Convention had even considered drawing a lottery of less than a dozen Electors from the House of Representatives and letting it chuse the President.

Objections were raised against every mode propozed, and every one that perhaps could be.

What to do?

Languish in Convention until the next epocha dawned?

Draw lots?

Flip specie?

Let Jemmy and Elbridge Gerry fight to expiration for their preference, like cocks in the Pit?

Though the Committee of Detail produced an admirable Draught of the Constitution, a number of Postponed Matters and Unfinished Parts still remained. These had been referred to The Committee on Postponed Matters on the final day of August, just over two weeks ago. It had been more than a trifle disconcerting that with the Convention having been convoked over three months and nearing conclusion, critical Decisions still languished unresolve-ed, including the mode of chusing the President.

The mode reading had been decided by the Committee on Postponed Matters. It had eleven Members, one Deputy from each of the eleven States in Convention when it was formed and met. The Committee on Postponed Matters had adapted the mode of chusing President from the Maryland Constitution, which specified that Senators be chosen by Electors chosen by The People. That is, Electors who were electored direct by The People.

Earlier in Convention, the mode of The People electoring the President direct had been proposed by Caledonia James and struck down. Caledonia had then proposed that The People at the least direct elector the Electors who would chuse the President, but this mode was also struck down.

Once it became apparent the mode of electoring President had to be indirect, and in truth well before, the Convention devolved into the same large-state Factions and little-state Factions it had when contending the Congress. Little States would not be overrun by the large States in proportional electoring. Large States would not be cheated by a mode of electoring by state. The objections underlying the debate about the Congress was regurgitate ad nauseum.

As expected when a matter was referred to Committee, Compromise had been wrought. The mode of electoring the Executive which the Committee of Postponed Matters proposed, and which the Convention approved, gave something to everyone. States, via Legislatures, would determine the mode of Elector selection, and were free to resort to The People chusing Electors direct, a possibility in theory in some states, yet one doubtful to happen in practice in all states as if made a provision in the Constitution. State Legislatures could, and most probably would, decide to chuse Electors themselves. Large States attained electoring largely proportional to population by the main mode, Electors. Little States had the number of Senators added to the number of Representatives in determining the number of Electors in the main mode, thereby diluting proportional Representation, and assuring that even the littlest States would have three Electors at the least. Little States also attained resolution of Ties by a Vote of States in the House, with each state having but one Vote, rather than some other more proportional mode.

The problem with giving something to everyone was that everything was often lost, and one ended up with Nothing. Franklin had oft seen laws passed by Parliament so altered to appeaze every Interest that the original Purpose of the Bill was not just pervert'd, but forsaken compleat. So it seemed here, perversion at the least. The mode of chusing the Executive would never have been approved without Alterations and Compromises. Yet 'twas impossible to view the wretched Construction and think it answered the needs of the question.

All Deputies knew it.

Debate on the mode of electing the President had still been taking place two Thursdays prior. The sixth of September was it? A mere eleven days ago. The Convention had hurryed through its compleation of the Constitution like some thick Harvard who had procrastinated on a Dissertation.

If the Convention were as brilliant as some suppose-ed, it would have found an answer to this seeming insoluble problem of electoring the President. Perhaps abandoned its intractible opposition to direct election or election by Congress.

Perhaps the absence of a mode even more odious was brilliance, a sterling Accomplishment.

Or perhaps no solution existed, and they groped for the impossible.

No one knew.

But as Jackson continued reading the Old Testament of a Clause—it contained no Revelations—Franklin could not see a single Deputy who looked pleased. Deputies seemed less troubled only when the Clause was behind them, words floating away like pipe smoke in a breeze.

"Section Two," Jackson read. "The President shall be Commander in Chief of the Army and Navy of the United States, and of the Militia of the several States,"

Franklin's gaze was drawn to Washington's sword. Virtual straight, the curve but slight. Grip of green-dyed ivory, extreme thin silver strip encircling it like a snake might a forearm. The worn leather scabbard, with dinged silver trim at the throat, locket, and tip.

The General disliked disarming, and the Sword hung casual at his side as he sat, a tool old and oft-used which he was comfortable with. He owned several ornate ceremonial Swords and was not averse to wearing them on singular Occasions, but for a Convention languishing months, he had favoured his more functional battle Sword.

Interesting though, that Washington had choze not to wear a ceremonial Sword on this the final day. Washington was obsessed with manners, comportment, ceremony, and Dress, military Dress especially, and gave careful consideration to the effect of what he wore. The simplicity and dogg-ed appearance of his battle Sword, as contrasted with the expected ceremonial sword, made it utter conspicuous. Washington doubtless realized that his battle Sword was the symbol of his military sacrifice for the nation, a tangible embodiment of his Prestige which made him seem more intimidating. Franklin envisioned Washington drawing the sword and running him through, those cold, wolfish Eyes peering into his without changing expression, the last Thing he ever saw.

Franklin pondered the opposite of Washington killing him.

Pondered Peace.

Precious Peace.

Elusive Peace.

As elusive as Liberty.

Franklin wanted the American historium to be one of peace! Not War.

Not ceaseless ruinous War.

Ever had War been the Excuse of Governments to encroach Liberty and then by inexorable Usurpations extinguish it.

Power to declare War. Power to command the Armies. What signify such Clauses in actuality? What forebode they? What when a President was at the Head of an Army fielded and standing, and asserted the right to exercise Command in a manner energetic? What when a Congress disputated, arguing that the President's actions would commit the nation to War, thereby usurping the Power of Congress to declare it?

The man commanding the Army made the Rules. The histories were emphatick on this point. Only the exemplar of Washington, his scrupulous Obedience to civil Authority, made anyone believe America would be different.

But what after Washington?

In most nations antient and modern, the Executive turned Tyrant and used the Army to browbeat the popular elective Branch into submission, often making an example of recalcitrant Defenders of Liberty and executing them. Thereafter, the Tyrant or Army were obey'd, the popular elective Branch and The People cowering.

'Twas impossible to ponder this sordid historium, and the American refutation of it, without again marvelling at Washington, who had been granted as much power as an Alexander, a Cæsar, a Cromwell, but rather than perverting by it and turning his sword upon The People, had returned it to them.

Yet in time all nations eventual elevated an Alexander, Cæsar, or Cromwell.

What then?

How to prevent such Ruin? How to redress it if not prevented?

The Convention tried, but the Constitution seemed to want for specificity and energy in this regard. The Congress and President were intended to consult not contend, working together in decisions about application of military Force. It was absurd to think a Congress declaring War would not first consult the President that would wage it. 'Twas less absurd to think a designing President and Army would ferment War which the Congress and The People desired not.

And what of changes in the character of War? Of Balloons used to reconnoiterer, gravitate Grenades, and deploy Grenadiers, as was already a contemplate? Of mighty great Steamships that could gallop oceans? Or the electric Fluid and Fire and the myriad revolutions in invention and aggression it seem'd destined to spawn?

The President would command the Army and Navy, and whatever other species of Forces might employ Balloons, air

Ships, electric Fire, and cetera. The Congress would declare War, determine—or limit—funding for the Army, Navy, and cetera, and make Rules for the government and regulation of the land and naval Forces, and perhaps those in the Air. In theory, the Power of War was counterbalanced between Congress and Executive. Yet a wide chasm of application lay between these two di-opposed grants of Power. What could the President do and do not with the Armies, in time of Peace or War? How much of the Presidential Power to make Treaties—of Peace especially—would devolve to a Senate that must positive them? The Constitution was silent on such questions. The absence of a Section in Article II explicit denying Powers to the President, as had been done for Congress and States, was right glaring to Franklin. Especially Powers of War. The Convention had flirted with such limitations, yet found its constructions wanting.

In crafting the Executive, the consuming Phobia of Deputies was a Constitution insecure against elective Monarchy. Curious then, that they had provided precious few direct limitations upon executive Power. All other Articles of the Constitution were shorter than Article I. This was thankful from the perspective of expedition of the grueling reading. Yet the shorter Articles might also signify that Powers were not enumerated—nor denied— with sufficient rigour. Would observers not in Convention draw this conclusion? Would futurity?

Had they struck the proper counterbalance in the quantum of Power granted the President and Congress? On War? On Treaties? On the full plenitude of Powers?

Late last week, Deputies had still been asking such questions and fiddling with constructions of the Constitution. No one felt certain the counterbalance was perfected. Nor did anyone know how to banish the haunting Spectre of War nor eradicate Evil from men's Hearts, especially not with a few addenda Clauses in a Constitution.

"Washington shall have Power," Jackson read, "by and with the Advice and Consent of the Senate, to make Treaties,"

Jackson's eyes grew large as he realized he had made an erratum. The Constitution was drawn to read, "He shall have Power." It said not, "Washington shall have Power."

Nothing to do but keep reading, which Jackson did.

Deputies simple smiled. A few chuckled. An easy errour to make, presuming Washington President.

The only person that seemed unamused was Washington himself. He still maintained the same vacant expression and indifferent posture, exhibiting Temper.

"Provided," Jackson continued, "two thirds of the Senators present c—"

Franklin felt as if a window had been shatter'd inside his kneepan, thrusting Shards into bone and flesh. He exhaled sharp. It took supreme effort not to whimper like a Sex. Franklin squinted so fierce an accoster might have been pressing against his eyes trying to crush them.

The words of the Constitution faded away as the Shards sliced Flesh. Dizziness engulfed Franklin. He breathed in through his nose, out his mouth, exhaling deep but trying to keep quiet. He massaged the exterior of his swollen Kneepan gentle, felt bumpy Ossifications, as if gravel had been stuff'd under his skin. Alas, these ossifications were not the cause of the current anguish. 'Twas the unseen Gout inside the joints that was right murderous.

Franklin suffered in Anguish for a time indeterminate. He took one extreme deep breath, and then kicked his leg forward, extending and straightening it. Instantaneous agony, as if Washington had run him through with a red-hot saber. The ossifications inside Franklin's kneepan shifted as the leg straighten'd, and in their new Positions they were no longer murderous. The agony vanished quicker than Parliament pass'd Taxes, and there was only that steady, less-intense throbbing that the Gout generated continual.

Franklin met the concern'd look of Governeur Morris with a playful pursing of his lips, and laughter in his eyes. Morris wasn't fooled and expressed sympathy with his eyes, until his Focus gradual shifted back to the reading.

"Section Four," Jackson read, "The President, Vice President and all civil Officers of the United States, shall be removed from Office on Impeachment for, and Conviction of, Treason, Bribery, or other high Crimes and Misdemeanors."

Another Clause of mighty Import. Deputies' severe expressions reflected it.

No man ought be above Justice. America had late thrown off a king who was.

If America endured, a corrupt Executive would someday elevate to office. Perhaps many corrupt Executives, though not on an Executive Council.

For the first time during the reading of Article II, attention shifted away from Washington, to Robert Morris. As Superintendent of Finance during the Revolution, he was the only approximate of Executive which the Confederacy had ever appointed, at least while Congress was convoked. The odious accusations of Profiteering still clung to Morris. He allowed a slight smile, yet kept his head high and level. His drooping Chins reminded Franklin of a bullfrog.

The Convention had wrestled mighty with the mode of removing a President, the Punishment, and most of all the threshold for Impeachment. Set the threshold too low, Deputies reasoned, and Impeachment would become a weapon of political Sport and Faction. In such case, the threat of Impeachment might prevent a President from vetoing Laws or otherwise exercising counterbalances against the Congress. Set the threshold too high, make the President nigh irremoveable, and the resort would be Assassination in which he was not only deprived of his Life but also the opportunity of vindicating his Character. It was best therefore to provide in the Constitution for the regular punishment of the Executive where his misconduct should deserve it, and for his honorable acquittal when he should be unjust accused.

So they had done. There had been much disagreement about which specific offences ought be enumerate as impeachable, and what degree of precision should be strove for in such enumeration. Some Deputies had wanted to enumerate more specific species of impeachable Abuses and a greater quantum of them. The custom of removal for Maladministration absent crime, as under english Law and several state Constitutions, had been negatived out of fear of impeachments of a political Species, devolving towards Executive Tenure at the pleasure of the Senate. If they had struck the proper accord none could say.

In british Government, Interest was the Rule. Lords, Members, and Monarch crafted law that aided Interests blatant, at the literal Expence of The People. To not constitute a more overt Protection against such Graft seem'd foolish to Franklin. Deputies supposed rotation in office sufficient, but what when Posts became such places of Profit as to corrupt nigh anyone rotated, and to attract Designers only? The Devilish Evil only?

Franklin would have preferred some broad construction which spoke to Posts of Honor that were perverted into Places of Profit. Franklin thought of Mr. Butler's proposal, Mr. Pierce Butler of South Carolina, who wanted Members of Congress ineligible for Offices not just during their tenure, but a year after. Franklin might have increased such Prohibition to well in excess of a year. Franklin thought of the Clause of the Pennsylvania Constitution which prevented Judges of the supreme Court from taking or receiving fees or Perquisites of any kind. Making a Fugitive of Perquisites, and defining their Abuse as a species of Bribery or high Crime using a construction exceeding broad, would have been Franklin's strong preference, not just for Justices of the supreme Court, but Representatives, Senators, Presidents, and cetera.

With no test on the competency of the President, there was no way to remove him should be become senile, or a Nero or Caligula ripe for Bedlam. This seemed imprudential to Franklin, though drawing a Clause that addressed this contingency with efficacy would have been difficult—much less securing Accord from Deputies upon it.

Franklin imagined Washington old and senile, eyes vacant in a more tragic manner, drooling into his Drink. Franklin imagined Washington being assassinated, as his Riflemen had so many british Officers.

A horrific thought, yet also incongruous, as Washington was not king. Senility, Insanity, Assassinations. These was endemic to monarchys, where Executives served for Life and could not be removed save by Death when they rendered themselves obnoxious. Assassinations especially.

The American historium was never to be one of Assassinations, though it warmed Franklin's heart to know a Senate had been added to the Constitution, so the fateful Precedents of Rome, of Julius Cæsar, might be replicate if America did succumb. It seemed incongruous to have lowling Representatives stab a President as he gave a speech providing information on the State of the Union. Only men of elevate Stature seemed appropriate for such a Censure, lofty Senators.

Tho' the mode of stabbing might be antiquate. How would futurity Assassinate? Poisons to the food? More advanced Riflemen? Munitions which hurled the electric Fire, as Zeus had lightning? Who could say? Perhaps futurity would simply lock obnoxious Executives in State Houses and read them Constitutions until they took their own Lives. Assassinations future might occur by some mode, by some Agency, the present could not conceive. No provision for a Lifeguard was in the Constitution. Was one needed?

There would be no American history devoid of Impeachments and Assassinations. To expect every Executive a Washington was to deny the innate Depravity of man, an act pitiful Naïve. The question was what mode would be used to remove Executives that had render'd themselves obnoxious, impeachment or Assassination. If the history be one of impeachments, perhaps even many, then America would be a Republic, the rule of law determining removal. If America made Assassination its creed, then there might be the mere Shadow of a Republic, but not the Substance of the thing.

Jackson paused a moment. He cleared this throat. The Impeachment Clause was the last of Article II. As Jackson concluded it, all eyes again returned to Washington. He conveyed not the slightest hint of discomfort under the scrutiny. Franklin wondered how many Deputies were pondering future Executives, as he was. Not many, in probability. Most Deputies probably pictured Washington taking the Oath of President.

Would historians and citizens of futurity find themselves oppressed by a President who was an elective Monarch, and condemn the Convention's want of foresight? Would America be trampled by foreign Powers or internal Convulsions because the Executive was too restrain'd and insufficient energetic autonomous? Was the Constitution drawn too much from the British medium? Had Deputies pendulum'd too far in response to the Tyranny of the king and his royal Governours, hampering the Executive unduly, denying him sufficient autonomy and Dispatch to secure Liberty? Franklin tended to think the Executive not constrained enough, but he had been proven wrong often in his life and had no Illusions of Infallibility. Nor of that of the Constitution reading.

Would another great Republic in a thousand annums, or two Thousand, or three, draw upon the wisdom of lessons provided by the American collapse and craft a Constitution of greater endurance? Might other Republics arise in interim and attempt different dilutions of Executive Power and Supremacy, providing precedent that could also be drawn upon? Was it possible that only a Convention with the wisdom of such empirickal example, that provided by a multitude of failed Republics comprehending epochas, as multitudinous as failed monarchies at present, might be able to glean the Wisdom needed to succeed? Or was some new Phylosophy of Government, of natural Rights, of Liberty, or political Œconomy, as of yet not promulgate, requisite? Perhaps no Convention at present, no matter how wise, could have succeeded in their futile task?

It was possible, to be sure.

Franklin felt only curdling Uncertainty. He was used to Experiments, even dang'rous ones with the electric Fire. But to hazard the fate of so many on a principle so untried, again, made any wise man necessarily nervous.

Grievous nervous.

The vagueness of Article II concerned Franklin. The executive Power vested in a President was scant defined, which would beget abuse.

The Power of War especially.

The division of said Power between Congress and President was enumerate insufficient. Franklin felt more Power ought devolve to the Legislature and that firm Negatives on Presidential usurpations should have been enumerate.

But they were not.

Thank Providence Washington would be President the First—assuming he condescended to suffer the Burden. Washington had the Character to buffer the errors of the Constitution and overcome them. Sure as the sun would a-rise, a horse would shite, or a wife would whine, any enterprize with Washington at its head would be Honest. As long as Washington was present, America would always be safe.

"Article Three," Jackson read. "Section One. The judicial Power of the United States shall be vested in one supreme Court, and in such inferior Courts as the Congress may from time to time ordain and establish."

Franklin continued to see the government they had design'd take Shape. The edifice had three pillars, Legislative, Executive, Judicial. A Legislative branch to create Laws. An Executive branch to execute Laws. A Judicial branch to resolve disputes concerning Laws and punish violations of Laws.

The Judiciary felt like an after Thought to Franklin. Article I enumerating the Legislature had been long, Article II enumerating the Executive shorter, and Article III enumerating the Judiciary was shorter yet. Though the original Virginia Plan included provisions for a Judiciary, the Judiciary had general been taken up only after wearisome debates on the Legislature and Executive. After dissipations on Representation, the Executive, Slavery, and a host of other provisions, Deputies were as worn as Roger Sherman's suit. There were brief Debates on the Judiciary in early June, and some again in middling July, but usually only when they impeded Progress on the Legislature or Executive. By late August, the Judiciary could not be procrastinated any longer and had to be compleated as best the Convention could manage.

There had been much Debate on the Power to establish inferior national Tribunals, national Courts that was inferior to the supreme Court. The Constitution decreed that the Congress might establish such inferior Courts, yet it did not have to, and some Deputies had wanted the language more energetic, enforcing Establishment. Other Deputies feared that such inferior national Tribunals would create jealousies and oppositions in the State tribunals, which they indeed would. There was fundamental disagreement over where the Power of Jurisdiction, the power of a Tribunal to hear and rule on different species of legal cases, should ultimate reside. Which species of cases should national Tribunals have jurisdiction over and which species of cases should state Tribunals have jurisdiction over? It was not an asking of whether national Tribunals would encroach on the jurisdiction of state Tribunals, but to what degree national Tribunals should do such.

The fœderal versus national argument, yet again.

Some Deputies wanted a virtual annihilation of state Tribunals, with nigh all jurisdiction consolidate in national Tribunals. Other Deputies wanted no inferior national Tribunals and wished jurisdiction devolved to Common Law in the States, where it was present resident. States preferred to retain their Jurisdiction, and the Power it imbued. What was best for The People was not manifest.

Though far removed from Ignorance of the Law, Franklin had never read it, so had general deferred to the litany of esteemed Jurists in Convention, many having served as Attorney Generals or been seated on state supreme Courts for considerable spans. Yet even the most scrupulous Jurist was not devoid of Interest, especially not when removed from the bench and placed in a political Assembly representing his State. State attorney Generals and state supreme Court Justices could be biased in favour of state Powers, and at times had been.

Slave Codes coloured the issue as well. Would each state continue to have Liberty to rule on Slavery and its many codifications as it pleased, with the result that distinct Common Laws continued to develop independent in each State? In the South, whites on plantations were prodigious outnumbred by Slaves, consumed by Terrour of Rebellion, and thus passed energetic Codes regulating Slaves, which deterred Insurrection.

Might the national Legislature pass a law making it legal to manumit Slaves in any State? Not enforcing Manumission, but mere granting slave Owners such Right? Southerners would oppose even this tepid Liberty, by the sword if need be. To say nothing of Codes making it legal for Slaves to learn to read or write, or laws sanctifying the legality of slave Marriages, or laws revoking the status of slaves as Property and recategorizing them as Human. Or, Providence forbid, laws manumitting Slaves. Slavery was a cunning legal Labyrinth, more arduous to invest than oft suppose-ed.

Would a south State have Tribunals it controuled make rulings on Slavery, or would inferior national Tribunals assume such jurisdiction? If inferior national Tribunals assumed the Jurisdiction, then the national Government might appoint men without a State to make rulings within it. In southern terms, the national Government might stock a southern inferior Tribunal with Abolitionists, who would then invest slavery via energetic Rulings.

The South would resort to the Sword in such instance. No President would be Fool enough to make such appointments, at Least under present circumstances. Certain not Washington, who owned nigh a hundred Slaves. As a matter of pure Politicks, with Congress specifying the mode of Appointment, Judges seated at inferior national Tribunals in a State would probably be jurists of that State, or at least the region. A jurist of Massachusetts would not be appointed to a national tribunal in Georgia, nor vice versa. At least not at present.

But a broader principle lurked. Such reasoning on slavery Jurisdiction, and its Fears, could be extrapolate to most any issue. Common Law was a sacrosanct tradition. An inferior state Court or county Court could hear a case and rule just, on an issue unforeseen or not enumerate by law. That ruling became Precedent, guiding other Courts in sim'l'r cases on the Issue. Without any formal Code created by Government or Legislature, which existed not in more primitive times, such accumulate Rulings became the Law.

As its nomenclature suggested, Common Law placed Power in the common People and their dispersed Tribunals. Common Law was intrinsic democratic in its Spirit. It allowed The People to appoint local Judges, and have Justice dispenced without the sophistrys, and often the Corruptions, of centralized Statute. Common Law also often allowed Judges rotatable by The People to override Statute, override Laws, should they deem such laws tyrannical or unjust.

Should a national Legislature passing a single Law or a national Tribunal making a single Ruling have the Power to negative long-established state Common Laws that reflected proclivities and traditions of States and their citizens?

Answers of Deputies varied.

'Twas tempting to envision a national Law manumitting slaves, or a supreme Court ruling slavery a Fugitive, as the Massachusetts supreme Court had in essence done, and laud such provision. Or whatever suppose-ed noble provision one's heart fancied. But even presuming such Powers enumerate in the Constitution and thus able to be exercised, which they were not, there might be equal abuse of such Power odious to Liberty. What of a national Law declaring slavery legal in all America, even the North? Or a supreme Court ruling declaring slavery sacrosanct? This would violate the rights and beliefs of the North as sure as manumission would the South. Keeping such Power resident in States was a rampart against Tyranny.

One could argue the matter from either mode, and Deputies had done so. Some Deputies saw turbulent variation in state Common Law and rulings of state Tribunals as an indispensable Liberty, a rampart against tyrannical Rulings of a national Tribunal, as well as the Spirit of judicial Encroachment and Consolidation. Others saw the imposition of Uniformity by a national Legislature as a remedy against tyrannical state policy. There was Truth in both Views and could be Liberty or Tyranny in either practice.

Lesser men fancy'd imposing their Views upon the whole of a Nation, Civilization, or World. Some Deputies had succumbed to this Corruption. Was this not the very sort of Absolutism that America had revolted against? The danger of such Absolutism was grievous plaguy with the Judiciary because Judges were not rotated in office as frequent as politicians.

Some allowance for diversity of Common Law was requisite, that people could freely cultivate Common Law suited to their peculiar local needs. Should America ever stretch to Las Californias or encompass Canada or the southern Americas, would national Tribunals presume jurisdiction in cases comprehending the whole of this vast region in every minute peculiar?

Prepost'rous.

The Anarchy of inviolate state Jurisdiction would produce disparate state policys on issues where a national Uniform was requisite. A small cabal of supreme national Tribunals decreeing policy with unity and uniformity in all Cases would be a judicial Despotism. The proper counterbalance between these Extremities had been sought.

But that did not signify it had been attain'd.

The question was where the Fulcrum between Extremities lay, and how different provisions for appointment of judges, terms of judges, removal of judges, and establishment of tribunals and jurisdictions would alter the centrum of Balance.

On this, opinions of Deputies also varied, and the ambiguity of Article III evidenced this fact.

The number of Judges on the United States supreme Court was undefined by the Constitution, determination left to Congress. Pennsylvania's supreme Court, which met in the West Room across the hall, had but three Judges, with a majority Opinion of two requisite for any Ruling. Presumably, the United States supreme Court would also vote by majority, but the Constitution made no specification. Congress the First would stipulate such provisions in a judiciary Law it would have to pass, presuming the Constitution could be ratified.

Might Congress require a two thirds Majority to render an opinion binding? Three quarters? Three fifths? Ruinous unanimity? Not at present. If the Constitution ratified, a simple majority requisite would probably be codified by Congress the First. But what of futurity? Might it alter this provision to increase or decrease the Power of the Court? Require greater unanimity to increase the threshold for rulings, especially in appellate Cases which might overturn lower Court rulings? How significant might such changes prove?

Would supreme Court decisions be issued seriatim, in series, each Judge drawing his own opinion? Or would there be a majority Opinion written by one Judge for the Court? What of dissident Judges? Would there be a majority Opinion and then seriatim Opinions of dissenters?

How much did any of these particulars signify at present? Would they signify in futurity?

A fœderal supreme Court would require more than Pennsylvania's three Justices. But how many? Five? Seven? One per State? Twenty-three? Five seemed a reasonable allocation at present, at least to Franklin. An odd number was prudential, to avoid equal-divided Votes on rulings, and two more than the minimum odd plurality of three seemed a wise starting Point. More judges meant less chance for the Consensus of a majority Opinion. Was this desired or detriment? Given the potency of the Power of a supreme Court, lessening application of its Power seemed prudential. More judges also diluted the Power each judge held. The same reasoning which under-rode an Executive Council might be argument for a larger supreme Court.

Once America large, the Burden on each Justice of the supreme Court in reviewing appellate Claims and writing Opinions might be immense, and a larger court would distribute and lessen this Burden. This tendency alone might beget shunning of seriatim opinions. Except that the number of cases the supreme Court would hear was necessarily small—at present. This was because the jurisdiction of the national Judiciary was purposeful minimal—at present.

A Chief Justice of the fœderal supreme Court had been specified in the Article I Clause on Impeachment of the President: When the President of the United States is tried, the Chief Justice shall preside.

The Chief Justice was not enumerated in Article III, however, which seemed unrigorous to Franklin. No method of chusing the Chief Justice was enumerate in the Constitution, save the Clause specifying that the President shall appoint Judges of the supreme Court. Would supreme Court Justices vote amongst themselves to select their Chief, in the mode of Executive Councils? If so, ought not a positive by the Senate or Legislature have been requisite, as with Executive Councils in Constitutions of some states? Or would Congress chuse the Chief Justice from amongst Justices seated on the supreme Court which the President had appoint'd and the Senate had positived? Would the President appoint a Judge as Chief Justice? From amongst Justices seated on the supreme Court? Or as a separate Appointment?

What other prerogatives would or ought the Chief Justice have, besides presiding over Impeachments? If the number of Justices be even, which was inadvise-ed, would his Vote decide equal divisions? Would he hear opinions of all other Justices, and vote last, chusing how close cases decided? Should the Chief Justice have such Power?

No one knew.

The Constitution was mute on all such questions.

Had they thirteen more years in Convention, such peculiars might have been attended with exactitude. Deputies had been unable to reach consensus, were exhausted and ready to intend home, and inclined to devolve latitude to Washington and Congress regardless. Would the precedent Washington and Congress established at the onset for the Courts be a binding precedent to futurity? Or would futurity vacillate in its selection process? Would the size of the Court itself vacillate? Grow as America sprawled westward? Be altered political, by designing Presidents and Congresses seeking to load the Court with Partizans? Would other changes be wrought for sim'l'r reasons? Other Perversions?

"The Judges," Jackson read, "both of the supreme and inferior Courts, shall hold their Offices during good Behaviour, and shall, at stated Times, receive for their Services, a Compensation, which shall not be diminished during their Continuance in Office."

Across the chambre, at the leftmost front table, Franklin saw John Langdon writhe slight, nigh as if shivering mild. He removed his wig right sudden, exposing his bald head. Langdon placed his wig upon the table, and reached for a Louse scurrying across his scalp. 'Twas smaller than a grain of rice, and whitish, or perhaps greyish, with a clearish aspect as well. Langdon worked his hand about his head, fumbling, but eventual gripped the Louse. He held it before his face, inspected it, and then squashed it and flicked it down onto the floor.

Langdon scowled prodigious as he began nit Picking his wig, picking out the Nit, the louse Eggs, which he began squashing within a small piece of parchment. No gentleman within chambre seemed suprized nor disgusted. Everyone present including Franklin had succumb'd to Louse numerate times, and at least a half dozen Deputies was probably Lousey at this instant. Langdon would need to have his wig boiled, but this would probably not be possible if he intended home in the morrow. Men not wealthy could never afford to discard a wig, but Langdon might, or have it shipped to him and boiled once home. Langdon might also just resign himself to Lousyness until he arrived home.

Langdon removed a small brownish apothecary Bottle from his suitcoat Pocket. Its glass stopper was uncommon, most stoppers being cork-ed. Langdon had tied string about the Bottle heightways, over the stopper, so as to secure it. Langdon opened the bottle, and poured a small portion of Tincture of Quicksilver onto his kerchief. Quicksilver's veneer and reflective quality were unmistakeable. Langdon rubbed the Quicksilver upon his scalp, as if larding a pan to prevent rust. The Quicksilver would repel Louse, confining them to Langdon's wig and preventing them from biting his Scalp again. 'Twould also kill many Louse resident within wig. Franklin was not enamoured of this Remedy, thinking that Quicksilver, which was to say mercury, tended to harm health, the mental Facultys especially. Franklin's was the minority View though, and reckoned mighty Contrarian.

Whilst Langdon resumed his nit Picking, Franklin continued to ruminate upon the Judiciary. The term and mode of appointing Judges was of supreme gravity. In the British model, the king simply removed Judges who issued not rulings he preferred. A President or Congress might easy do the same, perverting Justice. Judges had to be insulate from such pressures so as to remain disinterested—especially those of a supreme Court whose rulings would uniform the nation.

Representatives, Senators, and President were electored by The People, direct or indirect, but not Justices, a significant demarkation. Justices of the supreme Court, the only supreme Officers unelected, would hold their offices during good Behaviour. They could not be rotated out of office after a term of years as Representatives, Senators, and Presidents, save misbehaviour resulting in Impeachment, a high threshold indeed, encompassing but Treason, Bribery, and other high Crimes and Misdemeanors. In most instancys, the Justices of the supreme Court would thus serve nigh indefinite, until they died or chose to resign. The same would be true of Judges of all fœderal inferior Courts which the Congress might chuse to create, meaning that the entire fœderal Judiciary was immune to rotation and would serve for Life.

The basic thinking in England, at its noblest in both senses of the word, was that good Judges were difficult to find. If you had a good one, one excessive good especially, let him continue dispencing Justice, so long as he misbehaved not. The Convention had perpetuated this English tradition.

Some Deputies wanted the Legislature to appoint the Justices of the supreme Court, and fœderal inferior Courts, not the Executive. Some Deputies felt the Senate should appoint, others the House. Other Deputies preferenced other modes. The mode of chusing Justices had been debated prodigious, but there had been surprizing little contention or even consultation about the lack of Rotation and indefinite term of Justices.

In the Colonys prior to the Revolution, crown Court rulings were oft a savage lampoon of Justice. Deputies wanted to prohibit such Tyranny in America. They thus attempted construction of a Judiciary energetic in its independency from the Legislature and Executive. Measures such as indefinite Terms and fixed Pay were intended to accomplish this objective.

Deputies felt that Judges rotated in office and beholden to the Congress or Executive for reappointment would be corrupted, ruling to please the Congress or Executive in order to attain reappointment. Such policy had wrought not corruption in Pennsylvania, but most Deputies considered the Pennsylvania Constitution a Quackery radickal and democratic.

Deputies who presumed that re-eligibility wrought Corruption when Justices of the fœderal Court were chose by President and Congress had thus noosed themselves. They had little option but a term indefinite, or some other mode of Appointment or Rotation, and no other mode seemed prudencial. The only other mode available was Election, which would make judges into politicians, the antithesis of the Independency from politicks being sought.

Authority corrupted. Would not indefinite Appointment during good Behaviour represent a corruptive Authority bordering on absolute?

A Justice of the supreme Court, or a fœderal inferior Court, might hold office for more than a decade, surpassing the tenure a new birth'd child took to grow to manhood. What man could sit in Authority for so long a tenure and not be corrupted?

Washington perhaps, but Franklin could think of no other.

Why not rotate Justices, in a mode similar to Senators? In Pennsylvania, Justices of the supreme Court were appointed by the Assembly and served terms of seven years, with eligibility for reappointment by the Assembly.

With indefinite terms, would not Justices become habituate to Power, languishing on the bench until drooling Caricatures of senility, as Monarchs? Would this be the antithesis of good Behaviour, cause for removal?

Not in the Constitution reading, at least not as Franklin read it.

Would a future President and Congress have to strain and abuse Impeachment, misconstruing it to remove a senile Justice or one Ripe for Bedlam? Ought there not be some threshold below Impeachment yet above good Behaviour, however arduous, that allowed rotation of Judges in select instances? Perhaps also the Executive, and also Representatives and Senators? Yet add such Clause, would it not be abused to political ends by Designers?

Not in Pennsylvania, where good Behaviour was a way to remove Judges who had rendered themselves obnoxious but had stooped not to Treason, Bribery, and cetera. The Pennsylvania Assembly could remove Judges for deviation from good Behaviour, for misbehaviour, without Impeachment. It had been judicious in exercising such Power though. John Dickinson—or had it been Elbridge Gerry?—had wanted such construction in the fœderal Constitution, with any fœderal Judge removable by concurrence of House, Senate, and President. The measure had been reckont a Violation of judicial Independency and was nayed emphatick.

Were unjust Rulings, political Rulings, absent overt graft, a species of Misbehaviour? Were they high Crimes? Misdemeanors?

A devilish Ambiguity.

Franklin wondered if futurity would interpret good Behaviour as Deputies meant it, an indefinite term save Impeachment. Or would posterity interpret the construction more energetic, in the manner of the Pennsylvania Constitution? Franklin favoured the mode of the Pennsylvania Constitution, but not appropriation of said mode by energetic Deformities of meaning. He envisioned an explicit Enumeration of such Powers in the Constitution reading.

But 'twas not there.

Even if not incompetent with Age, how diligent could a Justice labour when he was as antient as Rome? Was it not preferable to have Justices not wearied with Age? Such arguments had been made against Franklin being President of the Executive Council. He had marshalled them in arguing he ought not be chose, though not with sufficient vigour to evade chusing, owing his age.

Franklin wanted to laugh. But this would be a breach of etiquette. And 'twas not funny.

Should the Republic be denied the Wisdom of its most antient yet wisest men? As Executive? As Senator? As Justice? Which was the greater Danger, rule by the senile or obnoxious, or rule by the unseasoned and unwise? How to best counterbalance the two? Would Franklin's more democratic notions prove more efficacious, or would the Convention's more republican? Franklin was too wise, had been too wrong too often in his life, to suppose his Sense that his notions superior might not be an Erratum.

When would Justices resign? In a gluttony, allowing a single President to appoint a disproportionate number of replacement Justices? Washington would appoint all Justices if the Republic inaugurate, but could any other person be entrusted with such Power? Would not an enforced rotation guard against this peril? Perhaps, yet if one President served long, an enforced rotation availed little. Only with a limit upon Presidential tenure would enforced rotation be certain to be efficacious, and even then, some Justices might expire before their term did. In such case, a President would appoint more than his intended apportionment of Justices. A term of rotation on the bench would nonetheless check the most egregious violations.

Would not men live longer over time? Might a Justice not be appointed when just thirty or forty and serve until seventy or eighty or longer? If men one day lived a century or more, like the mythologic antiquarians of the Bible, would Justices serve a half century or more? A century or more?

What term was too prodigious a duration?

Franklin agreed that long terms gave the Judiciary much needed Supremacy, independency from the Legislature and Executive. Yet it seemed imprudential to have any appointment be indefinite. Could not the sacred principle of Supremacy, of independency, be enacted without resorting to a term perpetual and bestowing immunity from rotation? Would not a term thrice that of Senators suffice? Or would appellate claimants hawk, a waiting the rotation of an unfavourable Justice? Was uncertainty about length of term a rampart against such concern?

Compensation of a judge was not to be diminished during his tenure, to prevent extortion under threat of pay diminution. Yet might not compensation be enlarged to provide effective Bribe in reward for Ruling? Should not the Clause prevent all alteration of Pay, diminishment and enlargement?

With pay nonamendable—at least in diminution—during the tenure of a Judge, salary alterations would effect new Judges only. With Judges serving indefinite terms, however, such changes might take decades to be effected in totality for all Judges. In the interim, might not corruptive pay Increases continue?

Franklin's rumination was interrupted by a great clacking of hooves and coach wheels. They was approaching, from what seemed to be the eastward. Franklin glanced out the north windows, and saw a Coach-and-Six race by fearsome rapid. Franklin saw but the darkish Blur of the horses followed by the reddish Blur of the Coach. He heard muffled Shouts from Promenaders, including one warm admonition to bloody well slow the Hell down. Franklin heard three distinct Sounds, the loudest and the most dominant being the percussive clacking of shoe-ed hooves on cobblestone, which formed a veritable cacophony, as there were six horses, each contacting the paving with two hooves per Second, approximate. Franklin also heard the softer Sound of the wooden wheels thumping against the Cobbles, as well as the even softer rattling and creaking of the frame of the Coach.

'Twas the great Speed of the Coach that made it so mighty loud, yet Franklin heard a slower Clacking that was equal loud, this time approaching from the west. He knew from Experience 'twas probably a supply wagon. The Clacking was more dominant, the thumping of the wheels and creaking of the wagon Frame scarce discernable. Franklin saw a massive fuel wagon pass by, moving slow enough that it was not a blur and could be clear discern-ed. The driver wore a whitish linen work shirt and a flapp-ed hat woven from straw or some other plant stalk, in the Stile of a farmer or labourer. Such uncocked hat with exceeding wide brim defended against the sun. The driver smoked a cobb-ed pipe. The wagon was nigh twice the length of a man, with side walls high and stout, and in excess of a corde of splite firewood stacked withinst it. The six draught Horses pulling the wagon were mammoth and frothy with sweat. Franklin's eye was drawn to the upward and downward movements of their cannons and heels.

The fuel wagon passed, relative quiet returned, and Franklin resumed his ruminations. Considered in their full plenitude, did these Constructions not deny The People the ability to reform the Judiciary with any degree of timeliness and energy? Was this imperfection tolerable, when weighed against the compelling Need for independency of Judges? They would be in a bad position if made to depend on every gust of Faction which might prevail in the government.

Indefinite terms of Justices of the fœderal supreme Court would have one other profound effect. Justices might remain in Power long after the Presidents, Representatives, and Senators who appointed them had been rotated out of office. At best, this was the infusion of Wisdom, at worst, it might confound the Will of The People nigh perpetual. If The People decided government ought reflect a new set of Principles, they ought have the Power to install leaders that adhered to them.

In theory, Judges were disinterested. In practice, all had politicks and phylosophys that coloured Judgements. The best Judges limited politicks and phylosophys and were disinterested and Just, yet even the best Judges might become interested and political over time. The People might need to cast out Judges interested and political, whose Rulings prevent'd Reformation, without waiting decades or longer for them to expire or resign.

Deputies having a Phobia of democratic Mobs, they viewed this repository of judicial Power immune to the will of The People as yet another desirable counterweight, but Franklin found it odious. Should Judges or even a supreme Court appointed decades prior or in a century prior, in possession of Opinions common past but at present obnoxious to The People, be able to sit decades rendering Judgments that impeded the Will of The People's? Franklin was not oblivious to the excesses of The Democracy, and the need for some security against them, but a Constitution need not stoop to indefinite Terms to attain to it.

Franklin fought the urge to cloze his eyes and rub them.

So many factors, so many contradictory arguments, each beguiling in portion, like a parade of belles. Which belle ought one wed? Chuse unwise, there would be no stable Marriage of compatible principles, no begetting Happiness, but rather convulsions and misery only.

The proper course was difficult to foretell.

"Section Two," Jackson read, "The judicial Power shall extend to all Cases, in Law and Equity, arising under this Constitution, the Laws of the United States, and Treaties made, or which shall be made, under their Authority;"

all Cases. in Law and Equity. arising under this Constitution. arising under the Laws of the United States. arising under Treaties made.

A broad grant of Power, indeed.

Especially if one were to interpret the language energetic.

At the table a front of Franklin, Colonel Mason once again seemed to fume. To him, there was no limitation whatsoever with respect to the Nature or Jurisdiction of the fœderal Courts.

Jackson continued to inch down the Constitution with his hands, letting more of the parchment droop in front of him. The inverted calligraphic "Article III." was visible two thirds the way down the parchment. Or was it up the parchment?

"To all Cases affecting Ambassadors, other public Ministers and Consuls," Jackson read. "To all Cases of admiralty and maritime Jurisdiction. To Controversies to which the United States shall be a Party. To Controversies between two or more States …"

In his mind's eye, Franklin imagined the words "The judicial Power shall extend" before each Clause beginning with To. This was a specific enumeration of the species of Cases over which the national Courts could exercise Jurisdiction.

Under the Articles of Confederacy, there was no Judiciary, just as there was no Executive, save a Tribunal to determine distribution of Prizes of War. States had jurisdiction over their Counties, were supreme to them, and could resolve Disputes among them or their residents. Yet there was no Court supreme to States, to resolve Disputes amongst them or their residents. At present, how were Massachusetts or Virginia to resolve legal Controversies between them? How was a citizen of one State to bring legal action against a citizen of a different State, or against that different state, save in the court of one State which might discriminate against the other State? And what of cases involving matters intrinsic fœderal, or fœderal Officials? No state Tribunal was competent to try such cases, and even if state Tribunals were incompetent not, chusing one state Tribunal to try such cases would raise it above the others, destroying coequality of States and creating fractious Jealousys.

'Twas a wretched State of Affairs.

Thus fœderal Tribunals with Jurisdiction were a mundane if requisite procedural framework a nation must have, at least in some Cases, which Jackson now enumerated. The list he read specified species of cases in which States were Parties; or the several States, the United States; or their Officers; or citizens in two different States; or foreign States; and cetera.

This was a narrow purview of Jurisdiction, as intended. It would not suffer the supreme Court or national Courts to stick their snouts into any matter they chose. If a case was not one of the species enumerate, the supreme Court and the national Courts had no Power to hear it.

In theory.

Any Clause above might be interpreted energetic by Designers. Virtually any Case might be construed as arising under the Constitution or Laws of the United States by unscrupulous Judges looking to expand judicial Reach. No Constitution could provide an unassailable Rampart against such sophistry, for any Powers or any Clause. A virtuous People was requisite to check such Abuses.

"In all Cases affecting Ambassadors," Jackson read, "other public Ministers and Consuls, and those in which a State shall be Party, the supreme Court shall have original Jurisdiction. In all the other Cases before mentioned, the supreme Court shall have appellate Jurisdiction, both as to Law and Fact, with such Exceptions, and under such Regulations as the Congress shall make."

Colonel Mason shook his head and exhalt yet again. Mason was nigh certain ired by the open-ended grant of Power, including Jurisdiction as to Fact, the ability to overturn findings of Fact by lower Courts. 'Twas one matter to negative how a lower Court had interpreted Law and applied it to Fact, but the Power to negative a finding of Fact itself made the supreme Court right energetic. Nothing curious about this provision, but 'twas an immence Power.

Yet what perhaps fuel'd Mason's foundry most, and was conspicuous to Franklin, was the same Section absent for the Executive, one analogous to Article I Sections 9 and 10 for the Congress, those negativing specific Powers. There was no List of Powers which the fœderal Courts could not exercise. The fœderal Courts were not denied Jurisdiction over any species of Case, nor explicit prohibited any tyrannic Practice, including dubious Warrants, unreasonable Searches nor Seizures, excessive Bail, cruel & unusual Punishments, religious Inquisitions, and cetera. Most all state Constitutions had such Prohibitions, often in the Declaration of Rights which prefix'd the Constitution.

Colonel Mason placed his porky hands flat on the table, and pressed down prodigious hard, as if trying to press it into Earth. Washington might have smashed the table to splinters, but not Mason. His entire body tensed yet seemed to vibrate, like a struck organ pipe.

As usual, one scarce needed a Prophet to conjecture Mason's thoughts. Absent negatives on species of Cases and Powers, they would be assumed and usurped by Designers. Mason's general View was that only those Powers explicit denied might not be exercised, judicial and otherwise, and history made him skeptical of even this. Governments would assume whatever Powers they could, Constitutions be damned. Mason thus considered it folly to have so few overt negatives on Power. Franklin doubted the Constitution would ever be ratifyed without a Declaration of Rights or a guarantee to ratify one, so fretted not this Count to point of nigh expiration as Mason.

Lawyers of competency were mindful of Details, however, and most of all planned for contingencys. Right glaring then, the absence of any Clause on negativing Laws, an inevitable contention. Though not so overt ominous as warrants, seizures, Bail, punishment, and cetera, 'twas a matter of similar gravity. The Constitution could not enumerate every Power denied or it would be endless and encourage assumption of Power unduly, but Franklin wished it were not mute on this mighty great Point.

A Majority of The People would elector Congress—the Tyranny of the disproportional Representation of the Senate notwithstanding—and it could pass laws implementing their majority Will, generally positived by the President who would give most Laws the sanction of his signature. The Congress and President would inevitable pass laws which Courts construed as violating the Constitution. In peculiar, the Majority might encroach the Natural Rights of the Minority, by having their Representatives and Senators in Congress legislate against the Minority, as with the Spirit of Levelling or Slaves. A few Deputies felt that in such cases, laws ought be set aside and voided, and wanted to grant Courts this Power to negative Laws. Other Deputies such as Jemmy were vehement that Courts ought never be granted such Power. With two Factions of Deputies in strenuous opposition on the issue, and no discernible Compromise, the Constitution defaulted to Silence.

A dangerous Silence.

If you knew nought what to do, was it better to do nought?

In Constitutions, the saying of nothing was the saying of something, to Designers of the sort Mason feared. Franklin had encountered such Designers in Assemblies and Courts the whole of his life. To Designers, the absence of a negative on Powers was by default a positive, an imply'd right to assume the Powers. The Constitution perhaps needed a general Clause which defaulted Powers not enumerate to The States and The People, to prevent rampant Assumption by Designers, as Mason wanted. Yet even such Clause might be designed around. Regardless, such Clause was not present in the Constitution reading.

Franklin reasoned that the Laws of Congress, generally positived by Executive, ought be Sovereign. Courts existed to interpret laws and adjudicate Disagreements about them, but that Power ought not extend to declaring laws invalid and of null Effect. A Court with such Power to negative Laws and keep Laws it preferenced only, would essentially Legislate, and such Power to Legislate ought lay with Congress. A supreme Tribunal of five or seven—or in some future time nigh a dozen?—unelectored Justices ought not have Power to negative the will of dozens—or in some future time hundreds?—of elected Rep-

resentatives and Senators that were the purest incarnation of
the Will of The People.

Yet oppression of the Minority was not a Danger to be
discarded trivial. The Senate was intended as a rampart to a
Majority of tyrannical intent, as it could not be rotated fully in
one election and would contain wise Elders who would in theory stand fast against obnoxious Legislation of the democratic
House. The Presidential Negative on Laws was also conceived
as a check on obnoxious or tyrannical legislation, and some
Deputies also wanted the Courts to have such Negative. They
thought the Judiciary ought to have an opportunity of remon-
strating against projected Encroachments on The People as well
as itself. Laws might be unjust, unwise, dangerous, destructive,
yet not violate the Constitution. Let the Judiciary have a share
of the revisionary Power, and they would have an opportunity of
taking notice of such Characteristics of the Law, and of coun-
teracting them by weight of their opinion.

Some state Constitutions included a Council of Revision,
comprised of supreme-court Justices and in some cases the Executive. The Council of Revision consulted with the Legislature
and review'd all Laws, making sure that they did not encroach
the principles of the Constitution, oppress the Minority, nor
specify provisions that were undue cumbersome and infeasible to execute. In many states, such Council of Revision could
negative proposed Bills before they became law. The result was
greater consultation and consensus amongst Legislature, Executive, and Judiciary when crafting Laws. The Legislature sought
to avoid the negativing of laws by the Council of Revision, and

thus crafted laws not obnoxious to Executive and Justices. The result was laws more just and practicable.

Many Deputies objected to a Council of Revision on the grounds that it was as violation of the principle of Supremacy. On its second day of meeting on the main business, the Convention had resolved to establish a national government consisting of a supreme Legislative, Executive, and Judiciary. Three branches each Supreme, their power Segregate, as Baron Montesquieu had advocated in his famed Spirit of the Laws. If Legislature, Executive, and Judiciary were to each be Supreme and have Independency of one another, then the Executive and Judiciary ought not partake of creating Laws, any more than the Executive or Legislature ought sit on the bench at Trials, or the Judiciary or Legislature ought command the Armies or execute the Laws. Franklin agreed not with this thinking in totality, but one might as well ask Christians to question the validity of the Bible as Deputies the Gospel of Montesquieu.

The king's Privy Council, dastard Bastards to the last man, had possessed the Power to negative laws of the Colonys. The memory of such Negativing made Deputies reticent to grant an American Council such power, lest they replicate British Tyranny inadvertent. Deputies had been happy to ditto the British Constitution nigh exact at times, yet was curious averse at other times, without seeming constancy of application.

The purest enumeration of the principle of Supremacy and segregation of Powers would have been a government in which the President acted not as a Council of Revision via his Power to negative Laws. The problem was that each Division of government was also supposed to counterbalance the other. Supreme yet counterbalanced. Like trying to be familiar but chaste, or guzzle strong Beer without becoming pissed. Supremacy had to be counterbalanced against other needs, including counterbalancing itself. Deputies were adamant about including constructions that guarded against a Legislature passing Laws which oppressed the Minority, namely them, and which also checked the Legislature's powerful tendency to absorb all power into its Vortex. Thus, an Executive Negative upon Laws was added.

The Congress would scarce have a sufficient Majority of Votes to ride over a Presidential Negative of a Law, especially given the ruinous Power bestowed upon Minoritys by the Senate. In Practice, this might often result in some consultation with the President during drawing of Laws, to ensure them complaisant to him, a de facto Council of Revision, albeit one absent a judicial Check.

Deputies deemed it imprudential to give the Judiciary a Negative akin to the President's, as they wanted the Judiciary to have the greatest independency of any of the divisions of government. Jurist Deputies also objected strenuous to Judges giving opinion on a Law before it came before them in Court, Dictator John especially. Jurists considered it paramount to maintain the precedent of this fundamental limitation on the exercise of judicial Power, lest Judges transmute into Inquisitors able to rule and exercise Power outside of Court in any locus.

Jemmy had nonetheless champion'd a Council of Revision so frequent Deputies wanted to drown him in the Delaware. Time and time again the measure was struck down, and time and time again Jemmy enforced it into debate.

Exasperating.

Bloody exasperating.

Jemmy envisioned a Council of Revision comprised of Executive and Justices of the supreme Court. If either Executive or a majority of Justices negatived a Law, it would take a two thirds vote of both Houses of Congress to positive the Law and ride over their Negative. If both Executive and a majority of Justices negatived a Law, it would take a three fourths vote of both Houses of Congress to ride over the Negative. The Power to negative a Law granting to the supreme Court prior to passage, the Power would be denyed after passage. Under this construct, laws would be cautious made, but then uncontroulable.

Franklin had served in enough Assemblies to know that even a simple Majority was often arduous to attain, and a two thirds or three quarters supra Majority was usual nigh Impossible. Jemmy's Council of Revision would have shifted too much law-making Power from the Legislature to the Executive and Court. In practice, Judges would become political, negativing not on Law, but on other factors, and the Congress would often be incapable of attaining the two thirds or three quarters supra Majority needed to ride over their Negative.

Strange that no Deputy had conceived a Council of Revision in which the supreme Court required a supra Majority to negative a Law, thereby rendering such Negatives arduous to attain. With some five Justices, a supra Majority would be four of five. There were scant few issues where such unanimity would be attained to. A two thirds or three quarters vote by a single Executive was impossible, unless he Ripe for Bedlam, yet was feasible with an Executive Council. Yet another argument for one.

Regardless, the root problem, by Franklin's mode of thinking, was that some Deputies fancyed the divisions of government supreme and coequal. Franklin envisioned three divisions of government supreme, which he hoped would prævent his Inquisition by Montesquieu zealots. Three divisions supreme, but not necessary coequal. The Legislature, the division controlled most direct by the sovereign People, rotated by them at the highest frequency, ought predominate. The Legislature ought pass what Laws it wished, and if The People were displeased, they could rotate the Legislature out and a new one would repeal Laws or pass new ones. The Executive and Judiciary needed Supremacy, and counterbalances among all Divisions was also requisite, but primary Power ought reside with the Legislature.

Franklin's thinking was again contrary on such question, as was the Pennsylvania Constitution relative to that of other States.

If the Power of negativing Laws was enumerate in a Constitution, as with Councils of Revision in state Constitutions, then it could be rightful exercised. Such explicit grants of Power not with standing, there was scant precedent for the Judiciary overruling a Statute, and rightful so. This would set the Judicial above the Legislative, the unelected above the elected, the unrotated above the rotated, thereby disempowering the sovereign People, making them incapable of effecting reformation by rotation, and perhaps overthrowing them and begetting a judicial Despotism.

The fact there was scant precedent at present did not mean there would never be. It seemed inconceiveable that a supreme Court would not attempt to negative a Law eventual, assuming the Power.

Usurping the Power, in point of fact.

The Constitution as read had no Council of Revision, save the Presidential Negative on Laws of Congress, and it was silent on the question of the fœderal supreme Court negativing Laws passed by the fœderal Congress.

Franklin would have preferenced a Clause in the Constitution negativing such Power explicit, preventing its assumption, its usurpation, so the that the Judicial would not be set above the Legislative, and could never attain to a Despotism. The absence of such Clause concerned Franklin.

Jurisdiction also concern'd Franklin. Original Jurisdiction meant the supreme Court heard a case first, before any other Court. For but two species of cases would the supreme Court have original Jurisdiction, those involving Ambassadors and other foreign Ministers, or those in which a State was a Party.

All other jurisdiction was appellate Jurisdiction, in which a party unsatisfied with an original Ruling, believing it erroneous or unjust, would appeal to a higher Court to reverse the ruling of the original lower Court. In the Constitution reading, fœderal Courts had appellate Jurisdiction on but a few species of cases.

In totality, the Jurisdiction granted to the fœderal Courts by the Constitution was limited. It would not constitute voluminous Cases of Law. The supreme Court would thus be a trifle relative to the Congress or Executive. This might displease designing Justices ravenous for Power and the Reputation, Esteem, and Emolument that often accompanied the exercise of it. Such Justices might scheme to expand Power, by expanding Jurisdiction.

How would the Powers of the Judiciary be constructed? Would the fœderal Courts be scrupulous and exercise Jurisdiction only in the specific species of cases enumerate, as intended? Or was future Justices to sit with designing smirks like the Little Lion, interpreting "The judicial Power shall extend to all Cases" as a boundless grant of Power?

Three species of fœderal Courts seemed necessitate: inferior Courts with original jurisdiction, inferior Courts with appellate jurisdiction, and a supreme Court with original and appellate jurisdiction. Congress was not required by the Constitution to create any Court save a supreme Court, but might create inferior fœderal Courts if it so wished. It probably would. Would one species of inferior fœderal Court have original and appellate Jurisdiction? Segregation into two species of courts seemed more prudential, but by this reckoning, there ought perhaps be two species of supreme Court, one for original Jurisdiction and one for appellate Jurisdiction, which there was not. Would a Court exercizing both original and appellate Jurisdiction prove corruptive? Was this a sphere where Deputies should have embraced Segregation with greater vigour? Was it friv'lous to have separate species of Courts when original Jurisdiction was so limited and the number of Causes such court would hear so small? Was this concern the fretting of minutiæ inconsequential, or an egregious erratum?

Franklin wondered about new theorys of government spawned by political Phylosophers. New customs, new practices, new inventions, new weapons, new modes of communication, perhaps with the electric Fire. Franklin envisiont the transmission of smoke Signals using lightning, but could not help but think of Mr. Pymer's recent debauch replicating his Philadelphia Experiment. Or perhaps signals transmitted via the spatially multiplexed Conductor of Mr. Le Sage, but with wires exceeding lengthy?

Franklin knew even this conceptualization was laughable primitive. Yet from his many Experiments with the electric Fire, he felt certain it would be apply'd by those cleverer and more ingenious than him to spawn mighty Advancement, via modes he was not perspicacious enough to deduce at present. Courts might have to apply extant principles of the Law to these novel begetments, and numerate others, a prodigious Power.

How would Congress specify the appellate, the appeals, process? If a person thought a ruling injust or in error, flawed in application of Law or determination of Fact, how would they request Appeal? If the process broad, might anyone bring any species of case before the fœderal Courts, facilitating usurpation of Jurisdiction from the states? Would fœderal inferior Courts or the fœderal supreme Court have to hear all appeal Causes, or could they chuse to hear only those that suited their fancy? Ought an external Council determine which Appeals heard? By abusive expance of Jurisdiction, would the fœderal Courts impose a tyrannical Uniform which oppugnant to The People and the several States?

The Constitution granted Congress the power to mandate Exceptions to the Jurisdiction of the fœderal Courts. In theory, the Congress could pass Regulations limiting Jurisdiction of a fœderal Court that was usurping Jurisdiction, even the supreme Court.

In theory.

Congress might legislate Exceptions that limited Jurisdiction of the fœderal Courts, but what of Expansions that
encreased Jurisdiction? The proper mode of expansion of the
Jurisdiction of fœderal Courts was Amendment. Would a designing or over zealous Congress seek to legislate an Expansion of
Jurisdiction without resorting to Amendment? Would a supreme
Court simple begin hearing cases which expanded Jurisdiction,
and the Congress stand idle and countenance Encroachment?

If the Supremacy of fœderal measures over state be presume-ed—that was in Article VI, which Jackson had not yet
read—then most any case could be heard or any Law review'd
under the appellate Jurisdiction of the supreme Court. The only
Power that seemed explicit denied to it was expanding original
jurisdiction. A supreme Court would have to wait for Appeals
to be brought to it to expand its Jurisdiction via such mode, yet
once it demonstrated itself energetic, appeals on every conceivable species of case might be brought. At such juncture, the
Court would be able to rule energetic on cases it chose and exert
political Dominion on any issue or in any sphere. It might very
well expound on the Constitution to ends Tyrannical.

Most Deputies envisioned a supreme Court that was to but
hear and Rule in the dernier Resort. Yet to Franklin, the Constitution seemed incompetent in constructing this intention and
insecure against Assumptions, Encroachments, and Usurpations,
by both the fœderal supreme Court and fœderal inferior Courts.

"The Trial of all Crimes," Jackson read, "except in Cases of
Impeachment, shall be by Jury; and such Trial shall be held in
the State where the said Crimes shall have been committed;

but when not committed within any State, the Trial shall be at such Place or Places as the Congress may by Law have directed."

Trial by Jury.

A palladium of Liberty.

No matter what ramparts against Tyranny a Constitution sought to provide, Tyranny would nonetheless arise. The paramount Power of a Court was its ability to convict People of Crimes, denying them Liberty, Property, and even Life. Judges might be corrupted, Congress and its Laws pervert'd, behaviour honest and moral made Fugitive. Trials would therefore resort to Juries. Juries drawn from The People, which were a Representative Assembly of The People, would make ultimate Determinations of Fact and Law when assaying if the Accused were Guilty of a Crime, and ultimate Determinations of Punishment when depriving the Accused of Life, Liberty, or Property. Juries were free to nullify any Law, negativing it by their Verdict, should the Law be at odds with Justice. They were equal free to ignore the instruction of any Judge or Court and render Verdicts oppugnant to the Bench. This was just. A government bottom'd on The People, springing from the well that was their bosom, should of necessity resort to them when depriving the Accused of their Natural Rights.

Mason shook his head again. No Deputy had to prognosticate Mason's dissatisfaction on this point, as he had made his views plain in Debate. Mason felt that grievous Abuses would occurr even with Trial by Jury, subverting Justice, unless said Abuses were negatived explicit. Mason was doubtless envisioning protections in the Virginia Constitution's Declaration of Rights, including the Right to be confronted by one's Accusers, the Right to call Evidence and Witnesses, the Right to not be compeled to give Evidence against one's Self, and cetera. Mason's views had strengthened since 1776 when he drew the Virginia Declaration of Rights, and he now favoured many additional Negatives of Abuses, including a Negative upon being twice put in Jeopardy for the same offence, a requirement of indictment by Grand Jury of The People for capital crime, a right to Counsel, a right to Jury in appellate supreme Court cases, and cetera.

Virginia had prefixed Mason's Declaration of Rights to its Constitution, and Thomas had mimick'd it in drawing the Declaration of Independency. Most all states had followed Virginia's example and prefixed their Constitutions with Declarations of Independency. Devoid of the indictment of the king which the Declaration of Independency contained, such Prefixes were more proper view'd as Declarations of Rights.

Some Deputies had wanted the supreme Court to try Impeachments, not the Senate with the Chief Justice presiding, as the Constitution specified. The resort to the Senate was chose because it savoured more of a Trial by Jury.

Trial by Jury.

A palladium of Liberty.

Franklin would never affix his name to a Constitution absent such Guarantee.

"Section Three," Jackson read, "Treason against the United States, shall consist only in levying War against them, or in adhering to their Enemies, giving them Aid and Comfort. No Person shall be convicted of Treason unless ..."

The Treason provisions, tho' much contested, were not complex. The definition of Treason in the Constitution was more limited than many Deputies would have preferenced, some desiring the inclusion of other species of Corruption. The standards of proof were to be exacting, to secure against false Accusation and unjust Conviction. No Corruption of Blood, no punishment against the Family or Posterity of a person convicted of Treason, would be permissible.

The problem was that a grievous plenitude of activity ruinous to Republics and Liberty was treasonous, yet not constituted as such. The lower the threshold for Prosecution, however, the more prone to Abuse for political ends. Franklin nonetheless wished the threshold had been lower. And that Bribery and Foreign Gold had been reckon'd explicit in the clause of Treason, and also perhaps Profiteering.

Franklin could not help but think of Benedict Arnold. All nations in history had been ravaged by Treason. America would not own Immunity on this count. Its future history would doubtless include the prosecution of many Benedicts, yet were such Trials absent, especially those of notoriety, it would probably not be evidence of absence of Treason, but rather of the absence of prosecution of it. Evidence of Corruption unpunished. As with so many provisions in the Constitution, Deputies had done their best, but few were certain they had struck the balance requisite to answer the need, least of all Franklin.

Section 3 enumerating Treason was the last of Article III. As Jackson drudged through it, Franklin pondered the Judiciary a final time. He thought of two of the Facts which Thomas had submitted to a candid world in his Declaration of Independency, which Franklin had helped revise. The king had obstructed the Administration of Justice by refusing his Assent to Laws for

establishing Judiciary Powers. The king had made Judges depen-
dent on his Will alone for the tenure of their offices, and the
amount and payment of their salaries. These ills were absent
in the Constitution reading, but Franklin still felt tremendous
uncertainty about the Judiciary. A queer personal Proclivity,
perhaps, owing his struggles against the Penns.

Franklin had fought a tyrannical Judiciary long before the
Revolution. In the late 1600s, king Charles II, of Britain, granted
land to William Penn to remedy a debt of £16,000. This land
became Pennsylvania. The Penns were Proprietors with significant Independency from the crown, but they assumed many of
the royal Prerogatives that precipitated the Revolution, including
the ability to negative Laws of the Legislature, absolute exemp-
tion from land Taxes, and the ability to appoint and remove any
Justice at their pleasure. Early in Franklin's life, The Penns abused
their Prerogatives and ruled as veritable Despots.

In 1748, turned of 42, having secured his Fortune as printer
and author, Franklin retired to the life of a Gentleman. He
promptly began his electric Fire experiments, which gain'd him
Fame through out the world by the early 1750s. This Fame
caused Franklin to be electored to the Pennsylvania Assembly by
1751. Most gratifying, as he had served as its Clerk from 1736
until 1751, from age 30 until 45, a span of nigh fifteen years. He
had grown tired of recording debates without ever partaking of
them and had developed a thirst to politick.

At times such as now, Franklin could not help but chuckle
at the exasperation of Deputies who felt long confined in the
State House. He had spent nigh three decades in this chambre,
beginning when the State House was semi-constructed nigh

half a century prior. Franklin had watched the State House grow, helped it grow, nurtured the growth of the City and State he loved, and also the Nation.

Fifty years of public service.

Bloody Hell.

No wonder he felt so worn.

In 1757, the Pennsylvania Assembly dispatched Franklin to England to politick Parliament, hoping to convince it to make Pennsylvania a royal Colony rather than a Penn fiefdom. Franklin had lived in England once before, from 1724 to 1726, so had familiarity. In 1757, he was also the only American of worldly Fame, a fact the Assembly was desirious to leverage.

Franklin failed to persuade Parliament. Repairing home five years later in 1762, he joined the Anti-Proprietary Party, was elect'd Speaker of the Pennsylvania Assembly, and continued to agitate for Pennsylvania to become a royal Colony. The People were affrightened of surrendering Liberty as a royal Colony, however, and rotated Franklin out of office at the sequel election, promoting him back to The People.

Franklin couldn't help but chuckle a bit as he thought back. In hindsight, his experience was pleasing Democratic, and proof of the wisdom of The People. At the time, he had been much chagrin'd at the publick's rebuking of his Views, and vigorous in denouncing them incorrect, but they had been correct. Right ironic that he had wanted Pennsylvania to become a royal Colony but a decade before the Colonys revolted. In those days Franklin had no conception of America as any Thing but British. At present, such episodes were stark reminder of his Fallibility, and that of all men, no matter how seeming wise. Franklin liked thinking of such Failures, for they imbued the Humility one must possess for an undertaking such as the Constitution.

The Assembly had dispatch'd Franklin back to England two years later, in 1764, as Agent to Parliament. He stayed until 1775, when undressed by the dastard Bastard privy Council and War inevitable. Thinking of the dastard Bastard privy Council made Franklin warm, even now, more than a decade later. During Franklin's eleven year stay in England as Pennsylvania Agent, other Colonys began to make him their Agent, gradual, until he was the de facto American Minister, even though no such formal office existed at the time. His status as de facto American Minister to Britain—and his Fame—led to his appointment as Minister Plenipotentiary to France during The War. Franklin sailed for France in 1776, and repaired not to Philadelphia until September 14, 1785, a Wednesday. Franklin was elected to Pennsylvania's Executive Council damn nigh immediate, just a month later, by especial Ballot, and the Convention convoked just twenty months from the moment his foot touched American soil again.

What a snaking road it had been. Franklin wish'd there were some simple yet overarching lesson from his experiences with application to the Judiciary, but knew such Hopes naïve and futile. His contemplation of the Judiciary had taken under a minute, but was right exacting. His analysis of Executive or Legislative had also been so, but the Judiciary felt peculiar different. Had the very brevity of Article III forced deeper contemplation? Franklin could not say certain.

Truth.

Justice.

Such elusive creatures.

The Law itself, the mechanism of Justice, was equal elusive. And effusive. It was vast, imposing, defy'd simplistic assailment. The Legislature and Executive, though superficial complexer than the Judiciary, were actual simpler in a manner, as Law could be so insidious complex. Nefarious complex. Common Law in peculiar was impossible to assimilate, much less corral. It was as vast as the continents, as Æthereal as the winds. Moulding it to Constitutional ends was like trying to grab smoke and form it into an object.

Yet form it they must.

Much thought had been given to how independent the Judiciary ought be and the ultimate character of American Jurisprudence. It was a calling to which many Deputies had devoted their Lives. Law ought be decided on honest interpretation of Facts, not be political. Make the Judiciary too subordinate to Congress or Executive, and rulings would focus on Politicks rather than Justice. Make it too Independent, the result would be a judicial Despotism. Even Deputies who had read not the Law needed no schooling in such Tyrannys. The British had provided ample Instruction.

Franklin assimilated these thoughts about the Judiciary and dozens of others. He felt satisfaction as he did so. His body might be crumbling like an antient Roman temple, but his mind remained nimble. As with so many other issues, the question of the Judiciary was delicate, complex, definitive right or wrong, correct or incorrectness, elusive.

Nigh two separate Nations, North and South. And other regions. Unifying their legal Codes was no trifle. Not something to be accomplish'd with rapidity, or perhaps ever in totality. Only through Time, by chisel strokes, as if trying to sculpt a face into a mountain. Chisel stroke by chisel stroke, ruling by ruling, the disparate Common Laws of the several States would evolve towards a more uniform structure—but never be absolute Uniform. The Law would adapt to changes in The People, and The People would adapt to changes in the Law. Over time, a portion of the Law of the several States would morph into a new species, not resident in States or Colonys or Countys, but rather reposit in the nation, a unitary fœderal Code more transcendent and singular American.

Minutes had passed. Then groups of minutes. Now more than a quarter hour.

And still Jackson read, ceaseless, tireless, his voice still booming with the constancy and vigour it possessed during the Preamble. As the procession of words and Clauses continued its ceaseless March, the sunlight from the south windows cut an ever wider Swath across the room, and eventual merged with sunlight from the north windows. Deputies lowered the operahouse curtains, preventing the Light from becoming blinding and forcing the entire room to squint, but Light nonetheless pierced the drapes, and the room grew substancial brighter. The grey east wall assumed a bluish tinge in the Light.

And it grew hotter. The air became stiller. Staler. More lifeless. Dust danced in the sunlight Beams, but except for this, the chambre might have been a mausolæum.

Sweat dripped off of Deputies like candle wax, falling onto table baize, droplets darkening the feltish green fabric. Fingers was pressed into cravats, loosening them on necks. Perspiration glisten'd on foreheads, tips of noses, lips, and chins. Franklin felt a sweat bead roll out his armpit and make the Pilgrimage down the front of his torso, towards his Plymouth Rocks.

The fowl-faced, beak-nose-ed William Johnson, of Connecticut, seated in the centre table of the front left row, scratch'd at his chest beneath his suitcoat. He did so vigorous, upon both sides his body. Johnson was perhaps Lousey, but more probably sweltering, and seemed to want to remove his suitcoat. Johnson glanced about at other Deputies, saw that no other was without coat, and seem'd to think better of it. On other days Deputies had removed suitcoats and even waistcoats, and in rare instances even their neckcloaths, but this seemed inappropriate upon the final day of execution.

Franklin reached within his suitcoat pocket, where he oft kept a Lady's hand Fan. 'Twas absent. Franklin cursed his forgetfulness. He knew from Experiment that Evapouration was the true mode of Cooling when sweating, the heat required to vapourate Sweat drawing from the body. Fanning tended to increase Evapouration, and thus heat removal and cooling. Franklin contented himself with use of the fresh struck Constitution of Government, and began fanning himself with it.

Other Deputies observed Franklin and aped him, also fanning with the fresh struck Constitution of Government. Even Colonel Mason did so, tho' he glared at the fresh struck Constitution with disdain. At least it served some practicable purpose, his indicting Glance seemed to say.

The longer one sat in the East Room, and the warmer it became, the more cramped it felt. 'Twas never so crowded when the Pennsylvania Assembly in session. And this was with just over half the appointed Deputies present. What if all 73 Deputies appointed by the several States had attended the Convention and were seated today?

Franklin tryed to envision the horrific overcrowding and the resulting Sufferance. With dozens more Deputies, they would have been cramm'd into the East Room like Felons on a Hulk. Perhaps some Deputies could have perched inverted upon the ceiling like bats? The Convention could have resorted to the Long Gallery above stairs, which ran the length of the building though but half its width, and it had done so upon occasion during the summer, but the Long Gallery was only a trifle larger than East Room.

Fortunate, and unfortunate, 18 of the 73 Deputies appointed to the Convention never seated. Some Deputies smelt an intention to create a new Constitution rather than mere revise the Articles of Confederacy and thought it Evil to participate in the design of an unauthorized and energetic government. Old Patriots such as John Hancock, Richard Henry Lee, and Benjamin West seemed to have boycotted the Convention for such reasons, as did planter Willie Jones. And perhaps Patrick Henry. John Pickering was building his legal practice and did not want to absent his clients. Henry Laurens was wealthy beyond reckon from ownership of the largest slave House in America and had retired from all public business. Abraham Clark and Thomas Nelson could not attend because of declining Health, Thomas Stone because his wife was grievous Ill. Erastus Wolcott feared he might contract the Smallpox in Philadelphia.

Other Gentlemen also refused Appointment, often without enumerating their reasons. George Walton, Chief Justice of the Georgia supreme Court. Francis Dana, Justice of the Massachusetts supreme Court. Robert Harrison, Chief Justice of the Maryland supreme Court. Richard Coswell, Governour of North Carolina. Thomas Lee, Governour of Maryland. Nathaniel Pendleton, former Attorney General of Georgia. Old Patriot Charles Carroll of Carollton, one of the richest men in America. Also jurist Gabriel Duvall, soldier John Neilson, and George Watson.

Many Appointees were busy with pressing local Affairs, especially Justices and Governours who laboured to keep society running amid the convulsions ravaging several States. Some Appointees were doubtless selfish, disinclined to absent themselves from their private Affairs at home for so long or undertake the arduous trip to Philadelphia. The mere addition of temporizing expedients to the Articles of Confederacy was also not momentous to many Appointees. Had the fugitive Plan to create a new Constitution been open expressed, many more Appointees certain would have seated, and in some cases different Gentlemen would probably have been chose.

The rule of Secrecy had proved right beneficial in this Regard. Had America learned of the Convention's fugitive activity, and the structure and character of government it intended, Agitations would have begun throughout the Land. Eminents would have rode to Philadelphia forthwith and seated in Convention, or exercised Influence to be appointed Deputies post facto. Agitations also might have been undertaken in Congress to revoke the Convention's sanction and disband it. In such case, to remain convoked, the Convention would have had to make itself brazen fugitive. Washington would never have countenanced this sullying of his Character, though he and Franklin might have stabiliz'd the vessel with the combined mass of their Reputations.

If the Convention had remained convoked under such conditions, a dozen or more Anti-Fœderalists would have been in state Deputations, voting down constructions of energetic government which the Convention had approved without them present. Anti-nationalists might also have sway'd other Deputies to vote down energetic constructions.

Patrick Henry came to thought.

So did Samuel Adams.

But Henry especially.

Bloody Patrick Henry.

The prospect of Henry speaking in Convention against the Constitution day after day filled Franklin with Fear. On the floor of the East Room, Give Me Liberty or Give Me Death might have become Give Me State Sovereignty or Give Me Anarchy. Had Henry heard of the radical Constitution planning, he would have been irate, probably would have mounted his horse that very instant and rode it direct to Philadelphia hard enough to kill it. Henry was revered in Virginia. When the Old Dominion appointed Deputies to Convention, only Washington received more Votes.

If there was a greater Orator in America than Patrick Henry, Franklin could not bring him to mind. Henry could probably connive a nun to part with her Virtue or a Quaker to fight. He would have view'd the Constitution crafting as a Subversion of the Revolution, one which sowed Tyranny, and might have swung the entire course of the Convention along an anti-nationalist Tack.

Fortunate, Henry had late stepped down from the Virginia Governourship, ending a long tenure of public Service, and was fixated on personal business. And he seem'd not to have smelt an Intention to create a new Constitution rather than mere revize the Articles of Confederacy. Old Patriots such as John Hancock, Henry Lee, and Benjamin West might also be categorized such.

Ever radical, Samuel Adams made his vehement Opposition to a strengthened fœderal government manifest, and since he was occupied as President of the Massachusetts Senate regardless, he was not appointed to the Convention by the Massachusetts Legislature. Adams was too busy governing and quelling Rebellion to incite yet another, a poetick Irony if ever there was one. Adams was a skilled orator, but no Henry.

Adams was a Rouser of the first order, however. His Power would have been felt without doors at the Convention, organizing malcontent Deputies and Deputations and energizing their Dissent. With Adams in Convention, opposition to fœderal Government would have been much more formidable and right intractable. Many of the Compromises the Convention wrought might have been nigh Impossible with him present. Franklin and Washington had sufficient Stature to overcome even Adams, but a Convention that had been right torturous without Adams would have been bloody Murd'rous with him. Adams was absolute indefatigable, prodigious cunning, and they would have had to battle him every Clause of the way.

Samuel Adams was also the type of Ruffian who might have violated the Oath of Secrecy and spilt to The People when a Constitution he disliked became inevitable, thereby scuttling the entire Convention. Better no Constitution than a bad one, he might have reasoned.

Henry, Adams, and cetera.

Treach'rous men.

Especially Henry.

Franklin saw an apparition of Henry at the Virginia table for an instant. Standing, speaking, a rousing. Franklin saw Henry's flat steeple nose, which cleaved his Face. And the theatrick lips, earnest and severe yet disappointed. Henry's expression conveyed a longing for something better and determination to hold fast for it, and this countenance effected audiences powerful.

Henry in Convention would have been a Nightmare.

An absolute bloody Nightmare.

The rule of Secrecy had prevented such Horror.

Right fortunate, that.

If the Constitution succeeded, the Secrecy would be an after thought. History would paint it as an honest Necessity rather than a Machination.

It had been both.

With observers, as at a trial, Deputies would have played for the Gallery and Publick and every utterance would have been tried in the Papers, making honest, impolitick Consultation impossible. Franklin pictured the Gallery behind him filled with spectators and the Fourth Estate, the Papermen, as well as enemy Spies, and saw Deputies altering their every syllable to avoid the appearance of Ignobility.

It had been especially critical to mislead Britain and Foreigners. Had they known how much the Convention tore at its own Vitals, how close it had come to Dissolution, foreign Gold or Invasion might have been encouraged.

In his mind's eye, Franklin saw a different Convention, with a dozen of the Deputies middling and plyable replaced by anti-fœderal Zealots.

Distressing.

Grievous distressing.

State Legislatures had appointed Deputies, often chusing eminent and qualifyed men without consideration for their willingness or ability to attend. But there had been exceptions. Thomas was America's Minister Plenipotentiary to France and John Adams was America's Minister Plenipotentiary to Britain, and as neither could vacate his post and cross the Atlantic, neither was appointed. Thomas Paine was resident in Europe, hoping to secure funds for his novel plan to use iron to arch rivers, could not attend, and had been appointed not. Paine's renowned Common Sense had explained the principles of the Revolution in simplify'd terms Aprons and Yeomen could grasp; it was probably the single most important writing of the Revolution because it created widespread popular Support for demanding Natural Rights and fighting for Independency. John Jay was serving as Secretary of Foreign Affairs in Congress and was indispensable there, and so was not appoint'd to the Convention, even though he was moderate, wise, and a strong supporter of a greatly strengthened fœderal government. If Franklin thought longer, other Eminents appointed not as Deputies would doubtless come to mind, but Thomas, both Adams, Henry, Paine, and Jay were the most glaring.

State Legislatures had been free to appoint as many Deputies as they wished, and space in the East Room notwithstanding, Franklin was tempted to wish that more Deputies had been appointed or attended, to provide a greater latitude of Wisdom to draw upon. Yet each new Deputy was a new Personality which might conflict with other Personalities. With many more Deputies, diversity of opinion might have been expanded so egregious that Compromise would have been impossible.

Some 73 Deputies appointed, 18 declining their appointments, leaving 55 Deputies who attended the Convention, though never all at once.

Attendance had been spotty.

The Convention was supposed to convoke on May 14, but only Virginia and Pennsylvania had Deputies present, and a quorum of seven states was required to conduct business.

Weather was blamed. In some instances this was true, as travel through the shoddy-roaded countryside and forests was arduous. America was a handful of disparate towns carved into the woodland. Most inter State roads were mere mudholes. And there were countless rivers and streams to ford, few with bridges. Drownings were a far from infrequent. On good roads in good conditions, a man might make forty miles a day, sixty at the absolute most if one were a rider fast and dext'rous like Washington. Twenty miles was considered a good day by most travelers. In poor conditions, or with a single severe delay such as an arduous river Crossing, a traveler would feel lucky to make ten miles in a day. 'Twas thus impossible to have dozens of Deputies depart from diff'rent locations, traverse hundreds of miles of wilderness via horseback or Coach, and arrive the same day.

Or even the same week.

Similar attendance problems had often plagued the Congress, which was infamous for its inaccomplishment. Having been called by the Congress, the Convention had been presumed by some Deputies to be a sim'l'r impotent affair.

In theory, Gentlemen would leave well in advance and arrive early, but in practice they were too busy to fritter idle days away from pressing business at home. 'Twas difficult to absent one's affairs, easy to envision the rigours of days or weeks of travel on horseback or in Coach, often in rain, or tossing about on a Ship, and put off leaving until the morrow. The further one was from Philadelphia, the longer one would be Absent, the more arduous the Travel would be, and the more tempting such procrastination became. Yet the most distant Deputies was most likely to be hampered for long durations by inclement Weather, broke coaches, lame horses, ocean Storms, or other mitigate circumstancys. Thus, the paradox of Deputies who should have left the earliest often leaving the latest.

Deputies planned on the tardiness of other Deputies, further feeding the tendency of procrastination. Why precipitate to the Convention only to a wait on other Deputies? Better to be fashionate tardy, as at a Ball.

Thus a quorum of seven States was not attained until 11 days after the official start Date of the Convention, on May 25. Fortuitous, as Virginia and Pennsylvania Deputies used the time to draft the Randolph Plan, the large-state Plan that became the starting point used by the Convention. Many Deputies arrived expecting open Consideration of all forms of government and were dismay'd to find themselves ambuscaded by the Randolph Plan.

Even with a quorum that allowed business to be conducted, the last state's Deputies, New Hampshire's, were two months late and didn't seat until nigh the end of July. Niggardly beyond all Reason as typical, the New Hampshire Legislature had refused to pay the expences of her Deputies, which delayed their departure. Wealthy Deputy John Langdon, a merchant associate of Robert Morris, finally paid his expences and those of Deputy Nicholas Gilman, and without his largesse New Hampshire might have absented the Convention entire.

Franklin considered it right selfish and reprehensible for any State to absent the Convention, out of mere parsimony especially, but New Hampshire had always been something of a castaway. In a Convention of States zealous of their Sovereignty, 'twas perhaps the most zealous. New Hampshire's casual indifference to the Convention, and glib willingness to absent it, surpriz'd few. Seating now, at the Convention compleation, most Deputies could sense that something historick had perhaps been wrought. But this had scarce been the impression from afar at the onset, especially to distant States removed from the cabal of Madison, Hamilton, and cetera, who conspired a new Constitution. States expecting temporizing expedients added to the Articles of Confederacy had no sense that a new Constitution would be wrought and thus no Reason to expect that that the Convention might be epochal.

The egregious delay in departure was especially costly for New Hampshire, as it was the northmost State. Its Deputies' journey of roughly 400 miles took more than a week on horseback under the most ideal conditions and could easy stretch to more than two weeks with inclement Weather.

The weather had been inclement the week prior to the Convention and the week it opened. Roads were trench-ed deep with mud, tiring or spraining horses, sinking wagon wheels, slowing travel immeasurable.

Deputies of some distant States had been serving in Congress in New York, a hundred miles from Philadelphia, and as the road between the two huge Cities was one of the few relyable in America, with regular coach service, including the Flying Machine, this allowed them to arrive in just days and provide the Deputies which many States needed to attain to a Quorum. Yet many of the more eminent and learned Deputies were not present early in the Convention despite the superficial appearance of ample Representation, as they had to travel from home. Georgia, the southmost State, had it worst, with a journey of more than 800 miles, nigh two weeks by land under the best of conditions, easily three weeks or four weeks if the weather was an adversary. Ships could precipitate the Journey, but sailing put one at the mercy of the raging sea, and shipping from the ports of the deep South to Philadelphia could still take weeks. Gentlemen intending to Places they would be long resident also often preferred to go by horse or they Coach, that they might have mobility at their destination.

The last Deputy to arrive had been John Francis Mercer of Maryland, in early August, and he was not present today for the Signing. Yet before all Deputies arrived, many vacated. Some, like New York's Deputies, were disgusted by the creation of a new Constitution and the energetic character of the resulting government, echoing the biases of their leader, Governour Clinton. Some Deputies had to quit because of pressing business or political Concerns back home, or because of illness of theyselves or they kin. Other Deputies who absented were mere apathetic or indolent, like William Paterson. Caleb Strong of Massachusetts, William Houston of New Jersey, Chancellor Wythe and James McClurg of Virginia, Oliver Ellsworth of Connecticut, Luther Martin of Maryland, William Davie and Alexander Martin of North Carolina, William Pierce and William Houston of Georgia. All had seated at Convention for a spell but had absented and repaired not.

Less than 30 Deputies had seated at the Convention early on and attended its entirety up to this moment.

Less than 30 men!

Intrusted with the staggering responsibility of resurrecting Republicanism.

And of these, less than two dozen had seated nigh every day. Virginia Deputies Washington, Jemmy, Mason, Edmund Randolph, and John Blair were in this clique, as were Pennsylvania Deputies Robert Morris, Caledonia James, Jared Ingersoll, George Clymer, and Thomas Fitzsimons. The four South Carolina Deputies, Dictator John, the pair of Pinckneys, and Pierce Butler, had seated every session, seeming unwilling to chance any machinations on slavery should they absent. Hugh Williamson of North Carolina was the only Deputy of that state present without respite, as was George Read of Delaware. The attendance of Nathaniel Gorham of Massachusetts had been nigh perfect, but like Franklin he had absented at least one day.

Connecticut had no individual Deputy in Convention continuous for its duration, nor did New Hampshire, New York, New Jersey, Maryland, Georgia, nor of course Rogue Island. That was seven of the thirteen states.

What was that in summation? But six States with even a single Deputy present for the whole of the Convention, and but sixteen or seventeen Deputies present for the entirety? And of these sixteen, perhaps a quarter had contributed minimal, Blair, Ingersoll, Clymer, and Fitzsimons among them. That decreased it to nigh a dozen.

Franklin resisted the urge to shake his head.

Easier to keep a Truant in school, than Deputies in Convention.

On the most overcrowded days like today, there had been about 45 Deputies, yet on most days less than 30 Deputies were present, making the Convention seem more like the Assembly of a single State. No more than eleven States had been represented at any time, never all twelve, at times scarce a quorum of seven.

With thirteen Tables each designed to seat two Deputies, the chambre could seat 26 Deputies without crowding, not including the Chair and the Secretary. For much of the Convention, each Deputy had a comfortable seat at a Table rather than lingering on the peripheries of tables. The Convention had scarce been overcrowded as 'twas today, with more than a dozen Deputies seated at the edges of tables, between two tables, or behind Deputies seated at tables. Deputies seated direct in front of tables tended to be the most Senior and Eminent, with more junior or less esteemed Deputies relegate to the edges of tables or between them.

As he had each day, Franklin computed the number of Deputies in attendance by summing the Deputies not seated direct in front of tables at primary Seats. Two Deputies at each of thirteen Tables plus Washington and Jackson was 28. If there were less than 28 Deputies, Franklin simply summed the open seats direct a front of tables and subtracted this amount from 28 to obtain the number of Deputies present. With more than 28 Deputies present, as was the case today, Franklin quickly tally'd those sitting at the edges of tables, between them, or behind them. He accounted 14. 28 plus 14 equaled 42. There were 41 Deputies present, including Washington. Plus Jackson, who had not been appointed by any State to its Deputation and was not a Deputy.

Franklin glanced about the room, tried to gulp in the Deputies in a single Glance. Most were Eminents in their States, and some were esteemed national. Well over half were Veterans of The War for Independency. More than half had read the Law and passed the Bar, though far less than a quarter supported themselves primary as lawyers. Most Deputies had sat in state Legislatures, at least a half dozen were or had been state Governours or Heads of state Executive Councils, and many had helped draft the Constitutions of their States after Independency was declared. Every Deputy had held some public office of significancy, and their single universal commonality was that all were property'd Politicians.

At the least, three fourths of Deputies had served in the Continental Congress, and two Deputies, Thomas Mifflin and Nathaniel Gorham, had presided it. This might be the most consequencial similitude. Most Deputies had experienced the impotency of the Continental Congress and the Articles of Confederacy and knew them inadequate. This was not an abstracted Theorization to most Deputies, but a Frustration they had suffered personal.

To survey the Deputies was to see a representation of the professions held by most gentlemen in America. At least a dozen Deputies were merchants or shippers, including Robert Morris and Elbridge Gerry. Roughly a half dozen were major land Speculators, including Robert Morris, William Blount, Jonathan Dayton, and James Wilson. Another dozen were Financiers and major holders of Stock and securitys, including Robert Morris, Rufus King, Charles Cotesworth Pinckney, and Jonathan Dayton. Franklin could also probably be account'd in this number, though he invested in useful enterprizes and was not some sordid stock Jobber nor Speculator.

About a dozen Deputies owned large Plantations and lived primary off the sweat of Slaves, including the pair of Pinckneys, George Mason, Jemmy, and Washington, who owned in excess of 100 Slaves. Mason owned a Corps of some 300 Slaves. Some two dozen of the 55 Deputies who had attended Convention owned slaves. By rough hazard, some dozen and a half Deputies in Convention today owned Slaves, a bit under half, including most every Deputy from the south States of Maryland, Virginia, North Carolina, South Carolina, and Georgia, as well as several Deputies from Delaware. Franklin glanced rightward, at the south Deputations, tried to locate a Deputy that owned not Slaves, and could not do so.

Some Deputies, and many Americans, resident in the North did not have plantations with legions of labouring Slaves, but owned a few as groomers, Cooks, valets, ladyservants, et cætera.

William Samuel Johnson of Connecticut was one such Deputy. Franklin had owned a few Slaves as house and shop servants, but had manumitted them all, the last being George in 1785. Franklin had named George after king George, having acquired the Slave when a loyal British citizen. Robert Morris had participated in the Traffick in Humans at least once, yet owned not a Slave. Franklin was unsure if Morris ever had owned a Slave, or what other Deputies of the North might have.

The American West was the last Frontier. As in crowded Europe, Land was wealth, but unlike Europe, the industrious could acquire Land with ease. Most Deputies had been industrious, had substantial land holdings which made them wealthy, and even those without substantial land holdings were comfortable wealthy. George Washington, Robert Morris, Daniel Carroll, Thomas Mifflin, and Daniel of St. Thomas Jenifer were among the richest Americans, Washington more from his voracious land Acquisitions than any acumen in overseeing Mount Vernon. Many Deputies like Washington were land Rich but cash Poor, despite their enormous Wealth, especially southern Planters who lived in opulence within plantations that were self-containt communities, yet were often scarce of Specie without such confines. Roger Sherman and William Few were probably the least wealthy Deputies, though even they lived in comfortable Stile and would be considered wealthy by any humble Apron or Yeoman.

Most Deputies employed freemen or Slaves. Missing business back home might be an inconveniency and impede the acquisition of wealth, but 'twould not impoverish Deputies the way it would a Yeoman or Apron who quit their Labour for a third a year.

Though some Deputies such as Franklin, Few, and Sherman had begun life as Aprons or Yeomen, this was not an assembly of Aprons or Yeomen, nor even ex-Aprons or ex-Yeomen. 'Twas a gathering of the Gentry, the property'd American Elite. Yet there was no idle class of wealthy nobility in America, as in Europe. Few Deputies had retired from their professions to live as Gentlemen, as Franklin had, and none was Dawdlers, to put it mild, including Franklin. He could only dream of dawdling. Many Deputies had advantageous Beginnings, but all had laboured mighty to attain to Fortunes or augment those inherit, and they intended to keep this Property. The present Convulsions in many States were concerning in this regard, even to a proponent of paper Money with democratic leanings such as Franklin. What mere concerned Franklin absolute petrified less democratic Deputies, which was nigh all.

In his famed Treatises of Government, promulgated in 1689, just under a century ago, John Locke had defined Natural Rights as the trinity of Life, Liberty, and Property. Thomas had drawn on some of Locke's non-Treatise writings which argued that the Pursuit of Happiness was a key Liberty. Was it Locke's Essays on the Law of Nature? Or his Essay Concerning Human Understanding? Franklin could not recollect certain. Hume was also profund with the Phraze. In the Virginia Constitution's Declaration of Rights, Mason had expounded the Natural Rights of Life, Liberty, Property, and Happiness. Thomas also drew from the Declaration of Rights, and included the Pursuit of Happiness in the Declaration of Independency, but not Property. Yet another concession to, and miring in, the quagmire of Slavery. Yet the Natural Right of Property had been forsaken not. The Pursuit of Happiness included Property, and Deputies were extreme cognizant of the sanctity of Locke's original trinity.

There were few Poor in America. In a nation with limitless Land in the West, and none of the tyrannial Trappings of Europe, a man who attained not to Property quite simply wanted for Industry. Labour was also scarce in America, and Wages thus high, and only Slothers or those ruled by Vice suffered poverty even if not propertied. Deputies who disagreed about nigh every Thing were unanimate in their hatred of democratical Levelling. Let those who wanted more labour for it, as all Deputies had, not pilfer the Propertied via the Pickpocketry of energetic Taxation or paper Money.

Most Deputies in attendance were in the upper tier of the American elite. 'Twas difficult to envision a future America that did not include most Deputies in prominent leadership roles, at both the state and fœderal Level, in politicks as well as the Judiciary, which were hopeful not the same calling.

If the Constitution succeeded, Deputies would be elevate in Eminence, and perhaps to Office, by mere having participated, and some of the more indifferent Deputies had doubtless come to the Convention for this reason. Power Jobbers. Office Jobbers, which was to say Officers. Coxcombs. The Convention had its Share of these. Jobbers, Officers, and Coxcombs aplenty in fact. Other Deputies had attended to exercise raw Interest, to ensure that their personal Interest or state Interest was cement'd in the Constitution, even if ruinous to the Whole.

Sometimes when Franklin gandered about at Deputies, he saw the assembly of Demigods men like Thomas had purported perceived. Other times the Convention looked decided more middling and mortal, a gluttony of Jobbers, Officers, and Coxcombs dragged along kicking and wailing by a few determined Geniuses such as Caledonia, Chancellor Wythe, Jemmy, and cetera. Franklin's perspective had tended to vacillate, both day to day and within days, depending upon who was speaking and his opinion of the wisdom of whatever measure the Convention was debating or adopting.

Caledonia James and Governeur Morris had contributed more to the Convention than any other Pennsylvania Deputies, yet they had been among the last Deputies appointed by the Assembly Caucus, and trailed lesser Deputies in the final Assembly Vote by a prodigious margin. The Caucus had met in the Half Moon Tavern direct across Market Street from the State House, which was general much cooler than the State House, not that such mattered early last December when they had met. The Pennsylvania Assembly's appointment of Deputies had been far less noble and principled, for more political, than 'twas comfortable to own, and the same was true in other states. How many men as brilliant as Caledonia or Governeur Morris had their positions filched by Jobbers, Officers, and Coxcombs? With even a few more Luminarys appointed by State Legislatures, might the Constitution have attained a success that would prove elusive? In darker moments, or perhaps more realistic moments, Franklin was troubled by questions such as these.

Usually when Franklin glanced around the East Room he focused on the Eminents, Influencials, or Luminarys. Washington, Caledonia James, Chancellor Wythe, Jemmy, Tall Boy, and cetera. In more frivolous or exasperate moods, Franklin focused on Deputies with physical stature or peculiarity of appearance and mannerism. Today Franklin's attention was drawn to the Dissidents.

Four Deputies present had either disavowed the Constitution or scrupled to sign: George Mason and Edmund Randolph of Virginia, Elbridge Gerry of Massachusetts, and William Blount of North Carolina. Blount was but a trifle. Gerry had indisputable Integrity, and though his opposition was vexsome, Mason and Randolph were the true Concern. They were two of the most eminent Deputies, and formidable enough to corrupt others.

Still, it might have been worse. There could have been a dozen or more Dissidents, rather than four, a manageable number. Yates and Lansing of New York, or Mercer and Luther Martin of Maryland, could have staid to harangue the Convention to its last instance rather than absenting. Mercer would have ranted, condemning the folly of suff'ring The People to participate in the election of members to the Legislature, and prophesizing the Tyranny liable to be wrought by the energetic centralized Government the Constitution would create. Luther Martin's drunken discourses were like a horse kick to one's Vitals, an affront no man of dignity wanted to countenance, especially not on the final day of the Convention. Nor any day, truly.

Franklin again thanked Providence that men like Governour Clinton, Samuel Adams, and Patrick Henry had absented. A crucial errour on their part. Especially Henry, who could talk a Fish into frying. Franklin wondered how much Deputies had reported back to Clinton, Henry, Adams, and cetera.

Not enough.

Governour Clinton had doubtless been briefed by the New York Deputies who absented Convention, and knew what was transpiring, yet what could he do? Condemn the Character of a Convention with the unassailable Washington at its head? Ride down and confront His Excellency?

Pshaw.

Henry had evidenced surprizing absence of curiousity about the Convention, according to reports of Virginians. Governour Caswell of North Carolina, the state of the Dissident Blount, had become impatient about the want of information on the Convention and taken to grumbling.

Good signs, these.

If men like Clinton, Adams, and Henry knew how tenuous support for the Constitution was, they and others might have ambuscaded the Convention and scuttled it. A primary Fear for much of the Convention had been never even reaching this juncture, when Dissidents were a manageable Minority whose rights could be violate. The Constitution had counterbalances guarding against Oppression of the Minority, but save the mode of voting by States, there were no such protections in rules governing the Convention itself. Thank Providence for that.

Had there been a dozen Dissidents present in Convention, unanimity could never have been pretended, nor could Votes which created the Constitution reading have been won. More concessions to anti-fœderal Interests would have been enforced to decrease Opposition, and the Constitution wrought perhaps devoted to fail certain. The Constitution reading had defects a-plenty, right certain. Proliferating defects in a structure so manifest flawed was imprudential. At what threshold the Defects wrought by political Compromise be fatal, none could say, but by Franklin's thinking, they had inched dangerous cluse to the equator of demarkation.

During the many heated months of Debate, it seemed probable that there would always be a large Minority objecting some aspect of the Constitution, and improbable that any final Charta would be acceptable to all Partys. To even be standing at the current Precipice with a manageable Minority of Dissidents was a Yorktown. All that remain'd was to cement the Treaty of Peace.

"Article Four," Jackson read. "Section One. Full Faith and Credit shall be given in each State to the public Acts, Records, and judicial Proceedings of every other State. And the—"

Jackson placed parchment the third of the Constitution down quick but careful and picked up the fourth. The parchment rustled as he did. Jackson cleared his throat once, gulping hard, and then gulped again as he switched pages.

Jackson switched from parchment the third to the fourth with the exact same sequence of movements used for previous switches.

His militant precision was impressive.

Right impressive.

Better than Temple might have managed.

"—Congress may by general Laws prescribe," Jackson read, "the Manner in which such Acts, Records and Proceedings shall be proved, and the Effect thereof."

Parchment the fourth.

Resolvements on parchment the fifth which were not a formal part of the Constitution notwithstanding, this was the final parchment!

Relief plastered the faces of many a Deputy.

The Constitution had seven Articles. Article I enumerated the Legislature; Article II the Executive; and Article III the Judiciary. Article IV enumerated state Powers; Article V Amendation; Article VI remaining Miscellany, including debts, oaths of office, and the Supremacy of United States laws and treaties; and Article VII the Ratification of the Constitution.

The four remaining Articles were all brief and a counted but half a parchment in totality.

Thank Providence!

Eyes of many Deputies remained fixated on the parchment, as if it were a strumpet exposing her Duggs. Franklin imagined a Constitution that stuck not to core Principles, one twenty parchments long reading. At about parchment eight, or thereabouts, Deputies fashion Nooses and begin hanging themselves to end the Misery.

Major Jackson continued to read, and read, and read, and read, adding to the Constitutional edifice, making it more complex and intertwined. This caused Franklin to reanalyze the delicate way in which the House, Senate, Executive, and Courts were counterposed to prevent Tyranny. Like trying to balance a teapot on the tip of quill. 'Twas easy to doubt the Wisdom of not just each single Measure, but the precarious totality. Yet the moment Franklin fretted severe, he found some reason for Optimism that dispelt doubt.

Other Deputies seemed to grapple sim'l'r. The reading elicited frowns and smiles, quiet sighs of contentment or chagrin, glances of concern or satisfaction from them, as portions they approved or disapproved were enumerate. The Constitution horrified each Deputy on some Level, often many Levels, yet when one gaped at the totality of the Edifice constructing, 'twas magnificent. Distant from Perfection, a far distant, yet still right magnificent.

Three branches, Legislative, Executive, Judicial. Congress, President, supreme Court. Different modes of elevation, terms of rotation. Myriad counterbalances of each Branch upon the other. Fœderal yet National, States and a Union. Sufficient energetic, but with Checks against tyrannick Taxation, Consolidation, and Levelling. A complex machine capable of performing the daunting task for which it was design'd. To secure Natural Rights, Liberty especially.

Franklin felt nigh lightheaded with Euphoria, as if he'd resorted too much Laudanum. An immense satisfaction filled him.

The Constitution.

The Constitution of the United States of America.

Humbling to behold.

Immature and insecure in portions, yet so much better than the expectation of most Deputies at the beginning of the Convention as to defy comprehension.

Miraculous was the only word that seemed appropriate.

Mirac—

A gash of pain tore at Franklin's lower abdomen. As his body attempted to evacuate fluids into the bladder, his kidney Stone moved, resettling that its jagged edges lacerated the neck of the bladder, stabbing like a Stalker.

Franklin's head pivoted erratic as Pain consumed him. The bluish walls behind Washington seemed grey again, and the table baizes bluish rather than green, as if the chambre were sudden drenched in shadow.

Curing the Gout and Stone. That would be the bloody Miracle.

Franklin grew dizzier. Stars spun in his vision, remarkable three dimensional, fireworks rather than mere stabs of Light. Franklin fancy'd there was thirteen Stars, as on the flag, and resisted the urge to chuckle morose. Who could doubt his Patriotism?

Franklin glanced up at the chandeler and pictured its glass tentacles flailing like the arms of an octopus. Franklin pictured glass suckers on the arms. He fancied Trolls living in the fireplaces, wanting to issue forth and devour the Convention, but afraid to battle Washington.

Anything to focus on, the more fancyful the better.

Anything but the Pain.

There was no Parole from it. Franklin clused his eyes involuntary, squint'd hard, as if walnuts had been pressed into his eye sockets and he was trying to crack them.

An endless black horizon filled Franklin's vision. Smell, sound, and taste vanished.

Squinting, senses blunted, time became meaningless. Every thing was reckoned in Pain.

The kidney Stone resettled that the daggers dug into the bladder neck much less. The agony abated, and though a residual pain persisted, it was that tolerable level to which Franklin was a customed.

When Franklin opened his eyes he saw Deputies peering at him with concern. Washington especially. Tenderness permeated the harsh features of his face.

Franklin wiped the tears from his eyes, glanced at Washington, and nodded. Deputies refocused on the reading.

As it once again became a Drone, Franklin fought boredom as much as pain. The reading of a Constitution was intrinsick monotonous, no matter how much contemplation, fretting, or euphoria accompanied it. By broader Reckon, so were all Assemblies. In Assemblies, time oft crawled slower than a crippled baby. All politicians developed ticks and tricks they utilized to deal with the boredom, and Franklin was no exception. During the Convention, he often peered at the sun on the back of the Speaker's throne. With Washington or Gorham oft seated, it was not always visible, but at present Washington had turned his throne rightward toward Jackson and was sitting forward on its edge. Washington was so straight postured natural he seemed to have little need of the back. His throne was stained cherry brown, and on the uppermost portion of the back was a carving of a half-Sun. The half-Sun was painted gold with rays radiating outwards, had eyes with brows and a nose, and was topped by a Phrygian Cap atop a pike, an antient symbol of Liberty. The Sol seemed to be peeking over the horizon. But was it a rising Sun or a setting Sun?

"No Person held to Service or Labour in one State," Jackson read, "under the Laws thereof, escaping into another, shall, in Consequence of any Law or Regulation therein, be discharged from such Service or Labour, but shall be delivered up on Claim of the Party to whom such Service or Labour may be due."

Several of the south Deputies smirked fractional, and some of the north Deputies sprouted glum expressions. At present, any Slave escaping to the North was free. North States general refused to deliver escaped Slaves back to the South.

Once the Constitution inaugurate, slaves escaping North must be delivered back to the South. Another particular where the Constitution would energize Slavery rather than explode it. This Clause was especially odious because it forced north States that opposed Slavery to enforce it.

Franklin felt Shame.

And that rare and disquieting sense that he was Devilish Evil.

Franklin try'd to imagine himself a Slave, having taken flight, endured months of harrowing tryals and sufferances to finally reach the North and suppose-ed freedom. Instead he is arrested and delivered back to his Master.

This Clause was indefencable yet indispensible.

Another of the Bribes requisite to unionize North and South.

Would north States turn a blind eye to fugitive Slaves in their territory? Would America elect a President of the deep South who would make fœderal officials enforce the Clause zealous? A delicate gambit, as such enforcement would render the South, the fœderal Government, and Slavery obnoxious to the North, perhaps provoking it to explode Slavery.

Franklin reminded himself yet again that they were not in Convention to cure every ill of humankind. Slavery was not an immediate impediment to the survival of America, as more pressing problems were. Slavery would be eradicated in time.

Perhaps not with the expedition hoped, yet whether it took decades or centuries, the injustice would be ended. This Clause, so oppugnant now, would be irrelevant in futurity, save perhaps as Testament of Slavery.

What bothered Franklin most was the disquieting sense that he ought be bothered more.

But he was not.

Jackson read Section 3, which governed the admission of new states to the Union. It was incontroversial. As was Section 4, empowering the government to guarantee Republican government to States, and protect them against Invasion and domestic Violence. Franklin hoped America would never suffer invasion, nor succumb to it, and wondered at the impetus and mode of future domestic Violence. Franklin could envision Thomas intoning that a nation absent domestic Violence from time to time was stagnant and had succumbed to Tyranny.

"Article Five," Jackson read. "The Congress, whenever two thirds of both Houses shall deem it necessary, shall propose Amendments to this Constitution, or, on the Application of the Legislatures of two thirds of the several States, shall call a Convention for proposing Amendments,"

More than any other Article or Clause, this one seemed to evoke expressions of perplexion or uncertainty from Deputies.

The Constitution formed was certain defective, as America's first Constitution the Articles of Confederacy had been found on trial to be. Amendments would be necessary. Better to provide for them in an easy, regular, and Constitutional way than to entrust to chance and violence.

But how easy ought Amending the Constitution be? Too easy, and ruinous Innovation would beget. Too arduous, and the chief failing of the Articles of Confederacy would be replicate. Amendment of the Articles required the unanimous assent of all States. The dissent of even a single State negatived Amendment, and in practicable terms this rendered the Articles of Confederacy nigh inalterable. They might as well have been etched in a stone tablet.

Bottoming a government on The People was so untry'd that the most fundamental principles of Constitution were subject to disputation, much less finer peculiars such as how best to adapt a Constitution over time. A modern Republic never having been constituted for a span sufficient to observe the efficacy of Amending provisions, there was no example to draw upon.

What was the proper Repository of the Power of Amendment? What was the proper threshold for Amendment? What was the most efficacious way to construct the Power?

As with so many other provisions, no one knew.

"When ratified by the Legislatures of three fourths of the several States," Jackson read, "or by Conventions in three fourths thereof, as the one or the other Mode of Ratification may be proposed by the Congress;"

Franklin doubted the modes of Amendment too lax. A two thirds vote of both Houses of Congress to propose an Amendment, and then ratification by three fourths of the several States, was right arduous. So too was the second mode, of Application by two thirds of the several States for a Convention which proposed Amendments, and then ratification by three fourths of the several States. Obtaining such majorities would be nigh impossible lest an Amendment enjoy broad publick support. This was especially true because ratification in each State would be by Legislatures or Conventions bottomed on The People.

Were the modes of Amendment too arduous? The Little Lion thought such, as did Caledonia James. Yet their views were the Contrary.

Most Congressional votes, such as those positiving Laws, was by simple Majority. Deputies thought this too lenient for Amending. They wanted the majority for Amending supra to that for approving Laws and other regular votes.

For the Congress.

Attaining supra Majorities in the Legislatures of the several States was more cumbersome and arduous, and caused Franklin concern. Especially the requisite for a three fourths supra Majority of the Legislatures or Conventions of the several States to ratify Amendments.

A Constitution fixed and unalterable must become unsuited to the circumstances of the Nation, rendered a veritable straitjacket that enforced Tyranny through its inadaptitude. Had the Convention wrought a straitjacket for futurity?

Or would the Constitution in futurity perhaps have dozens or hundreds of Amendments, Innovations a plenty, and the mode in hindsight be found not limiting enough?

With increases in the quantum of States, would Majorities and supra Majorities become easier to attain, or more arduous? Experience suggested more arduous. The Gospel of Montesquieu again. Montesquieu saw limits to the practicable size of Republics. Assemble more people across a larger geography, especially with diverse regional proclivities, and unanimity became harder to attain to.

This Article and Clause of the Constitution might have more effect on the security, durability, and endurance of the Constitution, and of America, than many other Clauses contested warm and given more attention by Deputies. The historium of an America whose People could not Amend the Constitution as it became antiquate might be one of bloody Convulsions. That or the quietest of Despotisms.

Pennsylvania had a Council of Censors. Electored every seventh Year direct by The People, it audited all actions of Government, ensuring that the Constitution was preserved inviolate in every part, that branches of government performed their duty as guardians of The People, and had assumed not to themselves, or exercised, other or greater Powers than entitled to by the Constitution. The Council of Censors had broad Powers to remedy Violations of the Constitution, including Censure, bringing Impeachments, recommending the repeal of Laws, and cetera. If the Council of Censors found any Article of the Constitution defective, they could call a Convention for amending the Constitution to remedy such defect, and could also propose remedial Amendments direct. Amendments had to be promulgate at Least six months before the day appointed for the election of a Convention, for the previous consideration of The People, that they would have opportunity to instruct their Deputies on the subject.

Franklin had chaired the Pennsylvania Constitutional Convention in 1776, helped draw the Constitution, and ensured that the Council of Censors construction was included. He would have preferred such a construction in the Constitution reading, one which enforced a regular audit of all actions of the fœderal Government. A Council of Censors? A Council of Amendment, at the least.

Alas, Deputies evidenced a curious aversion to any Council, be it Executive, of Revision, of Censors, of Amendment, of War, of Peace, or other wise. Such Councils were viewed as violation of the doctrine of Supremacy, of Legislative, Executive, and Judicial exercising Powers segregate. Councils were thought to intermingle these Powers hazardous.

Franklin was not clear how an auditory Council electored direct by The People, representing their sovereign Power, not a portion of any of the three branches of Government, violated the segregation of Powers. What was, or ought be, more Supreme than the sovereign Will of The People?

A Council of Amendment would have made the convocation of a future Convention much less arduous, though the Pennsylvania mode might have required adaptation. Franklin favoured the mode of a direct convocation of such Council by The People, at regular intervals or their leisure, and the direct electoring of such Council by The People. Direct electoring being infeasible fœderal because of the three fifths Compromise and little State fears of Hotchpotting, some other mode might have been resorted. Might a Council of Amendment have been convoked by the Legislatures of the several States, at their leisure, without any involvement of, or interference from, the fœderal Legislature? Via a simple Majority of the Legislatures of the several States, rather than a supra Majority?

Who knew?

All Franklin knew a certain was that the mode of Amendment made him uneasy, as so much of the Constitution.

Pennsylvania's Council of Censors had first been elector'd in 1783 and had counseled an upper House and executive Negative upon Laws. The War prevented such measures from taking up, but a Council of Censors would be electored again in 1790 and would nigh certain call for a Convention. Pennsylvania would draft a new Convention nigh certain in 1790.

How long until America did so? Men such as Mason wanted another Convention convoked nigh immediate. To Mason, the Constitution had been formed without the knowledge or idea of The People. Mason felt that a second Convention would know more of the sense of The People and be able to provide a system more consonant with it. Mason also felt it improper to say to The People, take this Constitution or nothing.

Deputies already knew the sense of The People and had insufficient respect for it, and them. There would be no Convention the Second nigh immediate, as Mason wanted.

When then?

When would America convoke a second Convention?

Six years after the Constitution ratified, as had been the case with the Articles of Confederacy? Fourteen years after ratified, as appear'd probable with the Pennsylvania Constitution?

The proposition of multiple individual Amendments comprising a Declaration of Rights seemed probable during Ratification or during Congress the First. Despite many Deputies' belief to the contrary, there would be no ratification of the Constitution by the requisite number of States, or perhaps any State, without a Declaration of Rights or guarantee of one being taken up by Congress the First.

At least one additional Amendment in the first decade of the life of the Republic also seem'd probable, to correct a defect, or defects, so egregious that the need for remedy was unanimous. Which defects would become manifest or obnoxious none could say certain.

But when would another Convention making major Amendations convoke? Decades? A half Century? A century? Nigh inconceivable, that the defective Charta reading would not require major Amendment by 1887, a hundred annums in futurity. If America even survived such span.

If no Convention as specified under Article V by 1887, Deputies' vision was far greater than anyone present suppose-ed, save perhaps Jemmy, who habitual overesteemed his. Either that, or Article V was flawed fatal, in which case the Constitution would be found outmoded yet incapable of Amendment, as Mason feared.

Tyranny then.

How wise were Caledonia James, Chancellor Wythe, Jemmy, and cetera, truly? Franklin wondered how wise he was truly?

The Articles of Confederacy were the best effort of man when drafted just a decade prior.

Had they really learned enough in just a decade, most of it spent warring, with the only new lessons the Hotch Potch of state Constitutions, to expect a Constitution of prodigious endurance?

If America endured a century, how many Amendments would be found at such time? Ten? None? Dozens? A hundred or more? An entire new Constitution? A third new Constitution? Constitution the Tenth? Mere Anarchy, Savages again exercising dominion, men revert'd to a State of Nature?

And what of a second fugitive Convention?

Precedents were precious.

The first precedents became Customs.

People did not cast off Customs lightly, even when ruinous.

One reason Washington condescending President the First was so crucial. To found precedents upon Principle. And cement such Principles.

In ignoring the mandate of Congress to mere amend the extant Constitution, and crafting a new Constitution, Deputies invited every Convention convoked for æternity by America to do likewise. Invited every Convention convoked for æternity to ignore the rule of Law, ignore instructions of the Congress and those of the States to their Deputations, make itself Fugitive, and do whatsoever it pleased.

Each future Convention might machinate around the old mode of Ratification and devize an expediential new mode, as the present Convention had. This was a proposition radical deviant from that of amending within the constraints of an extant Constitution. One liable to beget abuse and convulsions.

How much Right and Liberty did each new Convention have to discard the conventions of old? How much should the present shackle futurity?

Washington and Franklin abused not such Prerogatives. But a future America mightn't have men so principled at its head.

Overall, Franklin felt the mode of Amendment not direct enough, not democratic enough, and too arduous, in both the mode of proposing Amendments, and the mode of ratification of Amendments. This might prove ruinous, though not with immediacy. Over longer interim, Amendment was perhaps the most important provision of the Constitution, for 'twas the mechanism by which all other provisions would undergo adaptation. More than any other Article or Clause in the whole of the Constitution, this one might have sown the Republic with the seeds of its own destruction.

"Provided," Jackson read, "that no Amendment which may be made prior to the Year One thousand eight hundred and eight shall in any Manner affect the first and fourth Clauses in the Ninth Section of the first Article;"

Yet another fortification of Slavery enforced by southern States. Congress could not prohibit the Migration or Importation of slaves, the trade of Slaves, nor could such Clause be bypassed by Amendment. Congress could only lay Capitations, or other direct, Taxes in Proportion to the Census, the enumeration of the population. Slaves accounted three fifths a Person in said enumeration. Congress could not bypass these Clauses by Amendment, Taxing Slaves disproportionate as a flanking attack on Slavery.

Southern Gentlemen would have attached such ramparts to nigh every Clause in the Constitution, had they been given licence. This Clause was no more onerous than the Clauses it protected and was mere insurance against machinations which would subvert the Compromises which wrought the Constitution. Like or dislike said Compromises, they was a bargain broker'd candid, and Gentlemen honoured bargains.

This Clause insured that there would be no action against Slavery for two decades. Franklin despised all Clauses of the Constitution defending Slavery. He despised the absence of a clause exploding Slavery. But he was also a Realist, and an Optimist. As onerous as the slavery Clauses were, they could have been right worse. They could have extended to perpetuity, thereby consigning the nation to schism or to Civil War.

"And," Jackson read, "that no State, without its Consent, shall be deprived of its equal Suffrage in the Senate."

Jemmy's feet stopped a swinging and hung fruzen in the air momentary, like a duck just shot. At the Virginia table, the Massachusetts table, the Pennsylvania tables, and other large-state tables, Deputies stiffen'd. At the Delaware, Connecticut, and New Hampshire tables, and other little State tables, Deputies nodded curt or other wise evidenced satisfaction.

To Franklin this was the most obnoxious Clause of the entire Constitution, by prodigious margin. This Clause had been dictated by the circulating Murmurs of the little States. 'Twas a late inclusion, having been agreed to the week last without debate, no one opposing it, or on the question voting nay.

From the vantage of little States, 'twas far from absurd to think that if States added to the Union in futurity be large, the large States would attain the three fourths Majority needed to ratify an Amendment abolishing the Senate, thereby depriving little States of their equal Representation in the Legislature. This was the supreme Phobia of the little States, one which had reputed been causing some to harbour reservations about positiving the Constitution. A mode in which States had one to three Senators depending on population, with more populous states having more Senators, had been consider'd by the Convention, and even this Measure affrighted little States grievous. The Clause read made such measures Fugitive.

After 1808, Amendments on Slavery would no longer be Fugitive. Slavery would be eradicate after, whether in a year, decade, or century, the Blacks expellt back to Africa or the Carib, to live in a State of Nature as they seemed disposed by their Nature. But Amendments altering the mode of suffrage or representation in the Senate would be Fugitive for all time.

Any single State could negative Amendment of the Senate by not consenting to deprivation of its equal Suffrage, which meant every State would have to approve Amendment of the Senate. The ruinous unanimity of the Articles of Confederacy replicate—unless a Convention rejected the Constitution in totality and wrought an entire new Constitution. Perhaps in distant futurity attachment to States would atrophy and such result would be effected. Rank absurdity regardless, to have to discard an entire Constitution to Amend but a single Clause in it.

A Senate where States had equal suffrage. A House where People had equal suffrage. In one branch The People represented, in the other branch The States represented. A Constitution that recogniz'd The States as political societies armed with some power of self Defence, yet also treated The People as a sovereign entity, melding the two principles.

It sounded idyllic in theory but was apt to Tyranny in practice. For when it came to Voting in Congress, the Minority that could negative a Motion would hold Power.

At present, the population of the seven littlest States was nigh a third of America's total, yet would comprise a simple

Majority of Votes in the inaugural Senate. This meant that a third of population could negative the will of the Majority at any time in the Senate. It signify'd not if a Law passed the House, it could still be negatived in the Senate. In effect, a supra Majority of two thirds of population was requisite on any matter upon which little States unify'd, to attain a simple Majority of votes in the Senate.

And what of the two thirds supra Majority vote in the Senate for proposing Amendments? Assuming all thirteen States adjoined the Union, but five States could block any Amendment. Four states and one Senator from another state, to be more exacting. Franklin performed the Cipher in his mind with five States. The five smallest states totaling some 15 or 16 per cent of Population might prevent any Amendment proposing. The little States as constituted in the Senate were damn nigh an Oligarchy, a Minority effecting rule.

This was but the Tyranny at present. In futurity, there might be a prodigious number of little States, sufficient to effect greater injustice. Franklin feared that Deputies may have begot a system of piracy by Cabals of Senators.

Designers would analize the fortifications of the Constitution, seeking the weakest point for Investment. The densest Rube would rapid conclude the Senate easiest perverted, because of its empowerment of Minorities and infrequent Rotation. That or Justices of the supreme Court, but a few of who, if bribed else perverted or controuled, might be a nigh unassailable rampart. Senators would be easier to pervert or controul though.

Suppose the Republic corrupted. Its Congress ruled by Interests, not The People. Tyrants or Oligarchs might block all remedy nigh Perpetual, by mere Influence over a small Faction of Senators. Senators which it might take six years to rotate out of office, unless Impeachment or Expellation resorted to. But Impeachment or Expellation Votes would occur in the Senate and be subject to the very Corruption of which Remedy attempted. Yet another argument for a Council of Censors, though even this would not answer the need.

Damn the Senate! Damn this ruinous Clause cementing its Perpetuity! Damn the entire bloody mode of voting by States! What of The People?

Franklin once again glanced at Washington's throne, couldn't resolve whether the sun was a rising or setting, so return'd to more incumbent questions. Was there some fatal error in the Constitutional edifice that he had overlooked? Would his concerns prove fodder for laughter or prophecy? Would this Constitution transcend its Defects and truly secure Liberty?

Perhaps no government could overcome the innate Depravity of man. Perhaps no amount of study or knowledge or debate, perhaps not even the hand of Providence itself, could create a government that would secure Liberty in perpetuity.

Franklin knew not.

No one knew.

Franklin knew but one Thing a certain.

They had done their best.

Different colonys, formed at different times, by different peoples fleeing different regions of Europe with different cultures, religions, ideologies. Glancing about Convention, at the way Deputies even now grouped in cliques by region, made this apparent. The very cadence, customs, and character of life were disparate in different regions of America. A stranger from a faroff land thrust into Convention might not have guessed he was seeing residents of a single nation, but would probably discern at minimum two. Such stranger would be no fool, nor wholesome mistaken.

Most Americans lived and died within 50 miles of where they were brought to bed. North States knew little of slaving, rice, indigo, or tobacco, whilst the South knew little of codding, curing, and manufactures. Americans were more apt to be familiar with happenings and customs of distant Britain, especially its fashions, than goings on in even neighboring colonys, much less colonys hundreds of miles away in latitudes removed. Melding these different colonys freely, without the arousing fear of British absolutism to induce a sense of co-operation, had seemed impossible.

So much to overcome. Limited knowledge. The need to obtain compromize amongst myriad Factions. So many shifting, resurrecting Factions! Little State against large State. North against South. Merchant against Planter. Most of all, fanatickal Deputies determined that states should not cede any sovereignty, principled yet unwise men who understood not that to secure Liberty, some must inevitable be surrendered. This was the foundational axiom of Civilization itself, and the inability of so many Deputies to grasp it was vexing. Yet men had always been predisposed to favour their selfish personal Interest, and the local Interest, to that of the collective Interest, and the national Interest.

Pioneers had to abandon precedent and brave the unknown. They had done this.

Perhaps they had secured human Liberty. Or perhaps their names would be profane to Posterity. Regardless, they had given their all. There was satisfaction in that.

It was time.

It was done.

Nought left but to put a period to it.

Most Deputies felt it.

But not all. And it might take one Malcontent only to re-open the vein of vicissitude.

Which is why Franklin reached into his jacket and removed a piece of paper. 'Twas tannish coloured, and much lighter than the vellum parchment. Franklin paid extra for paper made from tan rags, rather than cheaper paper which was coffee coloured or grey, as the contrast between black ink and a tannish paper was easyer on his old eyes. The hemp-ed Paper was folded into thirds and had a red wax seal. Franklin broke the seal, felt it crack in his fingers like a gingerbread cake. He placed the letter on the table a front him.

Deputies were forbidden from reading whilst other Deputies were speaking, and even removing the letter skirted the bounds of protocol. But Franklin had the Prestige to probe the boundarys a bit.

Roger Sherman turned, rigid as buckram, the brown irises of his eyes swiveling rightward, exposing white which filled the left portions. Gash-like wrinkles sloped downward from the edges of Sherman's mouth, glistening with sweat. He glanced at the letter with approval. Jemmy then turnt and spied the letter, peering with blue eyes that should have seemed vibrant, but seemed not because the face they inhabited was so sickly and nervous.

Franklin had grown accustomed to seeing Jemmy's back and the bottoms of his swinging feet as he sat a front of him week after week transcribing the Convention. The face usual familiar seemed nigh foreign. Such a grave face for one so young, as if Jemmy had bore Washington's burdens.

Jemmy's face was long, his forehead dominant even before his hairline had retreated like a Militia. Yet a brave regiment of follicles front and centre had held their quarter, forming a phalanx. Jemmy's upper head was a trio of round tipp-ed triangles, with a tip of hair pointing downward, noseward, in the centre, with two triangles of exposed scalp on either side of it, rearward tips so deep upon the scalp they would intersect an æquator drawn between the ears. Jemmy's eye sockets were deep, tho' like Washington his eyes were set forward in them considerable, preventing an unattractive recess-ed appearance. But the eyebrows suffered, as they seemed to jut in a singular manner, even though trimmt short and not bushy. There was also a considerable distance between brow and eyelid, creating an underhang.

Jemmy had the barest beginnings of that misproportionality seen in midgets, where the face grew not to full size, and nature seemed unable to reconcile and find æsthetic balance. Yet Jemmy's face might have been endearing if he weren't so bloody serious.

Jemmy turned away quick, as if he feared Franklin's letter would leap across the table and slice his throat. Franklin couldn't help smirking. What grotesque irony for such a compulsive Scholar. Draw the Quill, Perish by the Quill? Hmmmm.

The Little Lion glanced at the letter next, exuding arrogance as always, though a bit less than typical, as usual with Franklin, whose ability to humiliate with sheer wit had always seemed to intimidate him a bit. The Little Lion seemed scrupulous in avoiding a rousement of Franklin, lest he become the Fodder of his Lampoons. As the Little Lion looked away, the staunchest Dissidents such as Mason, Randolph, and Gerry glared at the letter ominous, suspecting the crux. Soon all Deputies stared.

Except Washington.

The disruption was momentary, yet significant enough that Franklin wished he had waited to unpocket the letter. Focus thankful returned to Major Jackson, his voice still resounding, indefatigable, as if he could keep reading whilst seasons shuffled and years withered. How had he not grown hoarse?

As more and more clauses inexorable accumulated, and the end of the reading neared, the tension seemed to abate in some Deputies. They seemed to forget their objection to specific clauses and to consider the broader totality. Mentally, they seemed like sculptors washing the clay off their hands, standing back and surveying their work. Deputies began to nod slow, repeated. To glance at each other and allow modest smiles.

They had done it!

Almost.

"Article Six," Jackson read, "All Debts contracted and Engagements entered into, before the Adoption of this Constitution, shall be as valid against the United States under this Constitution, as under the Confederation."

Article VI was a Hotch Potch, the repository of Clauses without place in other Articles, and it contained some of the least contested Clauses of the Constitution. The Clause perpetuating Debts prevented a general Anarchy when the Constitution inaugurate. Without it, every contract and indenture in the whole of the land might be negatived, which was both impracticable and unjust.

At least to Deputies.

Many States was wracked by Convulsions over debts and foreclosures, with Yeomen and Aprons trying to suspend the enforcement of contracts and foreclosures upon land. The shortage of Specie with which debts had to be paid, the premium charged by Shavers and Speculators to lend or sell said Specie, as well as the degeneracy of commerce wrought by the want of Specie, made it nigh impossible for hundreds of thousands of Yeomen and Aprons throughout the several States to pay debts and honour contracts. Franklin understood the warmth of Yeomen and Aprons, but the solution was not universal negativing of contractual obligations—so long as Legislatures submitted to secured paper Money and suffered Yeomen and Aprons to make payments in it.

This Clause might displease Shayites and Levellers throughout the land, but it would be preposterous to absent it. The Constitution contained much of this sort of procedural minutiæ. Every Clause involved not a principle incumbent weighty, nor a contested Interest. Just most Clauses.

"This Constitution," Jackson read, "and the Laws of the United States which shall be made in Pursuance thereof; and all Treaties made, or which shall be made, under the Authority of the United States, shall be the supreme Law of the Land;"

Jemmy nodded appreciable at this. The Little Lion sprouted his designing Smirk. Colonel Mason fumed.

Franklin pondered the supreme Court negativing state Laws, invoking Supremacy. He imagined a future Tyrannical government which interpreted every open ended Clause energetic, including the Preamble, Power to make all laws necessary and proper, Power to lay and collect Taxes for the general Welfare, and cetera.

Yet 'twas impossible to envision a Constitution absent such Clause. If fœderal Law had Supremacy not, any State might negative it, with effect little different from the present turbulence tending towards Anarchy. 'Twas insensible for a Convention called to prevent a general Anarchy to perpetuate one.

"The Senators and Representatives before mentioned," Jackson read, "and the Members of the several State Legislatures, and all executive and judicial Officers, both of the United States and of the several States, shall be bound by Oath or Affirmation, to support this Constitution; but no religious Test shall ever be required as a Qualification to any Office or public Trust under the United States."

Deputies of all persuasions nodded emphatick at making religious tests Fugitive. Grievous Tyranny had been wrought throughout history by commingling religion and government. Inquisitions and Crusades galore. America would not retrod this Brutalia Absurdium. Religion and government would be staunch segregate. Men would be at Liberty to chuse their religion without disqualification or fear of oppression.

This clause was a departure from many state Constitutions. In Pennsylvania, a man could not serve office unless he subscribed to a belief in one God who was the creator and governour of the universe, and rewarder of the good and the punisher of the wicked. A man must also acknowledge the Scriptures of the Old and New Testament to be given by Divine inspiration. In Massachusetts, a man had to declare that he believed in the Christian religion and had a firm persuasion of its truth. In New York, no man could hold office unless he be of the Protestant religion.

And cetera.

Franklin was not a walking cyclopædia of Constitutions, as Jemmy and Caledonia James, and could not remember every religious qualification in every state Charta.

Most Deputies being rational, they were not Zealots for religion, though neither were they Atheists. Richard Basset of Delaware was the only Deputy rabid in his religion, and he appeared right glum. Basset was a Methodist and had been converted by Bishop Asbury.

Thomas would have approved were he present. He took as much pride in authoring the Virginia Statute for Religious Freedom as he did the Declaration of Independency.

This Clause was the only mention of religion in the whole of the Constitution. Which was perhaps why Mason looked dour again. He was desirious of more emphatick insurance against the perversion of government by Zealots. Mason wanted a firm negative upon the Establishment of Religion, and he felt that absent such negative the power would be assumed and America might devolve towards Theocracy.

As Jackson approached the end of Article VI and the Constitution, the State House clock struck eleven, its metalic gong penetrating the room, though not so full as it would have if the windows were open. The sound was still strong, something felt in the head and bones more than heard.

No one seemed surprized that an hour in Convention had passed.

It felt like longer.

Much longer.

Franklin was literal struck by the clock, as if a shot fired across his bow, a reminder that there was still a battle to be fought this day. He glanced at his paper, at his speech, and avoided the urge to look at Washington.

Washington's thoughts doubtless mirrored Franklin's. The Convention must not fail in this, the absolute final instance. Washington and Franklin were the two most eminent Deputies and Americans, The General and The Sage, and the ultimate responsibility for the success of the Convention was incumbent on them. The full brunt of their stature must be brought to bear to ensure success.

Franklin took measure of the Dissidents again. Of George Mason, who turned a moment, revealing a face that belonged at Versailles and the lips of an irritate wife. Of Edmund Randolph, face rectanglish, like a figurine chiseled out of a tree, the acreage dominated by a gargantuan nose and introspective yet indecisite eyes. Of the ghoulish, ever-squinting Elbridge Gerry, he of the endless forehead and indefatigate obstinancey.

No satisfaction on Dissident's faces, as with most Deputies.

All three men looked troubled.

Increasing troubled.

To be continued …

THE
FOUNDING
FATHERS
RETURN

Part the Second

For information about *The Founding Fathers Return: Part the Second* please visit LawrenceRowe.com.

To receive a notification when *The Founding Fathers Return: Part the Second* is released, sign up for Lawrence's e-mail list at his website.